W9-AOP-980

PROPHETIC REVERIE

"There is always the blue chair, waiting, welcoming, ready to whisk me away with magic carpet swiftness into the past, where the suspense of living is still strong and the simple curiosity about how it will all end is sufficient motivation to keep one going through the best and worst of times.

"There is John Powell (intriguing thought) somewhere in this city. . . .

"Yes, he has been on my mind. Damn it, he made me feel like a woman, exercised some invisible female organs that had begun to atrophy. I was, in short, the victim of his charm. And it was nice, to be so victimized. One should perhaps allow oneself to be taken in, or even used.

"If the rewards are sufficiently pleasant, who says they have to be real?"

THE BLUE CHAIR

A NOVEL BY

JOYCE THOMPSON

 AVON
PUBLISHERS OF BARD, CAMELOT AND DISCUS BOOKS

THE BLUE CHAIR is an original publication of Avon Books. This work has never before appeared in book form.

AVON BOOKS
A division of
The Hearst Corporation
959 Eighth Avenue
New York, New York 10019

Copyright © 1977 by Joyce Thompson
Published by arrangement with the author.
Library of Congress Catalog Card Number: 77-78140
ISBN: 0-380-01656-7

All rights reserved, which includes the right
to reproduce this book or portions thereof in
any form whatsoever. For information address
The Otte Company, 9 Park Street,
Boston, Massachusetts 02108

First Avon Printing, July, 1977

AVON TRADEMARK REG. U.S. PAT. OFF. AND IN
OTHER COUNTRIES, MARCA REGISTRADA,
HECHO EN U.S.A.

Printed in the U.S.A.

For Paul

1

My son's dry lips touch my forehead briefly. He does not want to kiss me; I can feel him recoil, instinctively, from my flesh. For myself, I would gladly delete this scene from the script. His uneasiness communicates itself to me, and I shrink from the contact, too, for different reasons. Well, I don't demand this charade of him. It is his own obsession with forms that makes him kiss me.

"Happy birthday, Mother," Jason says. He straightens quickly and heads for the sofa, glancing down at the cushion before he sits. He would like to brush it off, perhaps, but is too polite to do it.

Suli is standing in the doorway with the tea tray, motionless and discreet. When we have played our scene and Jason is settled, she advances, making the subtlest of sounds in her throat to advise us of her otherwise silent approach.

Our eyes meet briefly as she moves toward us, and I am struck again by the sharpness, the intelligence of her gaze. Suli does not let her eyes be eloquent; they simply collect impressions, to be pondered privately, and offer back no comment or response. Jason pays no attention to her, of course. It is his job, and a good one, to import such people to serve us. He has no desire to be confronted with their humanity.

But Suli has seen and understood, I think, what has taken place between my son and me. She distrusts Jason, I suspect. In his presence, she becomes even more inscrutable, less obtrusive, than she normally is. With a smile, I try to extort some sign from her, but she refuses the invitation to comment and drops her eyes quickly from mine.

"Anything else, ma'am?"

"No. Thank you, Suli."

Jason appears more easy when she is gone. I would like to impute this to conscience, but would, I think, be wrong. The Handbook that tells us how to treat our help is Jason's work, and it advises against discussing things in front of servants.

"How *is* the Ministry these days?" I ask my son. "I hear you're expanding your police force again."

"Strengthening it. Yes."

"That scares me. You'll have a private army soon."

"It's for your protection, Mother. We need a strong enforcement arm. Do you realize that in another five years, the importee population will exceed the number of citizens?"

"With a birth rate like this, it's not surprising."

"That's one factor. Yes," Jason says. "It's a potential powder keg. We have to prevent their numbers from giving them strength."

"That's a neat trick," I observe.

"With an adequate force, it can be done."

Somehow I think there would be less to fear from a warmer-blooded man. Jason's dispassion frightens me as much as his power does. "Let's hear it for oppression," I say, to get his goat.

"Mother, let's not discuss policy today. I know you disapprove of my work."

He's right. I *do* disapprove. Jason's Ministry imports people from the starving Third World to keep our homes immaculate, our own hands clean. He is, crudely put, a flesh merchant, though he despises flesh.

"What are you doing to celebrate?" he asks coolly. "I thought I might find Father at home, it being your birthday."

"I asked him not to make a fuss. Besides, he's very busy at the lab."

Jason replaces cup in saucer and sets both on the table before him. Since childhood, his movements have been like this, neat and precise. He was a clean child, never soiled his clothes or himself, and had, still has, a way of drawing back from dirt as though it caused him physical pain.

"I'm sorry to have missed him. What was his gift?"

"Seventy-five isn't the birthday for receiving gifts, Jason. In fact, it's time to give things back. I have to turn in my Health Card this afternoon, and register with the Bureau of Geriatrics."

Involuntarily, Jason winces.

"Sorry, Son. I know it pains you to contemplate your eventual loss." As soon as I say it, I am ashamed of myself. I bridle at the games we play, sometimes, and then abuse them. To make amends, I say, "If you want to see your father, you might have dinner with him Thursday. I have a reading that night. You could let him off the hook."

"Ah, good." Jason brightens a bit. "I hoped the Ministry would do something in honor of your retirement. But I'm sure Father wouldn't miss it. Nor would I."

Poor Jason. He has always wanted to profit from my small fame, though he's never liked or understood my poems. "My forced retirement? Actually, I have to go to the Ministry of Culture today, too, to turn in my Artist's Card. From now on, I'm an out-of-work poet. *Sic transit et cetera.*"

"But what about your reading?"

"It's not at the Ministry, Jason. I'm reading at the Poets' Guild."

An expression of disgust comes to rest on my son's face. He must think I've taken leave of my senses.

"That's very unwise, Mother. How can you associate yourself with those people? You know what they are."

It occurs to me that what Jason fears is guilt by association—that he will suffer for my transgressions. "Cheer up, Jason," I tell him. "No one will blame you. They know by now you haven't got a seditious thought in your head."

"I wasn't thinking of myself," he says coldly. "But what you do reflects on Father."

"Your father shines so brightly he practically runs the galaxy. It won't hurt him."

"Still," Jason says. "It can't be good for you. Do you want to end your career like that?"

"It's the Ministry of Culture that's ending my career, Jason. *I'm* not any less a poet today than I was yesterday.

The Poets' Guild doesn't give a damn if I *am* seventy-five. They want me to read."

"I think it's a mistake."

"Good. Think what you like."

"Age hasn't made you any less stubborn, I see."

I smile at him. "Probably more so." Not because he has a right to know, but because I have debated the issue myself at some length, I try to explain. "Look, Jason. I don't see how what I do now can have *any* consequences. Once I turn in my cards, that's it. They have nothing I want anymore. No carrot, no stick. They can't take away what's already gone."

"Have it your way, Mother. I *did* warn you."

"Thank you, Jason, for your concern."

It gets harder and harder to play the roles we've chosen for ourselves: loving mother, affectionate son. We both know it is foolish to try to play them for more than five minutes. Longer, and truth threatens illusion. Our history intercedes. Jason knows it as well as I. He rises now, smoothing imaginary wrinkles from his impeccable gray slacks.

As he stands before me, I am struck by how much he looks like Marcus. It's unnerving. Even though he's fifty now, Jason so strongly resembles my husband at twenty-five, when first I loved him, that it tears a little at my heart. Jason is tall and slim, with his father's dark hair and emphatic brows, his lean, rectangular face. Blue eyes dominate his unlined face—eyes that come from me, but are not mine. The worlds we perceive through them are vastly different. Jason has trained himself to see what he *should* see, while I, I like to think, look for what's really there.

"I must get back to the office, Mother. Can I drop you downtown on my way?"

"No, no. I'm not quite ready to go yet."

"I'd wait, but I have a three-thirty appointment."

"It's not necessary, Jason. I can get there on my own hook." I rise, though it is no longer entirely easy to rise, and walk with him toward the door.

He pauses beside it. "Well, felicitations."

"Thank you, Jason. Thank you for coming." I bite down on rising sarcasm and smile him out. When the door is closed behind him, I move to the window and watch him get in his car. The car is as well kept as Jason himself. It's a sign of his importance that he has a car at all, and Jason is nothing if not careful of the symbols of his rank.

With the tinted glass of the car window and the distance between us softening his expression, it is hard to believe that the man I see is not my husband, fifty years ago. It makes me shiver a little. When I turn from the window, I find Suli standing quietly behind me. I start a little, not meaning to.

"You surprised me."

"I'm sorry, Mrs. Harmon. Do you want me to clear the tea things now?"

We pass to the living room, and she heads at once toward the tray.

"Wait, Suli. I think I'd like another cup. Somehow it's hard to taste things properly when Jason's around."

I return to my chair, and it feels good to sit. From the heavy pot, I pour myself another cup.

"Is there anything else?" Suli asks.

If I say yes, she will be instantly in motion. Her stance, as always, is expectant, poised for action. "Yes, Suli. Get yourself a cup and join me."

"Ma'am?"

"Please have a cup of tea with me. I hate to drink alone."

I have thrown her off balance. She hesitates. I have never made this request before. "Please."

She goes to the kitchen and returns with a plain white cup, a humble cup. It is a survivor of the first set of dishes Marcus and I owned, a wedding gift, I think.

"You can use the good china, Suli," I tell her. Then, looking at the cup, at the simple integrity of its shape, I ask, "Is there another like that?"

She nods. "One."

"Where is it, Suli?"

"I'll get it for you."

"No, just tell me where."

She pauses, imagining the pantry, then gives me directions. In the pantry, I follow them like a treasure map until, on the highest shelf, I find the last white cup. My hands tremble a little, taking it down.

"I've always liked these dishes," I tell her, resuming my chair. She has waited for me, hands folded in her lap. "Cream? Sugar? Go ahead," I urge.

From the way she sits, unnaturally erect and close to the edge of the seat, I can see that Suli is nervous. She watches me closely, and watchfulness impinges on her dark beauty, creasing her forehead, making her seem harder and older than she usually does. The cup rattles slightly in its saucer when she picks it up to drink.

It was not my intention to make her uncomfortable. I wish I could put her at ease. Even in my own mind, what I want of her is unclear. For seven years, Suli has been part of our household, a silent presence mostly, solicitous and efficient, yet I know virtually nothing about her—not her age, not her history nor her interests. More specifically than the continent of Africa, I do not even know where she comes from, or who her people are. Humane as Marcus and I pretend to be, as different from the rest, we have become arrogant, too. The woman has lived seven years in my home and is a mystery to me.

Lately it has occurred to me that Suli is not equally ignorant of my life. It has played out carelessly before her these seven years, there for the seeing. Perhaps it is a measure of our insensitivity how little we have hidden from her, how unconscious of her presence we have become. Lately, for no good reason, I have begun to watch her, though, and found her watching me, absorbing my actions, my hesitations and mistakes with her large, dark, one-way eyes.

Quite simply, I guess, I want to know what she thinks of me.

I sip my tea and smile at her. "Yes, this is better. Jason puts me on edge a bit, I guess."

She keeps her eyes on me as she sips, warily, from the very rim of her cup.

"Jason and I have never been"—I look for an appropriate word, then choose a milder one—"close. As you may have guessed."

Suli gives me polite attention, but I cannot see below the surface of her eyes. By now, I regret forcing myself on her, but having done so, I carry on.

"Jason's homosexual, I think, if he's sexual at all. At any rate, he dislikes women. Doesn't seem to find us quite clean." I laugh nervously. "My fault, no doubt."

She continues to watch me, but does not respond. I try a direct question. "Well, what do you think of my bouncing boy-child?"

She looks at me speculatively, then surprises me by speaking. "Your son hates you, I think."

Her voice is soft and dispassionate, the same voice that tells me Marcus will be late for dinner, or that the laundry is back. It seems strange to hear a hard home truth so gently spoken. She's right, of course, though I have never said so, and learned to think so in small doses only.

"Why, do you think?"

She shrugs slightly. "I don't know. Perhaps because you are mortal."

"For that he should be grateful. If nothing else."

Suli speaks slowly, weighing her words, and giving equal emphasis to all. "I think it must be hard to be grateful for so great a gift. Especially because he will never pay the same price. It's hard to forgive people to whom one owes too much."

"Maybe," I tell her. "Maybe so." If she knew more of our story, I wonder if she'd change her mind. "It's awkward, anyway. I don't like it."

"No," she says. "I wouldn't think so."

I am amazed that Suli speaks to me. Encouraged, I ramble on, becoming vaguely aware as I do so that I must need an audience, a sounding board, a human ear.

"It hasn't turned out the way I thought it would, you know." I laugh. "I must have *outcome* on the brain today. The time has come to pay the piper. By now, the bargain seems less just than when I made it."

There is nothing Suli can say, but I think I can feel her sympathy, as well as her reserve. She cannot have missed the signs of erosion in our marriage, cannot have failed to see that as I've aged these last few years, my husband, only four months younger, has retained his health and his vitality. Our silences are longer than our conversations now, and she must know it. What she doesn't know is how much

I loved the man, how good it was for how long, or how much our current estrangement hurts and frightens me.

We were supposed to face this part of life together. Now, as the end draws near, I feel persistently that I am going it alone. On the surface of things, nothing has changed, but my nightmares tell me something has gone terribly wrong. Even waking, I am uneasy. Marcus spends more and more time at the lab; both of us look to this as an excuse for the distance that has grown between us.

Suli stirs uneasily, and my mind comes back to her. "I'm sorry," I tell her. "I'm just a capricious old woman. You'll have to pardon me. I think my mind's beginning to wander."

I watch for her reaction. Perhaps it will tell me something that I need to know. My mind *has* altered; I need to know if it shows yet, in social intercourse. I misplace whole blocks of years sometimes, and yet remember others in detail so exquisite it tears at me. More than remember: I have found I can, sitting in the blue chair in my room some afternoons when the house is quiet and the shades drawn, relive whole segments of my past.

It is strange and exhilarating. Everything is there—the rooms and their furnishings, the smells, the quality of light, sounds I half noticed then, and half hear now. Most of all, *I* am there. I do not watch myself replay the past, but actually relive it, behind my own eyes, inside my head, my body, perceiving directly and for the first time what I am living for the second. There is compelling magic in it. More and more, I withdraw to my room in the afternoon and conjure up the past.

Senility, I suppose. It happened to my mother, and to hers. I come from a family whose minds become unanchored with advancing age. Always I have known, and always feared, that it would happen to me in my turn. What I regret now is that I did not understand then that it is a compensation, too, a great gift among the devastations of age. Had I known that, I might have spent less time fearing it, and would be able now to enjoy it with less guilt. I am afraid to ask Marcus if it happens to him, too. I am almost certain it does not.

If Suli has noticed my lapses, she gives no sign. She has

been patient with me this afternoon, and now I try to focus my attention on her.

"How did you come to speak English so well, Suli? Are Jason's schools really that good?"

"I received instruction there," she says. "I also read. It has helped me." She looks embarrassed.

"What do you read?" I ask.

"Oh, many things," she tells me. "I read your poems."

It is my turn to be embarrassed. Not only does this woman see the show, she reads the program, too. Suddenly, I feel naked and vulnerable. I make a deprecating noise, and feel a blush rise on my neck. The old, odd conflict stirs in me—the passionate love I have for my work, and the intense pressure I feel to belittle it.

"Then you know what a fool I really am."

She shakes her head. "Don't think of yourself as your son thinks of you," she says.

Though I have brought about the encounter, I am ready to end it now. Suli has touched my tenderest spot.

"Well, I'd best get moving. I have to go downtown." Slowly I rise, and Suli becomes a servant once again.

"Will you want the car, ma'am?"

"No, Suli. I think I'll take the subway."

I wait for some comment, but she makes none. It occurs to me she already knows I take the subways, though I have never mentioned it. She knows everything about me. She must. Perhaps, someday, I will know her, too.

As I head for the stairs, I see she is already back at work, dropping the little silver tongs back in the sugar bowl, collecting our cups.

2

The subways are used almost exclusively by those of us who will die. I don't know if the Ministry of Transportation intended this, or if it just happened. In the last few years I have used them often, even though Marcus and I have each always had a car. Suddenly I realize that when I hand in my Artist's Card, I will probably have to relinquish the car as well. Such privileges are not wasted on the dying. But I don't mind; I have accustomed myself to the subways, rather enjoy riding them by now.

It grows hotter and hotter as I descend the stairs that lead to the trains. For much of my life, I felt a vague terror at the sight of subway entrances, at the gaping stairwells that appeared, suddenly, without sufficient warning, in the middle of normal, unremarkable sidewalks. Sounds and smells, drifting up from unimagined depths, frightened me with their richness and profusion. The first time I ventured down, I trembled most of the way.

Now a man hurries past me on the stairs and in passing brushes against the left side of me. The contact does not even make him pause, but the place where he has touched me remains alive with excitement when he is out of sight. Less and less am I touched as I grow old.

Unlike the first time I took the train, I am confident now about how to proceed, and stick my coin in the turnstile without a moment's hesitation, then push with my stomach against the wooden arms of the stile until they yield and let me pass inside. I savor the process, and so am slow, causing a break in the flow of traffic. Behind me, others mutter at my slowness.

The light is very dim, brighter now, though, than during the rush hours when workers travel to and from their jobs,

from houses like mine to the apartment cities that Jason's
Ministry has built to house them. I have always been glad
to spare Suli the trouble of commuting, the pressures of a
double way of life. Yet perhaps we have done her a dis-
service. The people on the platform beside me strike me
as being very interesting, very human. They do not have
Marcus' abstracted manner, or Jason's cold one. Some, like
Suli, are clearly African; others appear to be Indians. As
many, though, seem to be the products of genes crossed
and recrossed to create a striking hybrid beauty in face
and body. There are just enough other white mortals that
I myself am not conspicuous.

That is precisely why I have come to like the subways
these last few years. My face, my body, do not occasion
curiosity or comment. All around me have chosen or been
forced to choose the old lifestyle, the march to death. Here
my own death, as it approaches, is not exceptional. I embarrass no one; I am like the people around me. There are
no treatment-takers here.

An ancient train roars in, shaking the platform beneath
our feet. The tremors penetrate the soles of my shoes and
pass into my body, traveling upward to the knee. The air
grows even warmer as the doors groan open and expel
their human cargo. I stand aside, then light my flashlight
and board the train. The first time I rode the subway, I
didn't know there was no light inside the trains. I didn't
have a flashlight, and was terrified by the density of the
human shadows that surrounded me. I hugged the metal
pole so tightly I could scarcely pry open my fingers to let
it go when we reached my destination. Now I have a flashlight like the rest.

Once again I have been slow, coming too late to claim
a place on the molded plastic benches that run along the
walls. But I am willing to stand, and attach myself to one
of the kidney-shaped rings that hangs from the ceiling of
the train. The train starts volcanically and plunges into the
tunnel, leaving the dim lights of the station behind.

The white heads of flashlights punctuate the dark. I have
noticed before how beautifully this kind of light can sculpt
the human face, and now look hungrily around me, ready
to be moved. My gaze falls on a young man sitting just

below me and slightly to the left. He holds his flashlight close to his stomach, and its beams shine upward, illuminating the undersides of his features, casting their tops into dense shadow. Light strikes the prominent ridges of his brows and is thrust back downward into deep eyes. Quite by accident, we look at each other, and his expression changes as I watch. Then he stands up, a move made violent by the hurtling speed of the car, finds his balance, and offers the seat to me with a jagged sweep of his arm.

"You sit," he says.

I sit, humbly and at once. "Thank you so much," I tell him, but he looks away, rejecting my gratitude. The bench is still warm from his body, and the warmth he has left behind him, touching me, seems very intimate indeed. For a long time I stare at his back, and wonder what he saw in my face to move him to such kindness. I accept the mystery, as a birthday gift. For a moment, I let myself imagine that all the little flashlight beams are candles, lit for me, and feel well loved on my warm and plastic seat.

We pass one station, two. The makeup of the crowd changes, while its density remains the same. The young man who gave me his seat is gone, though I can still feel the warmth of his body against my buttocks and my thighs. The subway thunders on. At the third stop, I get off.

The station is somewhere below the last and deepest basement of the government complex, and I must ascend, level by level, sometimes on escalators, sometimes by elevator or by stair. On the first two levels, signs simply point upward, and say "Government." At the third, there is a free-standing sign post whose many arms guide people through the physical labyrinth of our tangled bureaucracy to the place where they have business with the appropriate minotaur.

The metaphor quickens my own passage through the maze. My heart accelerates a little, too, and a sense of urgency overwhelms me—all the poems I must yet write, all the little pieces stored up in my brain, waiting to be matched up with other pieces and be transformed into something a little bigger and more coherent than any is alone. I have not begun to tap the resources I've gathered, these seventy-five years, yet the time remaining to me is short. Much will be lost. I must work hard, unflaggingly, to use up as much as I can.

Even as, for perhaps the thousandth time in my life I promise myself to waste no more time, spend no more mornings in idle daydreams, no more afternoons at lunch with people who do not love me, I know that I will work no more and no less, these last years, than I ever have. Partly I know this because I know my muse, who is reliable and workmanlike, but will not succumb to pressure. And I know the appeal of my blue chair in the shaded bedroom, where I can summon up a past more interesting than the present, more inviting than my future. I know that I will suffer Jason gladly when he comes to tea; I have pretended affection for too long, and taken my mother's role too seriously, to abandon either now, even though I know my time and energy could be far better spent than on a son whom I must call, in some private, lucid recess of my heart, a failed experiment. No, I will work no more and possibly less than ever. Age makes its demands; being alive is sometimes enough to exhaust me.

So far, the Ministry of Health and the Ministry of Culture have lain in the same direction. Now, at the fourth level, I must choose to visit one before the other. Should I give up my Artist's Card or my Health Card first? Each is painful in its way. I choose the Ministry of Culture first, because it lies to the left, and all my life, in all things, I have listed slightly in that direction.

Inside the Ministry, there are more directions to be followed. Here life mirrors criticism rather than art. The bureaucracy divides itself into functional units by genre, first separating the Visual, Verbal, Cinematic, and Musical Arts, then continuing, within each category, to classify progressively smaller characteristics of art in order to administer the people who practice it.

Thank god I am no genius, but create only in one small form. A Renaissance man would have to spend whole weeks, going from window to window to be registered and carded for everything he was capable of doing. I picture Michelangelo in a porkpie hat, being licensed to draw, to paint, to write sonnets, to carve marble and cast in bronze, then running to the Ministry of Engineering to be certified as an architect as well. He who has the most cards is clearly the greatest man. The government makes it easy to know where one stands.

For the last time, I make my way to the Bureau of Verbal Arts, Division of Poetry. It does not sadden me that I will never walk these halls again; I have always mistrusted the spare sterility of this place, with its concrete walls paneled with slabs of what seems to be tangled, compressed spaghetti, meant to muffle the footsteps and mute the voices of the men and women who transact business here.

Miss Green sits in her window. When I have gone to the Division of Poetry, these fifty years, I have always gone to Miss Green's window. It is, of course, impossible to guess her age because she has not changed at all since I've been coming here—a pity, I think. Age might have helped her, might have brought some distinction to her reticent features. Miss Green has little color, save in her name. Her hair is colorless, leaning toward brown; her eyes colorless, leaning toward gray. Her skin has a yellowish cast (though might not, by the light of day), her lips, too, seem gray, with a slight inclination toward pink. Unlike mine, Miss Green's face has no wrinkles, no marks of age. Her hair is not shot with white, and her shapeless body is still the body of a young and shapeless woman.

"Good afternoon, Miss Green."

"Mrs. Harmon. It's nice to see you again. How can I help you?"

I like to imagine that, for the last twenty years or so, a little hint of warmth creeps into her even voice when she addresses me. I have always been very cordial to her.

"Today is my seventy-fifth birthday," I tell her. "I was supposed to report here today."

For once some emotion—dismay—is perceptible on Miss Green's plain, unchanging face. She makes several false starts before she manages to say, "You'll have to see the Director. I've never—that is to say, it's very seldom that we have to . . ."

"To take someone off the rolls. I know." I smile at her, as kindly as I can. There has been ample time for me to learn to deal with the embarrassment I cause others. The self-righteousness of my early years has mellowed; I am no longer so certain that my way is the right way, or the only one. This tends to make me apologetic; no longer proud of my differences, I am genuinely sorry for the trouble my differences cause others.

"I'm sure the Director will know what to do. May I see him now?"

"I think he's in his office. I'll see."

I realize as she retreats that I have never seen Miss Green's back before. She is gone for a few minutes, then comes through the low gate at the end of the counter and holds it open for me.

"He'll see you now. The third office along the wall."

She closes the gate behind me and returns to her window. From this side of the counter, I see that she sits on a tall stool. A number of clerks look up from their terminals to watch me cross the short distance to the Director's door. I stumble once, self-conscious.

The door to the Director's office is only slightly open. Outside it, I clear my throat two or three times, waiting for an invitation to enter, while the eyes of the clerks remain intent on me. Finally I advance, push the door open, and step inside. Over a large desk, I see the leather back of a swivel chair, with just the very crown of a human head protruding above it. I make polite noises, to announce myself.

At last the Director swings his chair around and we are face to face. He closes the book he has been reading carefully, and marks his place with a clean sheet of Mylar. When he puts the volume down on his desk, I see it is *Paradise Lost*. The binding appears, from this distance, to be real leather, and the title is stamped on the spine in gold. It must be a very valuable book. I would love to pick it up myself, weigh it in my hands, feel the stiff, creamy paper of its gilt-edged pages.

I point at the volume of Milton. "It's beautiful," I tell him. "That's how poetry should be read. I know it's old-fashioned of me, but I love to hold a book in my hand and feel it when I read."

The Director looks up at me. "Yes, so do I. Though

lexavision is a great thing," he adds quickly. "Inexpensive and efficient. And it leaves the forests intact."

"Oh yes. I know. I just have a predilection for the real thing."

He sighs. "So do I."

I have always rather liked the Director. It is more nearly possible to guess his age than Miss Green's. His voice and manner bear the marks of age, though his body, of course, does not. He sighs frequently and doesn't always say the kinds of things a Director of Poetry is supposed to say. Just to confess a preference for books, when the Ministry of Culture so strongly supports lexavision, is quite an admission.

I have always suspected the Director would like to be a poet himself, and not a bureaucrat. Perhaps he is. It isn't hard to imagine him searching for the right word, the right image to convey some feeling that wells up in him, though it *is* hard to imagine that he ever finds it. Therein, most likely, lies his tragedy. In earlier times, he might have been a professor of literature, quite an adequate one, or perhaps one of those slightly wistful book reviewers who wrote in magazines, mostly about what displeased them.

"Well, we'd best get on with it," I say. "This is my birthday. I'm seventy-five years old today."

"Miss Green told me. I'm sorry."

"Don't be sorry," I tell him.

The Director stands up, rather abruptly, leaving his chair to rock a little on its springs without him. He is shorter than I, and rotund, like a child's toy. An odd little moustache crawls like a caterpillar across his upper lip and becomes animated when he speaks. His round blue eyes are gentle, and perenially bemused, showing no signs of either malice or guile. If the Director has any public sin, it is, I suppose, just a touch of officiousness. But he is harmless and full of good will. The man wants desperately to be liked by the poets he registers. All too often, I fear, they, we, discount or despise him.

"I'm sorry that our laws are so arbitrary," he says. "A poet doesn't stop making poems because she's seventy-five. You must understand that I don't want to terminate your grant."

"Thank you," I say. "But you have to. I understand."

"We'll go on supporting charlatans like Everett Mac-Dougall forever. Literally. And if he ever stops posturing and turns out a decent poem, I'll be mightily surprised. It's a crazy system."

I smile. "I've thought that myself."

The Director jerks himself up to full pouter pigeon height.

"Well, if we must, we must, I suppose. To tell you the truth, I'm not too sure of the approved procedure. There must be one, though. Just give me your card, and I'll have it destroyed."

"The car?"

"Oh, yes. We'll have someone from the garage come round to pick it up. I'll try to make sure the idiots call first."

"It doesn't matter." I open my pocketbook and take out my card carrier. My Artist's Card is in the first slot. I take it out and offer it to the Director, who seems unwilling to take it.

"You won't stop writing, will you?" His little round eyes contract with concern.

"No," I tell him. "I won't stop because the Government doesn't pay me anymore. And I'll hold the rights to my poems now. That'll be nice." I pause. "Well, is that all? Are we through?"

"I wanted to do something to honor you," the Director says. "A big reading. Televised. You deserve it. But the Ministry wouldn't permit it."

"No," I say. "Thank you. Actually, I *do* have a reading coming up, anyway. No television, of course. Small time. It's at the Poets' Guild."

"I can't come, of course," the Director says. "I wish I could. But I'm glad." He crosses the room to where I stand and we shake hands.

"Goodbye," I tell him.

His little round eyes are clouding with tears; really, they are. One tear gathers in the corner of his eye and rolls, stupidly, down the side of his nose and into his moustache. I do not feel sad myself, only sorry for this silly little man. And now do something I am suddenly free to do: I put my arm around the Director's rounded shoulders and give them a gentle, motherly squeeze. "Goodbye," I say again.

I wave at Miss Green on my way out. Reflected in the glass panel of the door as I open it, I see the Director, staring wistfully after me. Walking is easy now. My feet and legs move smoothly, causing no pain. Somehow it feels as though, in surrendering my Artist's Card, I've also shed about twenty years. No such thing has happened, I know, but I give myself over to the illusion of youth, of well-being.

When I arrive at the Ministry of Health, I am still feeling fine. It is more crowded here than at the Ministry of Culture. I pick a line and stand in it. After almost twenty minutes, I reach the head.

"This is my seventy-fifth birthday," I inform the clerk. "I was told to report here."

"Wrong window," the clerk says. "You belong over there." He points to the most distant line, and I see that he is right. The line is made up of old people, like me, a slouching, shuffling, jagged line. I take up a position in it. It moves faster than the others. As I draw nearer to the front, I see that almost everyone is simply turning in his card. The man behind the window gives them something in return; I can't see what. None of the waiters speak to one another, yet there is a general impression of much noise, much talking in the room. Three places from the front, I take out my card case once again, in order to be ready when my turn comes.

The man takes it from me without ceremony, then hands me a red plastic tag on a metal chain.

"The law requires you to wear this on your person at all times."

"What's it for?"

"We call it a 'death's-head,' if you want to know. It's so if you get run over or something, and they take you to a hospital, the doctors'll know right off you're not entitled to any major medical. It saves a lot of time and money."

"I see."

"Well, put it on. There's others waiting. Now you have to go to the Bureau of Geriatrics and get registered with them. Room four-thirteen."

I do not thank the man for my death's-head, but do, since he is watching me, put it over my head and around my neck, then slip it down inside my blouse. It bounces against my breastbone as I walk, and the metal chain feels uncommonly cold around my neck.

The Bureau of Geriatrics, I learn, cannot be entered through the Ministry of Health. It is necessary to go outside, onto the street, and come back in. Although the two buildings are contiguous, they are not connected; I fail to appreciate this bit of architectural symbolism. It is carried on inside the building, too, which doesn't seem to have been quite finished. Here no one has attempted to soften the austerity of the concrete walls. They stretch floor to ceiling, an unrelieved gray, pocked with occasional knots from the pouring forms. The floors, too, are uncovered concrete, and electricity rationing seems to be especially tight here, as the lobby is poorly lit, and many of the fixtures hanging down from the gray ceiling do not have bulbs in them at all.

In the very center of the lobby, there is a round concrete booth, and inside it there is an old man, wearing a guard's uniform. I approach and explain to him what I have to do. From under his official cap, his small bright eyes take stock of me.

"Are you a Witness? You sure don't look like one."

"That's good," I tell him. "I'm not."

"Me either. I could have had them shots, you know. But I wouldn't take 'em. Would not. It's not natural to tamper with things like that."

"I quite agree. Where do I go?"

"You have kids?" he speculates. "You one of them?"

"I have a son."

"Only one? You mean your old man took the shots and you didn't? I never heard of a case like that before."

"We had two children," I tell him reluctantly. "One died."

"Now that *is* too bad," the old man clucks. "Between the devil and the deep blue sea. They always find a way to rip you off, I say."

I begin to realize he will keep me all afternoon if I let him. He is collecting me. I wonder how many stories he has pieced together this way. Each, I'm sure, seems unique, at least to its teller. Probably, none is. There must be patterns—need, response; problem, solution. We humans are a dull race. Out of a universe of possibilities, only a few ever present themselves to us. Given X, we will do Y, or possibly Z, without ever realizing that A through W exist. The old man probably knows about four standard variations.

Still, I sometimes like to think my story *is* unique—at least for the part that fate plays in it. Fate has got to be more creative, more imaginative than our brains conceive or dream of being. I love fate, though it can be cruel and sometimes has been, to me, as I love thunder and lightning because they defy all attempts to govern them and retain the power to surprise. It is nothing I do that makes me different from anyone else; it is the events, random and sometimes savage, that happen *to* me that make me what I am.

But I must not tarry with this gossipy old guard, must not let myself be collected and pinned to his board; I must do what I've come for, though I'm still not entirely sure just what that is.

"Where do I go to register?" I ask again, and reluctantly, the guard points out the way. My footsteps sound behind me as though I am being followed by something more substantial than my own ghost as I cross the cavernous lobby to the door he's shown me. I enter a large waiting room. Its smell confronts me first, a human smell, not rich and tumultuous like the subways, but stale and sad, as though pain itself had some odor, breathed out of the pores of the dying and the about-to-die.

The chairs in the waiting room are molded plastic and resemble cups. They stand on thin metal legs, at careless angles; many people have sat in them today, and morning's orderliness is gone. I speak to a nurse at the front of the room, and she tells me to sit and wait. Only a handful of others are waiting with me, and I study them, wondering about them, and wondering if they wonder about me.

Maybe not. Each seems absorbed in his or her own pain. An ancient African man, his face worn like old leather, bends so far forward in his chair that his chin almost touches his knees. He is asleep, perhaps. A fat woman, arms big as loaves of bread, waits too, buttocks spilling over the edges of her cupped chair. As I sit, I find my own hips have room to spare. The people around me seem very old.

At last a uniformed nurse comes in and calls my name. She leads me to a small cubicle, rather like those in the Clinics, and tells me to undress.

"Why?"

"You're registering today, aren't you? We take some tests to assess your physical condition. It's standard procedure. All your files will be transferred here."

She leaves me alone. The door is slightly open, and I can hear passing footsteps and the sounds, though not the sense, of distant conversations. I take off my shoes, my blouse and skirt, then look around for a gown to put on in their place. I can find none, so I wait in slip and pants for the nurse to reappear.

What happens next, though it takes a long time, is that a medic arrives, dressed in the customary white pajamas, and smiles his perfunctory doctor's smile at me. He carries a chart and consults it.

"Harmon, Mrs. Eve?"

I nod.

"What seems to be the trouble?"

"Old age," I tell him. "I'm here to register."

"I see," he says. "Damn nurses. All right. Finish undressing, please."

I do not want to finish undressing in this cold building, in front of this indifferent man. My body is seventy-five years old; the muscles have slackened and the skin grown taut. But still, it is my body, serviceable, cared for. I have tried to keep trim and can still remember days when my undressing was a matter of no indifference. Very slowly, I take off my slip and step out of my underpants. It pains me to display my sexual parts, parts that have given pleasure and received it, to the contempt of this perfectly preserved, totally bored man. He looks at me the way mechanics at the garage survey my car.

"You seem to be in pretty good shape. Lie down."

More humiliated still, I do. He finds a vein in my inner

elbow and inserts a syringe, ungently, to collect a plastic bagful of my blood, while he probes the private places of my body with various of his instruments—into my vagina, my mouth and throat, finally the anal opening, scraping off cells and smearing them on slides to tell their story later, under microscopes. He palpates my breasts. My nipples stand up under his touch, and I curse them for their stupidity. It has been too long since my husband touched them, and they are hungry for contact even now, on my seventy-fifth birthday. I wonder if doctors notice such things; I hope they do not.

The medic makes marks on his clipboard-mounted chart and labels each slide with a number. The plastic bag is full of my blood now, dark and bloated, with bubbles near the top. He pulls the needle from my arm and wipes away a little pearl of blood that oozes from the puncture. I raise my arm to stop the flow. The bag is labeled with my number, too.

Finally he tells me to stand up.

"Go down the hall, three doors to your left. We'll weigh and measure you, and take some X-rays."

"This is a very thorough physical. I'm surprised."

"The last one," he says tersely. "To patients seventy-five and more, we can only give palliative treatment. No surgery, no chemotherapy. You understand? Just pain-killers."

"Why bother with the physical then?"

"For the computer," he tells me. "It extends the data base. It's helpful in research. All of your health records will be fed in, along with a detailed autopsy report."

"I see."

"Yes. Being able to access such massive data has enabled research to advance incredibly. Much more efficient than trial and error. If you create the right program, you can test out virtually any hypothesis. You don't have to set up experiments and then wait fifty years to find out the results. It's all right there."

"You're interested in research yourself, aren't you?"

For the first time, the medic actually looks, not at my discrete anatomical parts, but at my face.

"Yes, I am. It's what I want to do. What I *will* do, when I finish my training here. How did you know?"

I smile. "Lucky guess. I suppose this is good training."

"Depressing," he says. "Now down the hall."

"Is there some kind of robe I could wear? Something?"

He looks up briefly from the chart. "It's not necessary," he says.

For a moment I'm poised between acute embarrassment and anger. I want to protest. I want to shout at him: Don't you know who I am? Even as I think it, I know I am no one. I climb down from the table and draw my thin, insulted poet's body up proudly as I can and walk past him to the door. My posture is so good my spine aches from stretching. Inside my head, I say over and over again: I am a human being. I am me. And walk naked down the hall, past three doors, and turn left, into a large room where my carcass is measured and weighed, my lungs and other organs scanned and photographed, electronically explored for the greater good of medical research.

When I return to the cubicle, the medic is still there. "You can get dressed now," he says.

With clothing on, I have more confidence.

"I don't really know the procedures here," I say. "Do I get some kind of card? What do I do if I get sick?"

"You can come as often as you like. We're free to dispense an unlimited number of various drugs to geriatrics. Including narcotics and hallucinogens, if you're interested. There's a substance called LSD, for example, a chemical compound that causes powerful psychic experiences. They used to use it in death therapy. Would you like to try it?" He looks at me again.

"No, thank you. At least, not right now."

"Suit yourself. You can ask for it anytime."

"What about a card?"

"All you need's your red tag. Your number is on it."

I lift the plastic tag to examine it more carefully. There *is* a small white number on the side I've placed against my chest.

"That's all the identification you'll need," he says. "You were told to wear it at all times?"

I nod.

"That's all, then. If the tests show any pathology, we'll be in touch with you."

Without saying goodbye, he leaves. I put my shoes on and finish buttoning my blouse, then leave.

The waiting room is empty now, and the digichron reads five-oh-three. Much later than I thought. I'd hoped to beat Marcus home and treat myself to an hour's reverie in my blue chair before my living husband was upon me. I much prefer the memory to the present man. He loved me then, and I knew it, and loved him back, reserving nothing. That made many hard things bearable, in our shared past. I am no longer so sure of anything as I used to be of that.

3

They're clapping. My god, they're clapping. For the first time I look at them, as people, and they smile back at me. I haven't humiliated myself. The practice in my bedroom, in front of the bathroom mirror, has paid off a thousand-fold. And these are *people*, not toilet bowls. Astounding, that's what it is. Miraculous. Unreal.

My face is very hot. My hands are trembling, now that it's over. The room swims with people, and other voices replace my voice, filling the terrible, attentive silence of a few minutes ago. I am not sure what I'm supposed to do.

The Director himself emerges from the crowd to shake my hand.

"Well done," he says. "Nice job. Welcome aboard."

I beam at him. "Was it really all right?"

"Excellent," he says. "After you calmed down, you gave a fine reading. Just fine."

A small knot of people, strangers to me, assembles around the Director. I assume they are waiting to speak to him, but when he moves away, they remain, wanting to shake *my* hand, to talk to me. I barely hear their words, though I try hard to listen, so I can store their comments away for later review.

"Thank you, thank you," is all I can say.

A tall blond man with a cleft in his chin, aggressively good-looking and vaguely familiar, elbows his way through the rest to stand in front of me.

"Very nice," he murmurs softly, and takes my hand in both of his so ceremoniously that if I were less excited, I would find it awkward. "Tell me. In the poem about your father, is the green water a symbol of death?"

I search my mind. "No, I don't think so. I didn't mean it to be."

"What did you mean it to be?" he asks.

I think again. "Green water."

The blond man laughs a suave baritone laugh. "You have a sense of humor, too. How delightful."

I smile weakly. That was no joke. Green water is green water.

"We must get together soon," he continues, still holding fast to my hand. "I'm Everett MacDougall. You might say we're members of the same club. Welcome."

"Thank you, Mr. MacDougall. Thank you for coming."

"Of course. I have a feeling I'll be privileged to come to many more."

"Well, I hope so."

"But I mustn't keep you from your other admirers. I'll be in touch." He bows over my hand before returning it to me. "Till we meet again."

MacDougall is well known already, and I'm flattered, but don't, in all honesty, like the man. I wish he had been more interested in my poems than in—what? Does he find me attractive? But I do not like him.

And there *are* other admirers; a mass of faces bobs before my tired, burning eyes. A seemingly inexhaustible supply of admirers. I cannot think about poetry myself, but wish some one of these strangers would say something about my poems.

"I really liked your reading," they say.

"Welcome," they say.

"Good performance," they say.

"Good luck."

"I like the way you use negative space. How what *doesn't* happen or what *isn't* there becomes as important as what is."

I start to mumble my standard thanks, but then the words sink in and I look up to see who says them.

"I'm a scientist myself," he goes on. "It's different, in specifics, but the concept is very important in my work, too."

I focus on his face. It fills my vision, suddenly becomes a little larger than life, and I can see every pore and every whisker on it. A kind of dizziness comes over me, and my senses are singing at their acutest pitch. I realize I am making a picture of this man's face that will stay in my brain for a very long time. Perhaps forever.

"Please tell me it's intentional," he says, "and not just something I made up because it's on my mind."

I find it hard to talk. "Oh, it is," I tell him. "I never called it that—negative space. I guess I've always thought of it as the holes. Or the invisible tensions, or something. A kind of ghost." I stop short, embarrassed. I've never told anyone about the ghosts in my poems and feel very silly, suddenly, speaking so earnestly to a stranger.

"They're nice," he says. "And real. I'm glad you see them."

"So am I."

Peripherally I am aware of others waiting to speak to me, moving restlessly to convey their impatience, which at last outweighs whatever need they have of me. Soon we are almost alone in the big room, except for a few maintenance men straightening chairs, collecting litter. My pocketbook leans up against the podium and I pick it up, making ready to leave.

"Well," I say, and can think of nothing to follow. His name, my mind says. You don't know his name. Must find it out. I want to seem independent, but am afraid of being cold; don't want to make a fool of myself, but want to know this man.

He loves someone else, my inner voice cautions. He must. How I wish I were good at flirting—one of those self-possessed women, confident of their appeal, who can make things run smoothly and never lose the advantage.

And then, not smoothly, but sincerely, not elegantly, but, thank god, he does it, he says, "My name is Marcus Harmon. Could I possibly persuade you to go somewhere with me? For coffee? A drink?"

"Eve. There you are. I've been looking all over for you."

The man's face changes in front of my eyes to become the face of a much older man, handsome still but lined and coarsened, worn.

"Marcus Harmon," I say. "That's a funny name."

"What?"

"Your name. It's funny. It sounds like a made-up name."

"Oh," he says. "That again. You've made fun of my

name for fifty years. You bitch." He leans over and kisses me on the cheek, a dry, chaste, friendly kiss. "Happy birthday, Eve. And dinner's ready. I asked Suli to make something special tonight."

Slowly I come back. The transition wearies me. "Oh, Marcus. It's you."

"You were expecting Shakespeare? Of course it's me. I was worried about you. Aren't you feeling well?"

"Me? I feel fine. Really. I just sat down for a minute to relax." I laugh. "It was a rather brutal day."

"It's past seven," Marcus says. "I didn't think to look for you up here."

Marcus is friendly, solicitous, a little too enthusiastic, so that I sense the whole is forced. I can feel sharp edges in the smooth flow of his words, and I wish he would show them to me now as he used to. There was a time when I was frightened by acrimony, afraid to disagree with my young husband, as though any small fissure between us might become a canyon of disharmony. And learned, as time went on, that there was nothing to fear in temporary lacks of synchrony—that life, in fact, is largely asynchronous. We made peace with each other's cycles, finally, not by forcing them to coincide, but by learning to accept some lack of fit.

Marcus told me what he was feeling, and when, until fear took another form entirely, and became the fear of his *not* telling me. I have been married to Marcus for fifty years, and now the last, the worst of my fears has come to pass. There are things in my husband's mind I cannot guess, and I cannot guess them because they are deliberately hidden from me.

"Come on," he says again, like a father who has, after much thought, brought home a new toy to his child, only to be met with indifference.

I take pity on him and get up from my chair, smiling at him while I look for a line of dialogue to fit his play. "What's for dinner?" I ask. "Or is that a surprise?" There. I have refined the plot a bit, suggested a new scene we can play on our way to the dining room.

Marcus takes his cue. "You'll see," he says, mysterious. "You'll like it. If you'll hurry up and come."

Our secret carries us downstairs in good humor; now each of us has a position to take that drives our chatter on.

A bowl of roses blooms on the table, warm against the white cloth, the white dishes with their silver rims, the cold gleam of crystal glasses and the silver candelabrum. The table is very beautiful. Although its beauty comes from things I am accustomed to take lightly, whose virtues I normally discount, still I am pleased that these things belong to me, and are beautiful, arranged just as they ought to be in honor of my birthday.

Marcus seats me at one end of the table and takes up his own place facing me. He nods at the silver bell beside my water glass, wanting me to summon Suli with his special meal. I have rung this bell thousands of times, but today my fingers are unwilling to take it up. I would rather call for Suli by her name, or even serve dinner myself, than shake this bell to call her, like a dog.

"Go on," Marcus says. "Everything is ready. It's waiting for you."

Reluctantly, I ring the bell. Its sweet tinkle sounds like an insult to me, and I put it down quickly. Across the snowy tablecloth, past the wild blush of the roses, I see Marcus' deep and steady smile.

"The roses are lovely," I tell him. "Thank you."

His smile pre-existed my words, but serves as response. Suli comes in from the kitchen with a silver tray. She serves the meal expertly, and her silence extends to us, so that it seems we are waiting to continue our conversation until she's gone. In reality, I'm grateful that her presence puts off the need for talk.

She moves between us with her bowls, her serving spoons, depositing shapely mounds of plump peas and halfmoon mushrooms on our plates, pink slabs of beef with brown edges and a darker juice that wells up in the ridges of the meat. She serves us rolls with silver tongs. Saliva springs up under my tongue at the sight, the aroma of the food. Ascetic pretensions to the contrary, I will enjoy this meal. All is fresh, all is real. To put it together has cost money, which Marcus has in abundance, and time and care that must have come from Suli. One cannot always find such things at any price.

So I am genuinely grateful to them both. I want to show Suli my appreciation, but can't catch her eye. In Marcus' presence, she conceals her humanity to an even greater extent than he ignores it. The thought of asking her to join us at the too big, too empty table flits across my mind. I wish there were something or someone that could fill the space looming between my husband and myself. But to ask Suli would be absurd. It would embarrass them both. There being no convenient stopgap, I must shout across the distance at my once-best friend.

"Jason stopped in today," I tell him, when Suli is gone. Marcus' reply is noncommittal—a noise.

"Yes," I go on, "Jason is good about the formalities." Then I go on some more, farther than I should. "It's the remarkable lack of content that always astounds me."

Marcus stops his fork between plate and mouth to look at me, but says nothing until the pink cube of beef has finished its journey, been chewed and swallowed down. The meat is such a rare treat that, despite the irritation I know he feels, he savors it, and a look of pleasure passes across his face, staying his rejoinder and, probably, softening it.

"Don't be so hard on Jason," he says at last. "He *did* come, after all. He takes his obligations very seriously."

"Yes, indeed." How can I tell him I would rather have a son who forgot me entirely for months, even years at a time, a real blackguard of a son, so long as when he thought of me, it was with love?

"He's very well thought of in his Ministry," Marcus says. "None better."

"A prince of the slave trade."

"Eve! I don't understand you."

"Of course you do." Something is driving me to tread on dangerous ground. We never talk anymore about the choice we made so many years ago, although before it was made, we talked about it incessantly, for hours, days on end. Today my note has come due. Perhaps it's self-indulgent, but I feel *entitled* to talk about it. I feel, too, Marcus' aversion to the subject, more painful to him these past few years than any other. Because of Jason, I am going to die.

As I think this, I become aware that I've used the pronoun "I" where "we" should be.

"The peas are done to perfection," Marcus says. "And the beef's superb. I must remember to compliment Suli."

But I am in no mood to let it pass. Tonight, for my birthday, I would rather have truth than roses. I am willing to go to great lengths to get me some.

"It's not that I mind dying," I tell him. "But I'm at the point where one sees some of the disadvantages of mortality." I pause to let my husband answer, go on when he does not. "The natural cycle of things seems very attractive when you're young—the old giving way to make room for the new. Of course! How sensible. But now I begin to perceive the frustration of seeing that the new generation has less right to live than oneself. It's painful to be made obsolete by a horse's ass."

To be just, it's possible that Shakespeare's mother felt the same. It's probably equally unpleasant to be supplanted by genius, or by goodness, as by mediocrity—I can't be sure. As a young woman, I was certain it would be easy to meet death graciously, without profanity or whimpering; I surely would have too much dignity to try to evade it, would not cringe or grovel before the scythe. Now, about to be reaped, I feel a good deal differently.

I wait for Marcus' answer. His face colors slightly; he will not look up from his plate. Instead of anger or philosophy, I seem to have called up embarrassment. Incredibly, he pretends not to have heard me at all.

"How do *you* feel about it, Marcus?"

He looks at me with theatrical innocence. "About what, Eve?"

"About dying, Marcus."

The china rings when he puts down his fork. "I don't really think about it much," he says. "There's no point. You shouldn't either. We're both strong and healthy."

It seems impossible to me that so thoughtful a man does not think about dying. The motives for his evasion are not clear to me. Somehow I want to make him share the day's discomfort. "Do you know what they make you do?" The question is purely rhetorical. "I'll tell you. First they take away your professional card. The Director cried today, taking mine. And then"—here I pull the red tag out from under my blouse and wave it at him—"then, at the Ministry of Health, they give you this. And do you know what it's called?" I have given too many poetry readings in my time not to make good use of a pause here. "It's a death's-head, Marcus. You have to wear it all the time, so that if something happens to you, they'll know they're not supposed to save you."

I let the tag drop back against my chest and lean forward, elbows on the table, demanding some response. I think I want to make my husband cry.

He does not. "Well," he says, "the government didn't choose for you. It just gave you the choice."

Pronouns. That's it. There has been something wrong with all our pronouns lately. The we's have split up into you's and I's, as though the decision we made together now applies only to me. This happens in my speech, as well as in his; my choice of language warns me that something is amiss.

Suddenly my desire to get Marcus is gone. I don't want to hurt him or make him uncomfortable anymore. A new desire, just as strong, replaces it, but I do not know the name for what I want. Tears gather in my eyes, stinging my lids, and I become limp and meek, like a deflated balloon.

I want to know what it is that Marcus and Jason and my unconscious seem to know. I want my husband to take me in his arms and hold me tight. I want to be close to him, so close I can feel his thoughts. I want to cut away the tumor that's grown on the body of our marriage and make it viable again.

I want these things desperately. Marcus, at his end of the table, looks handsome and composed, untroubled by my fears. His hands as they cut the beef are strong and sure. He holds himself erect, as though it cost no effort to do so, and his eyes are clear, move quickly. It is hard to imagine he is only four months younger than I. This man is vigorous, even at day's end, when my own energy is in short supply.

It would be impossible not to resent his vitality a little, when my own back aches, as though each year past fifty had lashed a kilogram's dead weight to me, and my eyes feel sandy just from being so long open.

"You're not eating, Eve." Marcus says, looking up.

"Come on. The meat's delicious. And who knows when we'll be able to get it again."

"Who knows?" I echo dully.

"Please enjoy it," he says, with the first emotion in his voice I have been able to believe for quite some time. "I tried hard to make this a special meal."

"The Last Supper."

"You *are* morbid tonight," he says. "Today wasn't easy, I suppose." His face softens, and his compassion warms me so I feel I might melt.

"It wasn't," I tell him. "I didn't know it would be like that. You know, I'd pictured today for a long time." My voice breaks unexpectedly, under pressure of tears recently fought back, now rising up again. "I was going to be brave, and even flippant, and show the bureaucrats I didn't give a damn. I wanted to give off such peace that all the immortals would envy me, and wonder what I knew that they didn't. For fifty years, I planned to be very *happy* today. Serene, and strong, and beautiful." Now I begin to laugh as well as cry, making a little hysterical rainbow in the dining room. "And you know what? I was lonely and afraid and ridiculous. No better and no different than anybody else who's going to die. The clerks stared at me, and the Director felt sorry for me, and the doctor at the Bureau of Geriatrics looked at me as if I were already dead." I stop for breath, stare at my husband. "Oh, Marcus. Why was it like that?"

His face becomes much more the face I love, planes and angles rounding into a softness, and sensitivity I've found rare in men. Suddenly Marcus looks older too, and I'm grateful for that. It makes me feel less aged and ugly, less expendable.

"I'm sorry," he says. "Forgive me, Eve. I should have come with you. I shouldn't have let you go through that alone." He stops to reflect. "I don't know why I didn't offer. I suppose because I don't like to think about it myself."

As my man turns vulnerable, I gather strength and, as always, become ashamed of my complaints, sorry to have put him in the wrong.

"Don't be silly," I tell him, wiping the tears from my

cheeks. "I wouldn't have let you anyway. I know how important this project is. Besides, it wasn't *that* bad. I survived it, didn't I?"

"But it hurt you," Marcus says. "It made you cry. I don't like that."

Oh, how much he sounds like the old Marcus. How I love to hear this tenderness—excessive tenderness—in his voice. It wraps me in a warm, soft blanket, protects me, in excess of my need for protection. I love it, and have missed it. Still, it is not my habit to let him feel he's failed me. For so many years I have been his apologist that it comes naturally now; I always see his actions in the best light possible.

"It's my own damn fault," I tell him. "*You* can't feel bad because reality didn't happen to live up to my elaborate fantasies."

"Still, I should have known."

"Don't be absurd. At seventy-five, I should be able to look out for myself. And you know you've always told me it's better just to let things come. Well, you're right. My fantasies betray me all the time."

"They also make you who you are. They make you a poet, for one thing. And a mother."

The shadow passes over both of us. I smile at Marcus, and just a touch of the happy sadness, or sad happiness, I have always expected to feel today colors my smile. For a moment, I let myself pretend that things have come to pass as I projected them. Then, overwhelmingly, I know they have not, and begin to cry in earnest.

From the far end of the table, Marcus calls my name.

I am ashamed of myself for blubbering like this. Nor can I stop.

"Are you sure you're not ill?"

I nod at him, and he lets me cry in silence for a while, respecting my sorrow, whatever it may be. But I don't want to be given room; that is not why I'm crying. No, I have too much room, these days, to entertain my death. I want my husband to fill the space with his warmth, to shut out loneliness with his love. Why do men never learn to read the meanings of tears? Perhaps they shed too few themselves to understand the subtleties of crying. At any rate,

I must tell my husband what my signal means, and find it is not so easy as it used to be.

"Marcus," I say, genuinely meek, "may I sit by you? Can I touch you? I need that very much, I think."

I do not move until he answers me.

"Sure. Of course."

As I stand, so does he. Each of us, in going to the other, starts to walk up a different side of the table, me left, and Marcus right. We stop and stare at each other across the twelve pink heads of the roses, then laugh.

"Your place or mine?" he asks.

"Yours."

So we meet at Marcus' end of the table and move close, without a meeting of the eyes. It has always struck me that when people embrace, they look in opposite directions and never share a view. In a poem once, I used it as a metaphor for the essential separation between people, even, especially lovers. Perhaps it's not that at all. I don't know.

My husband's arms feel good around me, taste better than the beef did to my tongue. This hunger is more real to me than any other, and I cling to him, as a woman starved must cling. He strokes my hair.

We say nothing for a long time. Then Marcus asks, "What can I do to make it better for you?" And I sense that he would really like to know.

"Be with me," I tell him. "Touch me. Hold me. It needn't be all night. Not even a very long time, if there are other things you want to do. Just for a little while."

"Fine," Marcus says, to the top of my head. "All right. Shall I ask Suli to bring your birthday cake upstairs?"

Marcus frees himself and walks down the table to ring the bell. Suli appears at once, and Marcus makes his request. Soon she brings all we will need on a tray.

"Were there any calls this afternoon?" I ask before she goes, because I want to prove I am in control of myself by now.

"Just one, Mrs. Harmon. A Mr. John Powell."

"Thank you, Suli."

She hesitates, and I raise my eyebrows at her, inviting her to speak.

"Is that the poet, Mrs. Harmon?"

"Yes, Suli, it is. Mr. Powell's asked me to read at the Poets' Guild this week."

"It was worth trying," Marcus says.

"It certainly was."

"Are you going to do it, Mrs. Harmon?"

"Yes. I am."

I do not look at Marcus. Suli leaves us alone with the cake. "Well, are you going to carry it, or shall I?"

"When did you decide to read at the Poets' Guild? That's pretty political."

"Poetry isn't political. At least, mine isn't."

"There could be trouble. I wish you'd said no."

"Why? There's nothing they can take away from me. Except maybe my life. And the last I heard, poetry wasn't considered a capital crime. Not even bad poetry."

"Well, you've got a point."

"Better than that, Marcus. I've got a reading Thursday night. Let's go upstairs."

"Aren't you going to call this Powell?" There is a slight edge in Marcus' voice.

"No, I've had enough excitement for one day. Let's get on with the party."

Marcus reaches the second floor considerably ahead of me. My breath is coming fast when I join him in the hall.

"Your place or mine?" he asks again.

"Yours, please. For a little while."

"All right."

Our rooms adjoin, but could not be more different. Each has a double bed; the theory was that we could each have space to ourselves, but sleep together. For a long time, we alternated beds, or simply settled in wherever we happened to be when sleep overtook us. In the last few years, we have slept mostly alone. I can't remember precisely when this became the pattern, or why. I don't like sleeping apart, but, taking it for Marcus' preference, do not complain, perhaps because I didn't want to make him say something I didn't want to hear.

Marcus puts the tray down on his big desk, the desk that belonged to his father, displacing several lexavision discs to make room. Suli has put brandy glasses and a decanter of dessert wine on the tray, and Marcus serves this first.

"Sit down. On the bed, if you like."

I do, tentative as a college girl in her boyfriend's room for the first time. It is hard to remember how casually I once put myself to bed here, how much at home I was. Once there was a mixing of our possessions, little colonies of Eve in Marcus' den, pairs of his shoes beside my bed. Now I find no signs of myself in his expensive spartan lair. His room is neat, neater probably than it would be if I were often here. So I sit as a visitor while Marcus cuts the cake, remembering not to put my shoes on the bedspread, sorry for the wrinkles I will make in the tautly pulled bed-clothes.

He brings me cake and wine, then goes back to the desk for his own. He sits on the opposite side of the bed, and uses the nightstand for a table. I am shy, as his guest, and wait for him to speak.

He raises his glass to mine.

"To your birthday," he toasts.

Our tiny glasses touch, ring. We drink from them, look-ing down. A thin orange stripe runs through the green-brown plaid of the bedspread; I follow it until it disappears beneath my husband's thigh.

"Try the cake."

I break off a corner with my fork and find rich yellow cake inside the case of swirling sugar frosting. The textures contrast nicely, but the taste is very sweet—the kind of unrelieved sweetness that delights children but is soon out-grown in favor of more subtle flavors. I swallow my bite of cake and a quick, unexpected shudder passes through me.

"Someone's walking on my grave."

"What?"

"Old wives' tale," I tell him. "When people shivered for no good reason, that's what they used to say."

"Did they believe it?"

"How should I know?"

There are no graveyards anymore, no cemeteries for a poet's morbid muse to wander through. Most of the old ones have been reclaimed, the land used for government buildings, or sometimes parks. The stones of the famous have been preserved in museums, the others used again in the foundations of new buildings. Since so few people die these days, there is little use for graveyards, and I suspect they were an unpleasant reminder to the immortals of the cruelty of the old nature they have defied. Those few who choose mortality are disposed of quietly and without ceremony, in some much more efficient way. I have never troubled to find out what it is, though I know that domestics, when they die, are incinerated in special furnaces that leave little residue.

"You know," I say to Marcus, "the elegy's become an obsolete form. As a poet, I rather regret it. Look how many great poems came out of grief."

"A lot of things have become obsolete," he says. "More will."

"Such as?" I sense that he has specific things in mind, but will not say them.

"Oh, I don't know. It's just that when you make such a massive change in the ground rules of society, the shock waves go on for centuries. In ways it's impossible to foresee. What a time the sociologists will have a hundred years from now, when they find their old theories torn to shreds. It'll take them that long, at least, to figure out that something's wrong. It'll be quite amusing to watch."

"No doubt. What staggers me is the thought of one person growing and changing indefinitely. My god. What poems would I write at a hundred and twenty?"

"I think," Marcus says, sipping his wine, "I think that dying is absolutely essential to poets. Not death itself, of course, but knowing it's coming. Necessary impetus. Why do today what can be put off a decade or two, while you rest on your laurels? You've been astoundingly prolific. Contrast someone like MacDougall."

"Oh, well. MacDougall." I don't like to think about MacDougall, arrested in early middle age, eternally callow, writing bad poems until the end of time, when I've become only an image on a lexavision disc. The phony. I sigh at the injustice of it; it tweaks my ego. Thinking this, I laugh at myself, smile at Marcus. My right knee has crept up on the bed, my body turned to look at Marcus across the bed. Whatever has been so tightly coiled inside me when I am with him lately has begun to unwind a little, bringing back some of the old easiness. It doesn't feel quite as it used to, quite as it should, yet it is close enough that I'm encouraged, full of hope. Maybe I'm not so alone as I've imagined myself to be, or maybe the estrangement has been my fault after all. At any rate, I'm comfortable now, and ease melts into sleepiness quickly, for a woman my age.

"Do you mind if I lie back?"

"Not at all," Marcus says. "Of course not. Here."

He leans over to pull a pillow out of the covering spread and props it up against the bedstead behind me. Gratefully I lean back into it, catching Marcus' hand before he can pull it away. I have always loved my husband's hands, large but slender, honest-looking, kind. As I hold his hand now, I examine it closely, seeing familiar shapes and creases, familiar lines, and also the changes of the last few years— new lines, new scars, a little thickening at the finger joints. Then I press his hand to my lips and kiss the back of it, glad to be enfranchised to touch him again, to be free to love him in my own no doubt silly way.

"Tell me about the project, Marcus. Catch me up. You hardly tell me anything about your work anymore."

"Sorry," he says. "Most of it's secret. Not that there's anything sinister about it. It's just the government and its peculiar ideas about what's important."

"But it *is* important," I urge. "It must be. You certainly take it seriously."

"Well, sure," Marcus says, noncommittal. "What do you expect? It's my baby. This is the first time ever I've launched a priority-A study. Unlimited funds. You can't imagine what a difference that makes, Eve."

"No, I guess I can't, really. Having been in the world's cheapest line of work myself."

"It's night and day. Everything can be done right, without the usual compromises and equivocations. And you wouldn't believe how much faster everything happens when you've got the money to spend."

For a moment I stop being selfish, and it occurs to me that Marcus' race with time is far more painful than my own. I don't need an Artist's Card to write, but Marcus quite literally *needs* his card to continue with his work. Some of the equipment he uses has been designed especially for him, to serve his needs, according to his specifications. Not exactly the kind of thing we could replicate in the basement when he's retired. I decide to say something I've been thinking for quite a while.

"Maybe they'll make an exception for you, Marcus. Extend your card, at least until this project's done. I know they're rigid, but my god, you're the best they've got, or are likely to have." I'm quite excited by the time I stop, sure that the Ministry of Science could be convinced, if only I can convince Marcus himself first. "Isn't it worth a try? Your work means so much."

He answers me gravely. "I have reason to believe my card will be extended, Eve. Perhaps indefinitely. Certainly until this project is complete."

"Marcus, how wonderful! Congratulations. You deserve it." Another thought follows. "Why didn't you tell me?"

Slowly, carefully, he replaces his plate on the bed table. The fork, tines down, chatters a little.

"It hasn't been certain till very recently," he says.

"That doesn't matter. I could at least have shared the suspense. No wonder you've seemed abstract." No wonder. I'm relieved. This, now settled, is what's been on his mind.

"Have I been? I'm sorry. Actually, I've known for some time, Eve. I didn't want to tell you. It seems so unfair— that I can keep on working while they take your card away."

"Marcus, Marcus. You know it's not the same. To the government, art's embellishment. It always has been. They're not going to pay me any longer than they have to. With you it's quite different. They *need* you."

"They need you too, Eve. If only they knew."

"Well, they don't. And I've had plenty of time to get used to it. On the other hand, people do. The Poets' Guild has asked me to join them."

"Will you?" Marcus asks.

"Maybe I will. Especially now I know *you'll* still be working. You won't have any more time to spend with me than you ever have." There is an edge in my voice I didn't mean to put there. I wish it could be taken back.

"I may be able to ease off a bit, Eve. I'm quite a senior citizen by now."

"That's all right, Marcus. The point is, I don't really have to stop either. I can go on. It wouldn't hurt you,

Marcus, if I get involved with the Guild? If they need you enough to extend your card, what I do can't make any difference? Can it?"

"No, dear. Don't worry. I doubt it can hurt me at all. It may give Jason apoplexy. But you can handle that."

It is warm in Marcus' room, and his voice soothes me. I have not slept well lately, and my dreams, when I have, have dwelt on estrangement, made it worse perhaps. Feeling in accord once more makes me want to sleep, makes me sure I will be able to. I lie back deeper into the pillow.

"It's been a hell of a day, Marcus. I'm worn out. Do you mind if I take a little nap?"

"Of course not. Go ahead." He takes a comforter from the foot of his bed, unfurls it and spreads it over me. It is a long time since I have felt so loved, so well looked after. My husband kisses me on the forehead. My heavy lids drift down.

"Lie down with me a while. I'd love to feel you close by."

"Maybe later, Eve," he says gently. "I'm not at all tired now, and there's some reading I want to do. I may even run back to the lab for an hour or so. You ring Suli if you want anything, okay?"

"Okay." I'm too overcome by sleep to argue. "But come back. Come back when you're done."

I feel him kiss me again, lightly, and soon after, I hear the careful closing of the door.

When I awake the next morning, it is in my own bed.

4

Like the wakings of girlhood, those of age have become a special, private time. For so many years between, there was a man beside me in the bed, to be touched and kissed and talked to when I opened my eyes. Now, as before, there is only me and my own thoughts, perhaps a book beside me that has lain all night under the blankets, put down only when sleep stole over me, waiting to be taken up again, or a Mylar notebook and stylus, with a presleep poem waiting to be evaluated in the harsher light of morning.

This morning there are neither books nor notebooks, but I awake with a feeling of purpose—excitement over Thursday's reading, and a desire to make it as good as I possibly can. I have never read at the Poets' Guild before, and as this new era of my life begins, it brings new challenges. Age *does* have limitations; I can no longer, for example, choose a program in an hour, as I used to do. Not only are there too many poems to choose from, but too many holes in my concentration, too, and I must give myself ample time to make my choices.

These are compensated, in a way, by a certain lack of fear. It takes a great deal of energy to be nervous or apprehensive, and I have spent too much of myself on both. As I learn to conserve my resources, though, I learn, too, to let what is going to happen, happen, since it will anyway, in spite of what I do. Instead of worrying in advance, I save that energy to help me deal with things as they unfold.

This morning I am neither hungry nor thirsty, and have no pressing business that must be carried on. Instead of going downstairs for breakfast right away, or asking Suli to bring it to my room, I decide I'll sit awhile and think, leaf through some poems, while the morning still belongs to me. There are copies of my poems, all, on Mylar in my desk. Over time, my book has become fat and full, turned into two books, three, five; currently, there are seven books in all, one for each decade of my life. They give me both pleasure and pain, as one's children ought to.

To be honest, in fact, these books are more my children than Jason has ever been, for all my great expectations, and all my mythic dreams. This is a metaphor, and yet is not. I am not so fond or senile as to believe they love me, or are anything more than they are—words, mine, laid down in rhythms, also mine, on sheets of Mylar. They are nothing more than that. But nothing less, either.

I get up, put on my dressing gown, and take my seven books from their place in the desk. They make a neat stack beside my blue chair, more than half a meter tall. I take a pad and stylus, too, to keep notes as my order begins to emerge, and settle in comfortably, my gown easy around me. Where to start? Where?

Delicately. Ever so delicately. My meaning is subtle; I must not crush it with heavy words, must not tread carelessly among these finest of distinctions. I *know* what I want to say. Could explain it, clearly, awkwardly, in conversation, so you would know what I meant in your head.

And now, by this window, distracted by the slight, scented breeze that ruffles the edges of my page, lifts the ends of my hair, by the shaft of beautiful, chill sunlight that seems to chase my stylus across the page, among all these treacherous distractions, I am trying to find a way to say what I want to say so that you feel it with your heart. Yes, I want to set you up, manipulate you, a little, touch rather than teach you. And so I string my images, weave my words carefully. Very carefully. Is this the one? The only one? One that will do well enough until a better comes along.

There is a knock at my door, a crisp and forthright knock.

"Who is it?" I call, my eyes still on the page, the stylus forming the last curves of that last word.

"It is I, Mother."

My son's voice. He is eight years old and doesn't say
"It's me"—through no fault of my own. It is an unexpected
visit; I put the poem by, willingly, even a little excited.

Small and erect, he stands before my door as I open
it to him.

"You could have just come in, Jason. I don't mind."

"I don't like to interrupt you," Jason says. The precision
of his final consonants is strange in his high boy's voice.

"Well, I'm glad you've come," I tell him. Reaching out
my arm, I try to shepherd him inside. He enters the room,
evading my touch.

"I've cut my finger, Mother. It should be cleaned and
bandaged."

"Oh dear. Let me see it." I move closer, instinctively,
and, equally by nature, he moves away even as he holds
out his injured hand. A red halfmoon outlines a crescent-
shaped cut on the third finger of his right hand.

"Let me see it, Jason. Is it very deep?"

Reluctantly he comes near enough to let me take his
hand in mine, and examine his finger. The bright blood,
arterial blood, and the torn flesh do not seem to belong
on this pale and shapely hand, so exquisitely groomed for
a small boy's hand, with its shaped fingernails (no dirt
underneath them), its pallor perfect and unstained. Jason's
skin is cool to the touch.

"Deep enough to hurt, I bet." I look into his cool blue
eyes. No tears in them, no pain. He bites his lip, though;
the finger does hurt him.

"Well, let's clean it up," I say. "Come to the bathroom
with me."

He sits on the toilet, his feet together, toes in line, while
I wet a clean cloth and put mild soap on it. My hands
tremble a little. My son has come to me for help. It makes
my heart sing; it makes me officious. I want to soothe him,
without offending. The part in his silky brown hair makes a
fine white line across his scalp below. I squat at his feet
and daub at his cut with my cloth. As blood is wiped away,
more rises up to fill the cut, to repaint the red crescent on
his white, white flesh.

"Am I hurting you, Jason? Tell me if I do."

He shakes his head.

I break a phial of antiseptic and let its sterile contents pour into the wound. A few drops roll around the back side of his finger and fall to his trousers, dark, round spots. He brushes at them with his free hand. A bandage now. Where are they? Damn! Too eager, I drop them. The metal box clatters on the tile floor, and Jason winces a little at the sound. My child loves harmony, pursues a perfection that is quite beyond my reach. I try, I try, but always, somehow, fall a little short.

"Sorry, Jason." I stoop to collect the spilled bandages, aware, as I would not be in dressing a wound of my own, that the bandages have lain for a moment on the bathroom floor.

My son says nothing as I pull back the plastic film and discard it, then try for a grip on the elusive flaps that cover the adhesive ends.

"Here we go." It has taken me a long time to perform so simple a task. "Has the antiseptic dried?"

Jason nods gravely. His patience at my fumbling is without flaw, maintained, I imagine, at some cost. I look at the bandage, and my fingers holding it, too big, too human, to be sufficiently deft. I squat beside him again and ask him for his hand. He lays it lightly across my palm, so I can't really feel its weight, only the peculiar persistent coolness of his skin.

"Okay," I say, "here goes," and try to position the small gauze pad to good effect over his cut. Carefully, carefully, I pull one tab, then the other, wrapping the ends of the bandage around his small finger, pressing the adhesive against his skin. He can't help a slight recoil from my touch—a little pulling back I might not notice if I were not his mother and had not experienced it many times before, since he was very small. Today I will try to ignore it, try not to be hurt by it. That's just Jason, I tell myself. That's Jason's way, his peculiar sensitivity, which has nothing to do with love. It means no more than the color of my hair, my pointed nose. His way.

Will I ever learn not to be hurt by my son's aversion to my touch?

In the worst of my nightmares, I see Jason in a roomful of people, men and women, children and adults. He gambols among them, brushing against arms and legs, stopping now and then to tug at a coat sleeve, or suffer himself to be hugged. Large men tousle his hair, and he smiles at them. Pretty women squeeze his fine-boned shoulders, and he does not flinch. There is some comfort, waking, to know that it is not just my touch that repels him, but all touching; it is the feel of flesh on flesh that he cannot abide.

"Is that too tight, Jason? Does it feel all right?"

Already my mind races ahead: Will I risk hugging him? Is there a way to make my son stay longer in my room, to talk with me, to share a part of this spring day with me?

"Thank you, Mother," he says, rising to go.

I don't stop to put things away, but follow him into my room, not wanting him to slip away so easily, while I'm detained by trivialities. Already he is halfway through the room, heading quickly for the door.

"I'm about ready for a break now, Jason. Stay awhile. Would you like some juice? Or tea?"

He turns to face me, to decline. "I don't think so, thank you."

"All right," I mutter weakly, trying to convince us both that I don't mind, that the offer was casually made. How can he know what it means, that I am willing to stop poems to be with him? It cannot signify to him. "All right," I say again, closing the door softly behind him.

When I return to my desk, the poem is not there. Very little was on Mylar yet; it was just beginning to take shape in my mind, and now that shape is gone, blown away, like the cloudships we see in the sky.

"Oh, you *are* up, Mrs. Harmon," Suli says. And, responding to her present voice, I become my present self and find that yes, I am.

"Good morning, Suli. Yes. I'm up."

"It's later than usual, I wanted to make sure you were well."

"All's well. Or seems to be." How long, I wonder, was she in the room before she spoke? I would not like others to learn the secret of my blue chair; like the masturbation of children, it is a covert pleasure, maybe more pleasurable because not shared. It is rather nice to have such shameful

secrets, or to imagine they are shameful, though quite likely
the world, if it were to discover them, would yawn once
and continue on its course.

"I wasn't hungry, Suli. So I decided to do some work on
my reading for the Poets' Guild." I point at my books, to
prove it. "It takes me longer than it used to. I tend to day-
dream, I suppose." I turn a page of the book that is open in
my lap, managing to cover the blank first page of the Mylar
tablet with it. "Last night's dinner was superb, Suli. Really
a treat. Thank you."

"Mr. Harmon ordered."

"Yes. Yes, I know. But you shopped, and saved, and
cooked. It wouldn't have been the same meal if Marcus
had done more than order it." I win one of Suli's rare
smiles. "The cake, too, Suli. You're a fine baker. It's a
pity we don't give you more practice."

Now Suli points at my desk, and I see she has brought
me coffee and a roll. "Would you like it now?"

"Thanks, Suli. I would. You're very good."

She absorbs my praise with her back turned as she leans
over the tray. Soon she hands me a cup. Newly struck by
her kindness, which so exceeds efficiency, I thank her
again, and then regret it, seeing that after seven years of
taking her more or less for granted, my sudden gratitude
nonplusses her. She is doing no more for me than she has
always done.

"If you'd like to work without interruptions, I can tell
callers you're not at home," she offers, knowing my pattern
on working days, not yet sure if this is to be one. Neither
am I.

"It's so unlikely anyone will call that I might as well
speak to anyone who does."

"Very well. And Mrs. Harmon, I told Mr. Powell you'd
speak with him. I told you last night, but I thought you
might have forgotten."

"I didn't forget, Suli. Am I so old I seem forgetful? Is
there a good reason to remind me of my calls?"

"Oh, it's not that. Not at all. Just that I mentioned it
when you were perhaps thinking of other things." She
speaks more rapidly than usual, anxious not to offend.

"Neatly done," I laugh. "A nice extraction. But if it's

true, if I am getting feebleminded, then I all the more appreciate your help. I sometimes suspect you know more about me than I do, at least sooner."

Suli says nothing, but her silence is tantalizing.

"And of course, you're objective, which one can't be about oneself. I'm sure you could tell me a great deal about myself."

"Perhaps, Mrs. Harmon. But that is not my job." Immediately, she begins to apologize.

"No, Suli. It's all right. Quite true. And sad, when you think about it. If you were my friend, rather than my housekeeper"—I choose the term deliberately, though Suli's license reads Domestic Servant—"I'd have full benefit of your insights. As it is, I don't. I'm sure the loss is mine."

Poor Suli. I keep changing the rules on her, so she is caught off guard. To be honest, though, I don't seem to know the rules myself anymore, and am often caught in unexpected squalls instead of sailing through these human seas with ease.

Though she has no functional excuse to stay longer in my room, Suli lingers, pretending to wipe a speck of dust from the desk top, looking about for little chores to be done.

"How did you know John Powell was a poet, Suli, and not a clerk from the Bureau of Geriatrics?"

Now she turns to look at me. "I like his poems. You and Dr. Harmon have been kind in letting me use your lexavision discs. You have much poetry."

"Yes, we do. I'm glad you enjoy it. When do you find the time?"

"At night sometimes," she says gravely, then pauses. "What I wanted to ask, Mrs. Harmon, is if you'd mind if I went to hear your reading at the Poets' Guild?"

After I'm surprised, I'm deeply moved. "Of course not, Suli. We'll go together."

Suli looks unconvinced, seems to question the propriety of this suggestion, so leaves that issue open and turns to another.

"I've watched you on the discs many times. I'd like to see you read in person."

"I'm flattered, Suli. And I'd be delighted to know you

were in the audience. It will give me confidence to see a familiar face."

"Then I will try to put my face where you can see it," she says. She puts the coffee on a low table beside my chair, then leaves me to my morning's work.

5

Is this a good one? That better? Where to put it? Start light and darken the mood, or vice versa, or don't, perhaps, manipulate at all, but rely on my own whim or the emotional logic of the moment to create some kind of working whole? And *her*. What will please her, gratify her, hold her, seem to her, a mirror of such high resolution, an adequate, an honest representation of myself?

Now that I know Suli will be there on Thursday, the task of shaping my program has taken on new meanings, too many, perhaps, to let me proceed with any assurance. I remember when I first knew Marcus, and knew that he would be coming to hear me read, how hard it became to choose the poems I'd read. They had to be just right, to work in perfect harmony, even if what they worked for happened to be disharmony. I wanted, not so much to impress him as to speak to him, imagining him the one just and sensitive listener, able to understand my words and, through them, to understand me. My readings were a gift to him then, handmade, presented with all that I possessed of sincerity and love.

Now Suli becomes my perfect listener, the one among many whom I care about reaching, the one among all others I hope will understand.

As the program begins to take shape, I see it is one of self-justification. From old notebooks I am picking poems that sprang from the high places of my personal mythology, from the crucial events and emotions of my early life. I have gone back to first loving Marcus, beyond, in fact, to find the woman I first was alone. To my parents, who are dead. To my children, and my middle age, loss and gain, disappointment and elation. All I have been is here, sometimes obscured, intentionally, by metaphor, so it would pass the censors of the Ministry of Culture as they enforced their strange taboos. I violated them in my poems as in my life, quietly, unobtrusively, hoping the right people would notice, the rest remain ignorant of my infractions.

The seven notebooks suck me in, and I see my images as artifacts, my self distorted by too many mirrors. Every time I think I have found some thread that will lead me to the heart of the maze, I find it is only the raveled end of some unfinished fabric. My loose ends appall me, they are so many and so random. Even the straightest thread, chronology, has many breaks.

I become tempted to burn everything, to become a poet without a past, a present person. It seems I would be more real if these books did not exist. What good are maps that show the way to places you will never go to again?

Yet, what would I be without my books? I would cease to exist if the world were wholly empty of the things I've made.

The telecom bleats distantly, and though I don't answer it, I stop my work and wait, ready for interruption.

Suli's voice comes through the intercom. "The Bureau of Geriatrics, Mrs. Harmon."

I pick up my silent extension.

"Eve Harmon, number four-eight-nine-one-oh?"

"Speaking. If numbers can."

"This is the Bureau of Geriatrics."

"I know."

"We have received the results of your registration tests." The voice is female, impersonal, vaguely metallic. I'm not sure if I'm speaking with a person or a computer tape; I've been fooled before. The voice quality and timing get better every year.

"We have received the results of your registration tests," the voice repeats. It *is* a tape. It will go on and on with the same thing until I answer it.

"We have received the results of . . ."

"Yes. All right. Go on."

There is a faint click somewhere in the system, in the electronic viscera of the computer.

"You are requested to appear in person at the Bureau for an interview with one of our staff."

"Can't you tell me over the phone?" It doesn't matter what I say; this computer, I deduce, is rather crudely programmed. It will respond to my voice, and continue to speak, but cannot take any meaning from my words.

"Your appointment is scheduled for Wednesday afternoon, November eighteenth, at three p.m. I repeat, Wednesday, the eighteenth, at three p.m."

"Damned inconvenient."

"If you are unable to keep this appointment for verifiable reasons, you may call XMF-four-three-one to arrange another."

"Uh huh."

"The number is XMF-four-three-one. Use it only if you are unable to keep your appointment."

"We are to the gods as flies to wanton boys," I tell the computer. "They kill us for their sport."

"Failure to comply with these instructions will result in a Class C fine," the voice informs me, without passion.

"Grapefruit."

"Thank you for listening. You are urged to comply with instructions."

"Good night, sweet prince."

"The line will clear following a spoken response from you. Goodbye."

"Up yours, too," I say delicately.

When a record is to be kept of a specific call, the law requires that the computer be programmed to tell you this. Otherwise, one is free to say anything, with no fear of recrimination. Some people have become great wits in this genre; I myself never seem to think of appropriate rejoinders except in retrospect.

The digichron on my desk tells me it is now Tuesday, the 17th, precisely 2:17 p.m. I think of calling Marcus at the lab. Yes, I'm a little afraid of what the medic will tell me, and just as afraid of how I'll handle it. Of course, if the one were resolved, I could worry exclusively about the other and perhaps requite myself well enough. But this double-edged uncertainty cuts deep, deeper because I know I won't call my husband, will not call him from his work to comfort my fears. Perhaps it's because I no longer believe he can. There is nothing he or anyone can do.

At least in twenty-four hours, or twenty-four hours and forty-three minutes, to be precise, the dilemma will be halved, and that will be a relief. Until then, I will be tight inside, with the tightness of deferred bitterness, of restrained fear. There is no sense in being anxious over imponderables. To suffer on conjecture, imagining each of the horrible possibilities that may or may not match up with reality, to agonize over each as though it were real, seems to me absurd.

Only a veteran worrier, of course, with an energetic imagination, might ever reach this view of things; it's from experience that I recognize the phenomenon, and on the basis of long experience that I reject it. No, I will try not to think about it until I walk in the door at the Bureau of Geriatrics, nor speak of it until I know whereof I speak.

Still, going back to the notebooks is hard. I am suddenly impatient with retrospect; this smug stock-taking doesn't please me. My sense of urgency grows strong again, as though death were imminent and I more in need than ever of making poems. My mind must not fall silent before I have said it all; before every last noun and verb gestating in me has been dug out of my brain and planted in a poem. Out! Out! I want to spew poems; I want to assemble every crumb of wisdom I've stored my whole life long and push them all, by force, into poetry.

Now I am thrown into false labor; I feel the insistent push of poems inside me. Perspiration coats my face, my heart beats fast, my hands begin to shake a little. A new headache hammers inside my right temple, crowded by words, by images. But I do not go to my desk, knowing if I do, I will miscarry. The feeling is ripe, but the form still missing. It will be some time yet—how long, I can't say— before I am able to bear a healthy poem.

To try now would produce a monster, a misshapen thing, resembling the ideal just closely enough to be especially horrible. No, I must wait patiently, because waiting is part of the process. I must let the embryo develop out of my sight, below the surface of my mind, and trust it to signal my consciousness when it has come to term.

Wait. Waiting. How much of my life has been spent this way?

I let the stylus drop out of my fingers and watch it fall to the floor. I will not be pressured now.

6

In the same cubicle, or one much like it, I wait for the medic, clothed this time and more alert than before to my surroundings. The white walls and floors are no longer entirely clean. Humanity passing through has left marks and stains, despoiled the clinical purity of the room. My nerves are tuned too finely, past the point where tension lends power to the stage where it betrays. My fifty years of planning to face this moment of my life with equanimity seem distant as a childhood dream, unspeakably naive.

The medic comes in, and his white suit, too, is a little soiled, his healer's face rumpled.

"Four-eight-nine-one-oh, Eve Harmon?"

"That's right."

He takes the only chair. I have been pacing, now am left to perch on the edge of the examination table. There is no way to mount it with dignity or grace; I leap up and catch its edge with my buttocks, then slide backward, feet dangling uneasily. Two metal stirrups, one by either knee, evoke memories of even greater indignities suffered at the hands of medical men.

The medic scans the printout on his clipboard, occasionally muttering something not meant for me to understand. One, two, five pages he pores over in this way, learning every secret of my metabolism, every peculiarity of my insides.

At last he looks at me.

"Well, Mrs. Harmon." His eyes pass quickly over my face and come to rest somewhere beyond my left ear. I check the impulse to turn around and see for myself what holds his attention there.

"Well?" I prompt.

"Yes." He hesitates and his eyes take refuge in the printout once again. "Your heart, pulse rate and blood pressure are all completely normal. Lungs sound. Liver and kidney functions adequate, left kidney slightly impaired. Endocrine system what it should be, in a woman your age."

He looks up to give me a swift, nervous smile. I smile back, pleased with my report card thus far, and genuinely hooked by the innate suspense of the situation.

"Brain scan reveals possible dysfunction in the memory quadrants. Once again, nothing uncommon, considering your age. Family medical data indicate that your mother became senile quite some time before death. Is that correct?"

I nod, suddenly remembering things I've chosen to forget for many years. There is a slight change in the cadence of my heart. "Yes, that's right."

"These things have a tendency to run in families, so to speak. Statistically, it's likely that someone with one or more senile parents will experience similar deterioration. The process isn't fully understood, largely because the IMM treatments seem to retard it completely. Are you currently aware of any change in your memory patterns? Forgetting recent things, or remembering the distant past with great clarity?"

Surprisingly, I feel myself blush as I think of my blue chair and journeys I take in it. My answer is evasive. "Perhaps so. I'm not sure."

"Well, it may become increasingly apparent. Don't be alarmed if it does. The process is organic, not psychological. You're not going crazy. Just getting old."

He confirms my own conclusion, without guessing, inside his armor of chemical youth, what secret joy this "process" is to me. I nod again. So far, so good. He has told me nothing I didn't know already.

"In fact, the entire examination reveals only one area of pathology. The heat scan—you remember the heat scan?"

"Yes. I know what it is." My mouth is suddenly dry.

"The heat scan shows the presence of an actively expanding mass in the left breast. Still small, but cell division appears to be occurring rapidly. Lymphatic involvement seems certain."

So. The ancient terror is upon me. Not meaning to, I lift my hand to my afflicted left breast. It feels no different; I feel no pain. A brief, false hope that the medical conglomerate might be in error rises up, then dies quickly.

The doctor goes on, his voice level and colorless. "Of course, if this had been discovered before your Health Card was revoked, it wouldn't have been a problem. As you may know, laser treatment enables us to excise such tumors completely without external mutilation. And we're able to arrest the pathological replication of malignant cells."

"Yes. I know the work. My husband is a biochemist."

His eyes move upward to the top of the printout, where my name appears. "Harmon. Of course. Oh my god." The doctor takes a savage swipe at the hair that overhangs his brow, pushing it away. It falls back in place, exactly as before. His voice is tighter when he speaks again.

"As you know, after revocation of your card, no curative treatment is provided." He fumbles with the collar of his white jacket, then puts the clipboard down on the cabinet beside him. "I have to tell you this shit. I'm sorry."

"I know. It's your job. Go on."

"Palliative treatment is provided. Painkillers, sedatives. I'll give you a prescription that can be refilled indefinitely, at our dispensary." His eyes move rapidly, a little wildly around the plain white room, trying to stay ahead of mine and thus avoid them. Normally I would make it easy for him, but now I follow doggedly. He is my oracle, my judge.

"You can also apply for euthanasia at any time. Or your family can, should you lose consciousness for a period of more than ninety-six hours. Application must be made in writing and submitted to the Department of Euthanasia."

"Does it hurt?" I ask stupidly, more for something to say than because I want to know.

"No," the doctor says. "I don't know. If it does, it's only a matter of seconds. It's very fast."

I slide down from the table onto unsteady feet. My knee joints pop loudly. It seems high time to leave. That there is much to think about, much to feel, becomes a steady imperative pressure inside my present numbness. Mostly, I want to be alone.

"Thank you, Doctor. If I can just be on my way now. . . ."

"Your prescriptions. Wait. I'll fill them out right now." He takes a Mylar pad from his pocket and inscribes the prescriptions. "Have you had any pain yet?" he asks.

"No. No, I don't think so."

"If you're not sure, you haven't had it. People differ in that, you know. In pain." He finishes writing and hands me the sheet. "Present this at the dispensary. It's on your left, coming in. They'll keep it in their files."

"Do you know how long, Doctor?"

He shakes his head. "People are different. It's hard to say."

I must get out of this room immediately. It's time to go. My hand is on the doorknob. As I turn it, I can see the doctor's discomfiture. He wants something from me, my absolution; his eyes ask me to tell him that I understand, that he is blameless, that I know he doesn't like what he has done. He is human, too, and suffering in his way. Part of me leans toward him, wanting to be generous, to offer him relief. Another part, the victim, forbids generosity; his pain is less than mine. My voice is cold when I tell him goodbye.

The corridor seems endless, and my footsteps very loud. As my legs and feet move in an approximation of my normal walk, the echo of my steps follows me, irregular, and tells me, objectively, that walking is difficult right now. This makes me so self-conscious that I concentrate too hard on walking, until it becomes nearly impossible, and I must stop, short of the lobby, to set myself straight. I lean against the concrete wall for a moment, and its coldness passes through my clothing to chill the flesh beneath. Feeling the gooseflesh rise, I shiver.

Deeply, deeply I breathe, long and slow. Calm, I tell myself. Be calm. My treasonous body shivers again, and even my hair roots prickle.

This is absurd, I tell myself. Walk on. Keep moving. You must get out of here.

It takes all my concentration to make my body move back into the corridor, away from the cold, ironic support of the wall. Step by step, like a child learning to walk, I make my unsteady way into the lobby.

The old guard salutes me. "I know you," he says. "You were here the other day. And now you're back again. Bad news?" His long, lined face bobs knowingly as he chews some unimaginable substance, and I feel a good, familiar, healthy surge of anger at his intrusion. His curiosity is the last thing I need, and his sympathy the last I want.

"Bad news," he confirms, after reading my face. "I know the signs."

The anger fades. I am only another bit player in the endless, meaningless tragedy that plays itself out here. Perhaps cumulatively, as the patterns emerge and repeat, the drama becomes funny, depersonalizes itself into comedy. The old man has learned to read our stories in the way we walk. Perhaps he, not I, should be the poet. In the end, his knowledge humbles me.

"You're right," I tell him. "Bad news."

He raises his right arm and points. "The dispensary's right through there. They'll take care of you, good as anybody can, considering."

"Good," I say, and my thin voice says back at me. My echo is not so robust or long-lived as the guard's; it flutters like a moth, then quickly dies. I turn my back to the guard and begin to walk toward the dispensary.

"You enjoy now. While you can. Me, I drink," he calls. I imagine his arm to be raised in salute. Hail and farewell, old man.

The door to the dispensary is heavy, and I have to use all my weight to pull it open. A little needle of pain pricks my chest—imaginary, I suspect—as I turn sideways through the slot of door I've managed to pry open.

The dispensary is a long rectangle, divided in half by a closed counter, like a wall, to about chest height, where it is met by thick glass with diamonds of wire inside it. At periodic intervals, there are windows in the wall of glass, pharmacy clerks behind them. Along the opposite wall, under the cold glare of the tube lights, a few people, old like myself, sit in solitary heaps on inhospitable benches.

I take my prescription to one of the windows. The woman behind it studies me for a moment before she slides the panel back.

"Yes?"

I hand her the sheet. She looks from it to me, then says. "Just a minute. You can sit down."

Before I can reply, she slides her window shut, and I turn back to join the others, grateful to sit. The sunken faces and slouched bodies of those who wait with me depress me until I realize that I am like them, that there is no need for pretense here. Already I sense there is a great effort ahead of me. I will, of course, be brave about it. That's how I've planned it all these years. A gracious death. An exemplary death.

There now. I've said the word, in my own mind. The doctor didn't use it. Nor did I, in my own thoughts, until this minute. I examine the word, its length and weight, its sound, the letters that make it up. In my mind, I walk all around it, inspecting each enormous letter. Still, I am somehow unable to reach beyond the word to its meaning. Right now it is a bit of language, five letters floating through my consciousness like animated butterflies. There is an awful satisfaction in having taken hold of the word itself. The meaning, I think, will come much harder.

For most of my adult life, it has been a word not spoken in polite society; the vocabulary of sex became enfranchised, while death became the ultimate obscenity. My parents' generation was the last to die, and the word was buried with them. My generation will not die. Only the servant classes, assorted religious fanatics, and a few isolated romantics will die. It has become a distasteful concept to society, a lonely terror for those of us outside it. It is a very long time since I looked into my mother's face and knew that she was dead, almost as long since I have thought of it, except for those times when it has taken shape, unbidden, in my dreams.

As I look around me now, at the two men and one woman who share my prospects, their faces freeze, turn into hers. I imagine each of them as they will look with their own deaths upon them.

My clerk returns to the counter and I am suddenly alert. She opens her window and reads a number. I fumble for my red tag, but before I've found it, one of the men rises painfully and hobbles to the window. He stands to about two-thirds of what must once have been his full height; the upper part of his spine is so bent that he looks perenially at the floor below. On the head of his cane, rootlike fingers are spurred and twisted. The toes of his old black shoes have been cut away, to accommodate the deformity of his feet.

At least *my* disease will not twist me up like that. There is some comfort in that.

I check the number on my tag, deciding to remember the last three digits only. When I hear them, I will know it is my turn. Finally it comes. I hear my numbers, and rise as I have planned.

"Tag, please."

I begin to pull it off, over my head, but she reaches out abruptly and takes the plastic pendant in her hand. My body follows as she pulls the tag inside her cage and inserts it in a slot in a small gray machine. There's a faint click, then she releases the tag and lets it fall back to my chest.

"The chains were longer, before the metal shortage got so bad," she comments. "Here." She shoves a sack at me. "Your prescriptions are refillable. They're in the computer, under your number. Use it when refilling."

I pick up the bag, and she pushes her window shut again.

7

In the entrance hall, I listen to my house, trying to locate Suli, but it is very still. I want to get upstairs, safe to my own room, without encountering her. If I'm lucky, she hasn't heard me come in. Softly as I can, I walk to the staircase and begin to climb. The Mylar bag rustles, and I hold it tight against my body to silence it. On the third stair from the top, I stop to listen again. Hearing nothing, I climb to the top and turn into the carpeted hallway.

Just as I pass Marcus' room, one door short of my own, Suli emerges from the bathroom, arms full of soiled towels.

"Mrs. Harmon. You're home."

"Yes." Realizing I must look foolish, I loosen my grip on the bag. I continue to head for my room.

"Can I get you anything, Mrs. Harmon?" Suli searches my face. I feel her other questions, the ones she is too polite to pose, and am grateful for her concern, sure somehow that it transcends mere curiosity. But it is too soon to talk to anyone else, before I have had a chance to talk to myself.

"No thank you, Suli. I'll be in my room. I still have some work to do, for tomorrow night."

She nods, still motionless on the same spot. I look for words that will uproot her. "Maybe a cup of tea would be nice. Please."

And Suli is in motion once again, heading for the stairs.

"There's no hurry," I call after her, knowing that the tea will appear even sooner than seems possible.

What I told her was no lie: I *do* have work to do before tomorrow night. Notebooks and pads are scattered everywhere, on my bed, my desk, the table by my chair. All over there are signs of a task in progress, hotly pursued. The room is as I left it, several hours ago. For the moment, though, it no longer seems to be my room, or my task. These endless sheets of Mylar must belong to someone else; this writing, so absurdly clear and childish, must be another woman's hand.

I sit on the edge of the bed and put my package down beside me. A sheet of notes, my outline for the reading, is close at hand, and I study it, decoding the hasty abbreviations. Yes, they are all words I might use, in orders I might use them. There is a simple logic in the program they describe that reminds me of my own sense of order. It is the excitement, the energy behind the words that seems foreign and incomprehensible.

Tossing the pad aside, I open the bag. An instruction booklet, a bottle and a box spill out across the spread. Inside the brown glass of the bottle there are capsules, hundreds of them. Opening the lid, I find they are green on one end, yellow on the other. Rather pretty, in fact. These are the sedatives. All right.

My heart sinks as I open the box. Just as I do, Suli's knock sounds at the door. Have I locked it? I don't remember. "Just a minute," I call, stuffing my medicines under the spread, then, "All right."

She brings the tea on a tray. I pick up the notebook again, and pretend to be engrossed in reading it. "On the desk, please."

She puts it down.

"Are you cold, Mrs. Harmon?"

"No, not especially. Are you?" I look up from the notebook. "You can turn up the heat if you like."

"I just wondered, ma'am, since you're still wearing your coat."

"I am? So I am. I'll take it off."

I unbutton the coat, take it off and lay it over the bedpost. Suli moves to hang it up.

"That's all right, Suli. I can do it myself. Thanks."

With manic energy, I fly to the closet for a hanger.

"Is there anything else?"

"No, Suli. No. I've got a lot to do. Silly of me to leave my coat on. Glad you noticed. I might have worn it to dinner."

She moves toward the door. I usher her out with a smile.
"Nerves, I guess. I must really be more excited than I thought."

When the door closes behind her, I bring the box out of hiding and examine its contents. There are maybe fifty small, disposable syringes inside, each with a gleaming needle, each with a dose of medication in a clear plastic phial. My skin crawls at the sight of them; I have always hated needles, have never been able to use them. When Jason was ill, as a boy, it was Marcus who had to give him his daily injections. I hope the pain doesn't start for a long, long time.

I choose my desk for a hiding place; no one ever opens it but me. The second drawer down, on the right. It should be safe. As I hide the medication under some magazines, I realize I have already decided to tell no one about my cancer. Not until I have to ask for help, anyway.

In the meantime, what to do? Thinking, it seems, is imperative. I must let my feelings come, and feel them fully. Somewhere beyond that, I must lay plans and make decisions. I sit on the bed and wait for the process to begin, willing to give myself over to it, because I must. I wait for the appropriate, powerful emotions to surge over me, sweep through me, to leave me clean and ready to cope.

I wait and wait, but nothing happens.

Pieces of thought, hard as marbles, rattle around in my brain, hit against each other and bounce back into their separate orbits. Normally full, my mind seems disastrously open, and the tools I use to marshall thought, put away somewhere I cannot find them. The words roll by and I try to catch them, to squeeze some meaning, literal or symbolic, from them, but it is like trying to make stones bleed. I think little, feel less. Grief, rage, self-pity, fear, sadness, fear, courage; I look for a way to be.

Numb, blank, empty, light is how I am.

For the moment, I give up trying to feel and lie back on the bed, telling the tight muscles of my neck to relax. My face is pinched tight, knotted with trying, and I concentrate on making its flesh relax and smooth out, as it should, over my bones. My feet stick straight up, perpendicular to the bed, and I make slow circles with them, trying to loosen the taut grip of my muscles. When my body is forcibly relaxed, my mind remains vengefully wakeful, not productive, but empty and alert.

Now, almost absently, I put my hand to my breast and explore it with my fingertips in small, concentric circles, trying to find my death. There are firm places and soft ones, as there have always been. At last I find a small hardness, no bigger than a pea, carefully hiding itself underneath a ledge of cartilage. This must be it. I try to take it between two fingers and in doing so, lose it again. But I know now it is there, small, hard, lethal, the seed of disease. Now I believe.

And the first of many feelings comes: If Marcus were still interested in my body, so would I have been. If he still touched my neglected breasts, we might have found this together, before it was too late. Tears, warm and welcome, fill my eyes, just a few small, stinging tears, not enough, really, to relieve the nameless pressures inside me. They do not overflow but, like gas escaping from a full balloon, leave me just a little less in danger of exploding.

Slowly, I get up from the bed and go to sit in my blue chair, perhaps intending to sort my poems, perhaps meaning to think myself into a new one that will let me reach my feelings through the circuitous path of art. Whatever I intend, or pretend to, once my ankles are crossed in front of me, and my arms spread comfortably across the blue arms of my chair, I let pass and give myself up to the beckoning journey.

〰〰〰〰〰〰〰〰

First times are always exciting. I have had enough of them to know that almost any man's touch can inflame at least once, aided by novelty, sparked by curiosity. And if there has been time between men, then one's own flesh is like tinder, needing only the tiniest of sparks to ignite it.

Still, this is a little different than before. A certain measure of awe is mixed up with my lust, and some impulse almost religious helps inspire my breathlessness. I wouldn't tell him this, of course, not being sure of how he feels, but I will let this new, strange, holy feeling participate in my own pleasure.

He is being very cautious with me, and I like it, am flattered by it, despite the impatience of my body. Maybe he doesn't know yet that we'll make love tonight, for the first time. There are no demands in his touch, only questions. I answer him honestly, holding nothing back.

He puts his hand on my thigh and strokes it gently. Under his warm hand, my nerves light up like tiny candles, and I let my whole body incline more toward him, so more of me is touching more of him. My cheek is on his shoulder now, my shoulder, underneath his arm. From torso to thigh, we are contiguous, and I am aware of his body's heat through our two interceding layers of clothes.

Marcus lifts his hand from my thigh to the top button of my shirt. For a while he toys with it intently, not undoing it. I say and do nothing to discourage him, too shy to undo it myself but willing, longing, to be undone. My nipples stiffen and stand up inside my shirt, waiting for him to uncover them.

He looks up at me. "Should I turn off the light?"

Only one lamp is lighted, and it is on the far side of the room. Its dim, mellow light carves his handsome face out of the shadows, makes both our flesh seem sleek and gold.

"No," I tell him. "Leave it on. Unless you prefer the dark."

"I like to see you," he says simply, finally pushing my button through its hole and, after a little pause, moving on to the one below it.

One button, two, three, four, and a fifth. Looking down, I see a half-inch-wide stripe of my own flesh. On either side of it, my breasts are waiting to be bared.

Slowly, exquisitely, he pulls one side of the blouse, the right side, away from one breast. Both of us watch it emerge, like a surprised eye. Around the stiff nipple, the aureole wrinkles with excitement.

I laugh a little, and look up at him, at this Marcus who makes my flesh change visibly. With perfect grace, he leans over to kiss the just-uncovered breast. His moustache is delicious, and I am warmly frozen, unable to imagine, for the moment, any feeling that could surpass the beauty of this.

Soon enough, the unsurpassable is surpassed, again and again. Now my two breasts are bare before him, and he slips off the sofa to kneel in front of me. Timid and determined, I fumble with the buttons of his shirt, until it is open and I see the dark hair that climbs in a straight line from his navel to blossom on his chest. We press ourselves together, stand, in fact, to do it better, and my chest against his feels like all good things suddenly happening at once, a homecoming, a welcoming of flesh.

He no longer doubts that I want him, and with new boldness, unhooks my pants and draws them down over my hips. Once past the widest part, they drop of their own accord, with a little sigh, to the floor. I am momentarily embarrassed by my plain white briefs, but soon they, too, are gone and I step out of the clothes piled at my feet to stand naked before him.

He puts his hands on my shoulders and spins me around slowly, runs a hand along the curve of my back and gently lifts one lobe of my ass a little, making a soft, admiring sound.

And now I face him, and follow his eyes as they pass over me. What next? I cannot wait to know. I am unbearably anxious to see him, too. I feel a rush of moisture drop down out of my body, to ease his way.

He pulls off his shirt and throws it on the sofa, then undoes his buckle and his fly, not slowly, as he undid mine, but with a rough and careless speed that excites me. Pants and briefs pull down together, and his penis springs out of them, free at last. It stands up straight to salute me, perpendicular to the vertical planes of his pale, hard body, wreathed with coarse, curly hair at the base. A drop of moisture gleams at its tip, and makes me smile, as I reach out to take it in my hand. It is hard and very warm, the skin itself smooth and soft as a baby's. I feel a little surge, and it grows in my hand, stretching the smooth skin taut. Softly, softly I trace the plump lip of its head with my fingertip, until we move together and I feel it hot against my thigh.

8

"So you're really going to do it, Mother," Jason says.

"Do what?"

"Go on with this reading at the Poets' Guild?"

"Of course she is, Jason," Marcus says. "Your mother is still a vital, productive woman. You can't expect her to stop dead in a fifty-year career because the Ministry takes her card away." Marcus leaps to my defense, and it surprises me. I smile over my plate at him.

Jason lifts his fork and holds it in midair as he speaks. I can't help but admire the steadiness of his tapering hands.

"I should think she'd have more concern for you than that, is all," he says, and guides the fork to his mouth.

"They're not likely to reprimand your father, Jason. He doesn't think so, I don't think so. We've been through all this. It's been decided."

He daubs at his lip with the napkin. "Even so," he says.

"Why do you object so, Jason?"

Suli comes in from the kitchen to refill our wine glasses.

"Frankly, Mother, it doesn't help me or my associates a bit. There are reasons the Ministry prohibits domestics from attending cultural affairs. And things like this Poets' Guild fly in the face of the system. What am I supposed to say when asked to explain why my own mother totally disregards our policies?"

Jason watches the red wine climb inside his glass without looking at Suli, without thanking her. When she moves on to Marcus, Jason picks his glass up between his slender fingers and, arching his wrist with grace, brings the glass to his lips for a noiseless sip.

"Why Jason, there are any number of things you can say," I tell him. I am a little drunk with tension and with wine. "Say I'm mortal. Say I'm getting old and unwise. Say poetry never started a revolution. Or say you simply don't know. Which is the truth."

"It's true, you know, Jason," Marcus chides gently. "No one will imagine that you condone it. You're not responsible for your mother, to the Ministry or anybody else. Don't say anything at all."

"That's right, Jason. And I'm not responsible for the work *you* choose to do. I have never apologized to anyone for your work."

Jason is no fool; he hears the mockery in my voice. "You've never respected my work, have you, Mother?" he says bitterly. "You've cherished your fine moral reservations. But my Ministry helps keep this society alive, far more than any poem you've ever written, or hoped to write. I'd think you'd be proud to have a son named Director of his Division."

"Jason!" Marcus says. "When did this happen?"

"I received the appointment yesterday," Jason says stiffly.

"Well, this calls for a toast," his father says. "The Ministry must value you a great deal."

Jason nods a sulky assent, while Marcus raises his glass. "To your career," he toasts. Then, "Eve, you'll toast your son's success, won't you?"

"Of course," I murmur, raising my own glass and taking a generous swallow. The wine of Jason's success threatens to choke me; the back of my throat closes against it, and I have to force it down. I cough a little, then say, "Of course. Congratulations, Jason. You're deserving, I'm sure."

My son looks coldly at me. I take more wine, and it goes down easily this time, not poisoned by the slave trade.

Marcus, self-cast in the role of peacekeeper, says, "It's nice to see competence rewarded. Does it mean a lot more money?"

"A generous raise, yes."

Even when Jason was a very young man, his earnings far outstripped mine. The Government pays most for what it values most, and Jason's icy, uncompromising ways must be very valuable indeed. A more humane man could never do his work so well. It's time to change the subject before my rancor grows.

"What do you two plan for the evening?" I ask.

"We haven't discussed it yet," Marcus says. "I should look in at the lab sometime."

Jason nods agreement.

"That's after our adventure, Jason," Marcus goes on. "We're going to wash the dishes."

"What," says Jason. "Is your servant ill? I can arrange for a temporary replacement." He puts down his napkin and starts to get up.

"Sit down, Jason," Marcus says. "It's all right. Suli is going to your mother's reading. So I agreed to do my bit."

"That's ridiculous," Jason says. "Is this her usual night off?"

"No. This is special," Marcus tells him.

"Haven't you read the Handbook? We specifically advise against special dispensations of any kind. A spoiled servant is not a good servant."

"After seven years, Jason, I think we can afford a few kindnesses."

"That's precisely when they're most apt to take undue advantage—after people have become accustomed to them, developed some kind of fondness."

"We *are* getting fond of Suli," I say, mostly to annoy Jason. "At least, I am. What about you, Marcus?"

"I hadn't thought about it much," he says. "She *is* good, of course. I'd miss her if we had to change."

"I'm glad she's satisfactory," Jason says. "You know I selected her myself."

"Yes, Jason," I tell him. "You did well. And *she's* done well, too."

"All the more reason to avoid becoming too lenient at this point."

"Look at it this way," Marcus says. "I can't take your mother to the Poets' Guild. I have to go back to the lab. And from the looks of it, *you're* not going with her. Personally, I'm glad she'll have an escort to and from."

The door swings open and Suli appears. "Will that be all?"

"Just bring some coffee for me and Jason," Marcus says. "Then you can go."

"Yes, sir."

Apparently Suli had the coffee waiting, because she comes back with it immediately.

I get up from my place. "I just have to collect my things, Suli. Then we can go. The car should be here very soon."

As I climb the stairs to my room, I hear the horn blast of the hire-car. Marcus talked me out of the subway, though I thought it would be safe, even at night, if Suli was with me. I ordered a car this afternoon.

Suli waits for me in the hall. I rarely see her in her own clothes; she looks quite handsome, and more real, somehow, than in her uniform. The coat she puts on is an old one of mine, and she has improved it considerably by adding a belt and drawing in the sides so they follow the line of her body.

"You look lovely, Suli." While she thanks me, I try to beat her to the door, but she gets there before me and holds it open.

The driver loads us, and I give him the address, then we're underway, down streets I rarely travel, past the well-groomed public parts of the city into those neighborhoods where servants, students and a few eccentrics live in apartment buildings, some new and forbidding, others old and in poor repair. Once we pass the Government complex, there are no lights in the streets, only the light that escapes, in tiers, from the insides of surrounding buildings.

Suli sits by one window, I by the other. We peer out into the dark streets, not sharing our thoughts. My pile of poems is on the seat between us. I wish Suli would initiate a conversation, but know it is not her way. I can think of nothing to say, especially since I know that the driver, who took careful stock of us as we got in, will overhear our every word.

At last I say, "I'm looking forward to meeting John Powell. I hope I don't disappoint him."

Suli makes a soft noise, signifying nothing but her politeness. The ride seems, and probably is, very long. If I had to get home by myself, I would be lost. The car is chilly, and it is colder out; we are on the brink of winter. Somewhat absently, I think of spring beyond, and wonder if I will be here to enjoy it. I don't *think* the disease could strike me down so fast, but I know little about it. All I find among Marcus' discs is the literature of cures, inaccessible to me, and nothing that describes the unchecked course of the disease.

My breath veils the window with little clouds and makes it seem a great fog is slipping through the streets.

"This is it, I think," the driver says. He slows, then stops the car.

The building before us is an abandoned school, brick, with small barred windows along the street and tall steps leading to a heavy door. I pay the driver and we get out of the car. My clothing has been disarranged by sitting, and tugs at my body in strange, uncomfortable ways. I try to shake it right before we climb the stairs.

Suddenly alarmed, I realize I have left my poems in the car, but when I turn, I see they are safe in Suli's hand. She gives them to me.

"Thank god, you're here. I must be older than I feel."

"You're excited."

"Yes."

We climb the stairs together and stop to read the sign above the door:

> Artists' Guild
> Dance Guild
> Drama Guild
> Musicians' Guild
> Poets' Guild.

An empty corridor stretches out beyond the door, dimly lit, with an ancient tile floor. Inside I find that all the sundry arts named above the door have not succeeded in exorcising the old school smell of chalk dust and sweaty children. My own education began in a building much like this, and I can easily imagine noisy hordes of children in the now silent hall, clotted around—yes, there it is, a white enamel water cooler in a little alcove cut out of the beige-brown wall. The memories induced are not unpleasant, but a certain panic begins in me, a first-day-of-school panic, not knowing where to go, or what to do.

"I hear voices down there, Mrs. Harmon," Suli says, and

I gratefully follow her lead to the head of a broad lighted stair that leads down to the bowels of the building.

"Of course. The auditorium."

We descend. Our intuition is confirmed by a small sign at the landing, just before a second flight of stairs reverses our direction. We come to a matched set of swinging doors, one propped open, wearing loose coats of metal with chipping paint, windowed with opaque glass reinforced inside with cross-hatched wire. We enter tentatively, and find a small group of people clustered at the edge of the old school stage. We are almost upon them before anyone takes note of us.

Then a tall man in a white sweater leaves the group and comes toward us, his hand already out in greeting.

"Mrs. Harmon. Right on time." He takes my hand, shakes it heartily, pulling us into the circle of light.

"I'm glad to meet you, Mr. Powell. I've admired your work."

He smiles broadly and seems genuinely pleased. Powell is a handsome man, not much younger than I, if chronology matters. He took the treatments, though, long before his activities brought him into disfavor with the Government, and so looks to be about thirty-five, or forty, in his prime. His hair is a gentle brown and his eyes surprisingly blue. The lines of his face are the lines of a good man; I see humor and the tread of many smiles on him.

I draw Suli into the light beside me, introduce her, and am pleased when Powell takes her hand and shakes it. He offers us wine in plastic cups. I gladly accept. Suli hesitates a bit, and I nudge her with my elbow, imperceptibly, I hope, until she too takes a cup.

"To your reading," Powell says. "May it be the first of many here."

We touch our cups. Then I look into the auditorium, where rows upon rows of empty folding chairs march backward into shadows, not a soul among them.

"I don't know," I say doubtfully. "I don't seem to be pulling much of a crowd for you."

Powell laughs.

"The reading starts at nine. I asked you to come early,

so I could meet you, and set things up the way you like them. Also, to give you a chance to case the place."

Now I laugh too, with relief. "Thank god. I thought I'd bombed before I started."

"I suspect it will be a successful evening," he says. "It's quite an event for us."

"For me, too," I tell him. "I handed in my cards last week."

"So they took them."

"Of course."

"I thought perhaps they might relent, since your husband's so important. There have been rumors."

"Really? I haven't heard them. They certainly took me off the rolls with great dispatch."

"I'm sorry," Powell says. "I wish it were me. But you can't give back the questionable gift of immortality."

"No, I suppose not. I never took it in the first place." Here I laugh. "As you can tell. I look like the old woman I am."

"Some women are beautiful at any age," Powell says softly.

The funny thing is, I believe he means it. Vague changes in my body tell me his words are deeply felt, by me, if not by him. Absurdly, I blush, and find I have been looking too long into his eyes.

I find this man attractive, a small voice informs me, and I begin at once to apologize for my reading.

"I had a nice, logical, retrospective order all worked out, till yesterday. Then something happened, and I scrapped it."

"What happened?" he asks, going to the heart of the matter, and I find I want to tell him what I am unwilling to tell my own husband, but sense prevails and I ride roughshod over his question.

"So what I have now is no order at all, just a lot of poems that felt right, about noon today."

"An order of the heart," Powell says. "Good."

By now a few people have begun to filter in, and Powell excuses himself to raise the lights in the back of the room. When he returns, I ask what happened to the people who were with him when we arrived.

"Oh, they're dancers. They'd just been practicing on the stage. They've gone home now."

More and more people arrive. They are of all races, and seeing the mix excites and frightens me. I hope I will not be despised for my long dalliance with the Ministry of Culture, my privileged home, important husband and despicable son. I wouldn't be surprised if they stoned me. Suddenly, I am not so glad I have come.

Powell returns from greeting those who arrive. "I think it's time to hide you away until curtain time." He laughs, pointing upward at the bare hooks and pulley across the ceiling in front of the stage. "I use the term loosely, of course. They rotted away long ago."

"Green plush and always dusty," I say, remembering.

"That's right. Come on. We'll bring the wine."

I let him lead me across the room, then turn. "Are you coming, Suli? You're welcome to."

"I've seen some friends come in. I'll sit with them, and meet you afterwards."

I nod.

"Good luck, Mrs. Harmon." She disappears into the crowd.

Backstage, made voluble by yet another glass of wine, I say, "Do you realize this is the first time that Suli has been able to come to one of my readings? In seven years. It's criminal."

"Yes," Powell says. "That's why the Guilds exist."

"I wish I'd known that before. I've been far too complacent."

"Too isolated," Powell says. "There's a sense of community in the Guilds. Reinforcement. And not much politics. I think you'll prefer us to the Division of Poetry."

"You sound as though you'd recruited me."

"I have. At least, I hope so. You're here now."

"So I am."

"More wine?"

"I shouldn't. I can't think of a more appalling spectacle than a drunken old witch swallowing consonants in public."

"You're hardly that," Powell says, pouring more wine in my cup. He checks his watch. "I'd better go and help make sure things start on time. I'll be back to get you. Would you rather stand, or have a stool?"

"The stool, please. I think I need it."

"You have it then."

He leaves me in the wings, crouched on a folding chair, the victim of increasing nervousness. I wish Suli were still with me, but she was right to join her friends. Oddly, I have never thought of Suli as having friends before, only selfishly, as an appendage of my life. I wonder who her friends are, what sorts of people.

It seems I have been narrow about many things, am now coming, too late, to many causes. What makes me different from Jason, whom I so conveniently despise? Not much, I fear. Not nearly enough. It doesn't seem that I have always been so stuffy, so insensitive. Until this recent reexamination, I imagined myself to be humane, concerned, unusual, rebellious even. Perhaps at one time I really was. When it stopped being true I'm not sure, but it is now clear to me that I have stepped over the line between questioning and complacence, that, in short, I have been bought and paid for, and did not even know the transaction had taken place. Even now, my regrets are far from selfless; I am struck by what a bad bargain I've made.

In the auditorium, I hear a sudden burst of applause. It must be starting now. Powell's voice—already, I recognize it—overrides the clapping and silences the crowd. He is talking about me, though I can only catch every third or fourth word of what he says. It is just as well, I think, to be ignorant of my introduction.

I stand up, shaky, and hold my poems close. My heart pounds, but the rest of my body seems to be asleep. I am light-headed from the wine, with the beginnings of headache in my susceptible right temple. Suddenly, I am terrified of the crowd I've come to face.

Then Powell comes in, through a door I have not seen before, and says, "All ready. You're on."

A smile breaks in two on my face. He has me by the arm, is pulling me toward the door.

"Wait," I whisper to him, pulling back. "I'm scared."

He laughs easily. "Good. That means you'll do a good job."

"But what if they hate me?" I resist him, trying to stop our march to the door, and look beseechingly at him.

"You really are scared, aren't you?" he says, because my face has told him so. A little of my own fear passes, reflected, over his face, and then he says, "Think of Suli. Read for her. She loves you."

The thought is new to me. "She does? Does she?"

"Don't keep her waiting," Powell says.

We approach the door together.

"Would you like me to come with you? Get you settled?"

Because he is unsure of me, I become sure of myself. "No, thank you. I'll be all right. For Suli."

I stride bravely though the door. The stage lights are blinding at first, until my pupils narrow against the assault and I can see that the podium and stool are at the far side of the stage. It is one of the longest, loneliest walks I have ever taken, to reach that stool. A disturbing din rings in my ears, which I don't realize, until I have taken precarious possession of my seat, is the sound of many hands clapping.

I put my poems on the podium and try to see beyond it, to Suli. Of course, I can't find her; even the first row is plunged into deep shadows that wipe expression from the faces there. From the mass of shadows, sounds and warmth, I sense, rather than see, that the crowd is very large. I will not be able to see in their faces how they respond; I will have to feel the crowd. My nerves tune up.

I must begin. Must not embarrass Suli. I face the crowd, and their warmth flows back to me.

I grip the edges of the podium to steady my trembling hands and say, into the new silence, "Hello." It comes out like a croak and drifts into the darkness before me, is lost out there. I clear my throat and try again, louder this time.

"HELLO."

It comes back to me clearly, sounds surer than I thought it was, saying it. I think of Suli once again, and feel the enabling surge of power, never expected but always welcome, steal over me. It makes me into a performer, lets me leave behind the small and frightened person that is my daily self.

"I'm very, very happy to be here," I say because suddenly I am. "I've been too long coming, I'm afraid, but at least I'm here at last. I turned seventy-five last week, and according to the Ministry of Culture, my career as a poet is over. This crowd tells me that's not entirely true. Thank you."

I did not mean to be political, only spoke what was in my heart. The audience greets my words with warm applause.

To quiet them, I open my folder and begin to read.

9

Elation carries me off the stage, an hour or more later. It was good. I had the crowd. They followed me, helped me. All I could, I sent out to them, into the darkness, and felt it come back to me, a hundredfold. The affect flowed both ways. We helped each other.

The dim light of the anteroom relieves my tired eyes. Almost immediately, I begin to wind down, to shrink into myself again. The special tension of performance flows out of me, leaving me light, clean, exhausted.

John Powell steps out of the shadows and grasps my hand, then drops it to move closer, encircles my shoulders with his arm and hugs me tight. It feels good, better than words. His physical warmth seems to incarnate the warmth of the crowd, my own warm feelings. Happy, careless, I squeeze him back, then move away.

"Thank you," I tell him. "Thank you. I needed that." A few inappropriate tears fill my eyes; his smile wavers in them.

"Come on," Powell says. "Meet your admirers. Are you up to it?"

"Yes. I think so. I'm very tired. I can't promise I'll be coherent."

"Just let them—us—take your hand and shake it then."

"I'll try."

I follow Powell from the anteroom into the auditorium, smiling, rather stupidly, because I cannot stop. He leads me through the crowd to a little clear place in front of the stage. The house lights are up now, and for the first time, the people I have felt so keenly have faces and bodies, a physical form. Eyes scan my face and make me shy. Somehow onstage, I lose my vulnerability, perhaps by institutionalizing it. Because I can't see them, I make the illogical and helpful assumption that my audience, too, is blind. I don't think about the movements of my face then, or the messages in my eyes.

It is different now. Soon Powell and I are at the heart of a rough semicircle. People mill around us, wanting to speak, afraid their words will be unwelcome. I have been there often enough myself, hanging back and asking myself what I can say that will make any difference. I have been there often enough, reluctant to impose, to sympathize. I try to help with smiles. Powell calls out cheerfully to people he knows until finally the circle tightens around us. A black man approaches, a little uncertainly, to tell me he enjoyed the reading. I take his hand and shake it, let myself look straight into his eyes. There is little I can say now beyond "Thank you," I let my eyes speak for me, trust them to say what I mean.

More hands, more pairs of eyes, more faces follow. These are generous people, kind people. Names, when given, elude me. I have never seen any of these people before, but I know that if I see them again, on the street, in the subway, I will know them well enough to smile. I seem to be photographing them; they will be on record permanently in my brain.

It takes a long time for the crowd to thin. It is a long time before I spot Suli at its shrinking edge. Powell hovers nearby, large and reassuring. I catch Suli's eye and try to signal her in. Next to her stands a very tall black man, lightly bearded, lean and attractive. I think they are strangers until she moves closer to say something to him that makes him smile. As they advance, I see his hand under her elbow, guiding her. At first I am surprised, but it passes quickly; there is a rightness in how they look, how they move together, that pleases first my eye, and then my heart. Finally they stand before me.

"Mrs. Harmon, this is Alan Wills. A friend."

There is a little awkwardness before our hands come together, mine lost in the bigness of his.

"I'm very glad to meet you, Mr. Wills."

"It was a fine reading, Mrs. Harmon. I enjoyed it very much." His voice is low and melodic. I find myself hoping this man is Suli's lover, though of course it is no business of mine.

I turn to Suli. What will she say? What does she think of me now? When I see the fullness of tears in her eyes, I move toward her and soon, somehow, we are embracing. For the first time in seven years, I am close enough to this woman to feel her skin against mine, and the surprising fineness of her underlying bones, to smell the smell that is uniquely Suli's.

We say nothing. When we move apart, I see that Powell is beaming down on us, beneficent and pleased, as though he felt responsible. Maybe he is.

"It's past ten, Mrs. Harmon," Suli tells me. "We should call for a car."

Her concern embarrasses me a little; I don't like the thought of separating her from Wills to take me home.

"I will, Suli. But you needn't come now. Stay out later, if you like."

"I'll come with you," she says.

"Don't be silly. I'm not a child. I can certainly get home by myself. Go on. Enjoy yourself."

"Mrs. Harmon, please."

Wills chuckles softly.

"All right then. Could you show me to a telecom, Mr. Powell?"

"Sure. There's one upstairs." He has been leaning against the stage, now stands.

"It'll take some time, Suli. I'll meet you upstairs in half an hour."

I follow Powell up the stairs and can't help noticing how lean and trim his backside is. I chide myself for being a dirty old woman, but damn, I *do* notice. I do still feel. Unexpectedly, I find myself wondering what things would happen if I *had* taken the treatments, were still a physically young woman.

From the office I call for a hire-car and find there will be some delay.

When I disconnect, Powell asks, "How long?"

"Three quarters of an hour, more or less."

"Good. That gives us time to talk." He indicates a swivel

chair, upholstery cracked, behind the old desk. "You might as well be comfortable."

I sit. Powell perches on the edge of the desk.

"This is one of the most successful evenings we've had here," he says. "You brought a lot of people in."

"It *was* a good crowd, wasn't it? I had no idea so many people were interested in poetry."

Powell laughs. "When you forbid people something, it naturally becomes very attractive. In a sick sort of way, it's actually good for the arts."

"I see your point."

"And then, the Ministry of Domestic Labor gives importees excellent training in the language. The methods are somewhat dehumanizing, but the results are fine."

"I know. Suli speaks better than I do, I often think."

Powell has brought the wine bottle with him. Miraculously, it is still half full. He opens it and takes a swig, then offers it to me.

"Pardon the informality. I don't have anything catching, do you?"

I shake my head. "I'm not sure. I'd best not."

"Come, now."

"No, really."

"You're not worried about being unladylike, are you?"

"No. I'm worried about communicable disease. Mine."

"All right, then." He climbs down from the desk and goes for a moment into the office behind us, comes back with a chipped mug. "This should allay your fears."

"Yes. Thanks. As long as you wash it very well before anyone uses it again."

He fills the mug with wine.

I take it from him and sigh. "Maybe I'm being over-cautious. I'm not sure. But I'd rather not take chances."

"You're being mysterious," Powell says. "Tell me what the problem is."

"No."

"Well then." Powell resumes his seat on the desk. "Back to my pitch. There's an amazing lot of talent around. More than the Ministries ever dreamed."

"Where?"

"Here. Everywhere. Among the importees, the dissenters. The mortals. There's something about knowing one's going to die that feeds the artistic impulse, I think. And it seems to be a comfort, too, a kind of redemption." Powell looks me embarrassingly in the eye. I rock on the old chair springs a little, to relieve the intensity of his gaze. "You'd know that better than I, of course," he says. "Isn't it odd how things work themselves out? Those damn discoveries have botched a lot of lives." He drinks from the bottle again. "I envy you, Eve."

I feel a little thrill of pleasure, hearing him use my name. I smile at him. "I envy you."

"Why? Why? You made the right choice. That took courage, and foresight. You're a remarkable woman, Eve."

"I'm an old woman, John." Suddenly I feel I must stand up, move around. The chair springs protest. I pace the narrow perimeter of the office.

"That's the beauty of it. Of you. Don't you see?"

I have to laugh, more at us than at him, each wanting what the other has. "Maybe no one's ever satisfied," I say. Then, my old refrain, "It hasn't turned out at all as I'd imagined."

"No? Why not?"

I realize I can't tell him. It would be a betrayal of Marcus, and of the self I've always presented to the world, and to myself. I stick by my choices. I don't complain. Powell is dangerous, because he makes me want to say too much. Nor do I know him well enough to trust him. He's a radical, a political man, and I don't want to be used for politics, another pointless missile hurled at the unyielding Government. Cautious, I tell myself. Go slow. Shut up.

Now he, too, stands. "Well, that's all beside the point, really. I must be feeling the effects of the wine. What I wanted to talk to you about was teaching here."

A number of quick images flash into my mind—myself, useful and admired; human contact; a chance to help; a challenge; working with Powell, coming to know him well—to create the net impression of wanting to say yes. Another set—myself dying; Marcus; Jason; even the police—rise up to tell me no. In the end, the two impulses come into perfect balance and leave me paralyzed.

"Oh, I couldn't," I say lamely.

"Why not? I think you'd enjoy it. You'd certainly be good. What have you got to lose?"

I was right; Powell is dangerous, if only because he asks the right questions.

"I'm not sure," I answer honestly.

"Think about it, Eve," he tells me. "You have a lot to give. And you owe the Government nothing. They exploited your talent, then turned you out. They don't want you anymore. But we need you."

"Is it dangerous?" I ask, feeling stupid.

"Not really." Powell smiles. "The Government still has to pay some kind of lip service to the old constitution, you know. I'll admit, there are a lot of loopholes. But they can't really do you any harm. Just withdraw privileges, withold the rewards." He pauses. "For me, it was hard at first. But after a while I found they hadn't taken away too much I really wanted."

Now Suli and Alan Wills appear in the doorway. Powell motions them inside.

"I've just been trying to railroad Eve into teaching here at the Guilds," he says good-naturedly. "If you'd given me another ten minutes, I think I might have had her."

He offers them wine, but both decline it.

"I'm very glad you turned up when you did," I tell them. "Have you changed your mind about coming home, Suli?"

She smiles and shakes her head.

"That's two men with limited powers of persuasion," Wills says.

In the street, the car's horn bleats for us.

"Yes. You both lose, for the moment." I put on my coat and Powell hands me my poems.

"Only for the moment, I hope," he says. "You think about it, Eve. I'll be in touch."

"All right."

Suli and Wills walk arm in arm up the corridor before us.

"They make a handsome couple," Powell comments, offering me his arm. I shift my poems to take it, find it pleasant to walk with him, if a little strange. After so many years, I am used to Marcus' way of walking. Powell moves differently, limbs looser. He trims his stride to mine.

Once in the car, I feel my age, held in abeyance for a while, catch up to me again. Suli and I keep our own counsel on the long ride home.

10

Except for a night light in the hallway, the downstairs of the house is dark when we get home. Suli's quarters are on the first floor, and we bid each other good night. I climb the dark stairs toward the lighted upstairs hall. The house seems very quiet, but listening carefully, I hear the little shifts and sighs that signify Marcus is still awake. The door to his room is slightly ajar, and on impulse, I knock softly, then push it open, curious to see the husband who is such a presence in my mind, yet sometimes so hard to conjure up in human form.

He sits at his desk, in front of the lexavision viewer, wearing an old plaid bathrobe I gave him many years ago. "Hello there," I say.

He swings his chair around. "It's you."

"Uh huh."

"Well, you look pleased with yourself. It must have gone well."

It's warm in here; I unbutton my coat and pull it off. "As a matter of fact, it did. Very well. The crowd was very responsive."

"I'm glad," he says, rubbing his eyes.

"Were you waiting up for me?" I tease.

He looks embarrassed. "Well, since I'm up, I'll take credit for it. Sure."

"How sweet." I go to kiss him on the forehead.

"You *are* in a fine mood."

"Am I?"

He puts an arm around my waist. I respond by sitting on his lap, and kicking off my shoes. Marcus, I think, doesn't look so very much older than John Powell. His hair and beard have turned partially gray, of course, but this becomes him; it matches the seriousness in his eyes.

He groans under my weight. "Oof. I wasn't expecting that."

"Cheer up. It's good for you."

"I'm an old man."

"So? I'm an old woman."

"For an old woman, you don't look so bad."

"Thanks." I ruffle his hair. "John Powell said something similar. This must be my lucky day."

"What?"

"What what?"

"What did Powell say?"

"Oh. He said some women are beautiful at any age. Something like that."

"A real cavalier poet," Marcus says.

"He's a very nice man, I think." I am enjoying myself immensely. Even if Marcus' signs of jealousy are sham, they please me. It's a long time since he's had any reason to be jealous of me.

"You're rather late getting home."

"What time is it?"

"Going for midnight. Way past your bedtime. And mine."

"That late. Goodness. It feels like ten."

Marcus smiles. "To me, it feels like three in the morning."

I nod gravely. "Jason does have that effect."

"Eve!" Marcus laughs. "You know it's not that. Jason dropped me at the lab before nine. I've been working ever since."

I pat his cheek. "That's very virtuous."

He makes to tickle me. "Hey, lay off. We're close to a breakthrough. I want to watch this happen very carefully."

"Tell me what it is."

He puts a finger to my lips. "Can't. Sorry. Sooner or later, maybe."

"I guess I'll just have to wait."

"That's right."

I put my arms around my husband's neck. After so much touching tonight, I am hungry for more; I want to touch this man. He wriggles in my embrace, and some of my customary shyness rushes back.

"Am I bothering you, Marcus? I'm sorry. I'll leave you alone." I start to slide off his lap, but he holds me there.

"No. It's not that. I'm just tired. It *is* time for bed."

"Can I sleep with you tonight, Marcus? Please?"

He hesitates before answering, then smiles. "All right. But don't expect any miracles."

"Oh, no," I assure him. "No miracles. Just sleep."

"You won't be disappointed?"

"Heavens no. It'll be a treat just to lie next to you."

"All right. Get up then. Let's go to bed."

"Loan me some pajamas?" I move toward his dresser.

Marcus is beside me in an instant. "No, wait. I'll get them for you." His voice calms. "You sit on the bed. Relax."

Obediently, I cross the room and sit, watching him with curiosity. He seems to probe carefully, then pulls out a pair of pajamas and tosses them to me.

I begin to undress, glad I have stayed slim, at least, in case Marcus should choose to look at me. He doesn't, but turns the covers down and climbs into bed himself. When I join him, he turns off the light. I settle into the crook of his arm, my head pillowed on his chest, long my favorite position.

"Sleep now," he tells me, patting my head with his free hand. Home now, I drift off easily.

Later, I wake up frightened, from a dream. I've lost Marcus; he is curled in a tight ball away from me. We do not touch. My breath comes fast and shallow; I really am afraid, though of what, it's hard to say.

Marcus and I sat at a table, in my dream, and I saw a woman coming toward us, then looked again, recognizing her. She stopped to greet some other people, at another table, then came to us. And I explained to Marcus that she was an old friend, a roommate from my college days. He greeted her cordially, saying, "See what good care I've taken of Eve." I searched for her married name, and was proud of myself for remembering.

My friend used to be rather heavy, but in my dream she was slim, and must have taken the treatments, because she did not seem old, though neither was she so young as when I knew her. There was a little web of wrinkles around her eyes.

I think what must have frightened me was her voice. She was a lively, effusive girl, who spoke quickly and with great energy, the way some people hit tennis balls. In my dream, her voice was flat and expressionless, and her words came very slow, as though it was hard for her to concentrate on our conversation. She seemed to be overcome by some profound ennui, not bored by us specifically but by all things, too exhausted by living to be glad to see us, or to produce even the small social tokens, the simple words we expected of her.

She was so very different, so sad.

I inch my way across the bed, until I am touching Marcus once again. We don't fit very conveniently this way, and his back is somehow less reassuring than his front, but still it is better than being alone with my fears.

11

The first thing I see, waking up, is that my prodigious stomach is gone, no longer domed. The next is Marcus, sitting beside the bed.

"Hi," I greet him. My voice is very small.

He gets up to stand above me, smiling down. "Hi."

"What happened?"

"Good things. We have a daughter now."

"Oh, Marcus. And she's all right?"

"Better than all right. She's beautiful."

"Does she look like you?"

"Like both of us. Do you hurt?"

"I don't know. Should I? Why was I asleep?" I try to concentrate on my body. It *is* sore, very. "Ouch."

"A cesarean. The little lady wasn't in there right."

"Oh. Can I see her?"

"I'll ask the doctor."

"What did they do to me? It really does hurt."

"Well, since they were inside anyway, and this is our second child, they did the hysterectomy, too."

A chill passes over me. "Ugh. No wonder I feel rotten."

"Yeah. The baby will help. She's gorgeous."

"Well, hurry up then. Get her. Even if you have to cosh a nurse."

"I'll see what I can do."

I hear the door close behind him. My eyelids are almost irresistibly heavy. In spite of my good intentions, I let them drop.

Then suddenly I hear Marcus' voice nearby, and the unmistakable cooing of my new daughter. They're like a vision, when I open my eyes. It is either early morning or late afternoon; the sun comes in at a golden slant and

plays around them. With one big finger, Marcus chucks the
baby on the chin. He is so enormous, and the bundle in
his arms so small.

"Oh, give her to me."

"Okay. Put out your arm."

I make a circle of my arm, and he puts the baby down
inside it. I manage to jack myself up a little on my other
elbow so I can look at her. "She *is* beautiful."

"Uhm hmmm."

I stroke my baby's face with my finger, then dig into her
blanket to see her other tiny, perfect parts, exclaiming at
her little rosy hands and feet, the small, round stomach,
that helpless, tender slit between her legs. Our daughter is
heartbreakingly beautiful.

"Come on, Daddy. Move your chair up here by us. We
have to name the lady."

Marcus slides his chair up to the head of the bed, sits
very close, and I rearrange the baby so I can see both of
my treasures at once.

There is a soft, persistent knocking at the door. Who
would want to interrupt us now? The knock goes on.

"All right. Okay. Come in," I call. I hear the door open,
but the footfalls are soft.

"Mrs. Harmon?"

"Yes, what is it? Come here where I can see you."

In a moment, Suli stands before me, smiling down. She
carries a breakfast tray. I see I am sitting in my chair.

"Good morning, Suli."

"Good morning, Mrs. Harmon. How are you today?"

"Fine, I think. Feeling the effects of last night's wine
perhaps. Nothing serious. And you?"

"Oh, I'm well." She stands a moment, smiling still, before
she puts down the tray. "Anything else, Mrs. Harmon?"

"Yes. Absolutely. Sit down and postmortem with me."

"Postmortem?"

"Certainly. Dissect the body. I want to talk about last
night. Pull up a chair and humor an old woman."

"Very well." She moves toward the desk chair. "This
one?"

I nod. She draws it nearer and sits down.

"Would you like coffee, too? I probably have another cup hidden away somewhere."

"I've already had breakfast."

"Well, I'll go ahead with mine, if you don't mind." I am somewhat heartier than usual, partly to help cover my lapse, partly because I find I genuinely *feel* very fine this morning. It makes me bold. I've found a certain role, the nosy dowager, that pleases me.

"Now tell me about Alan Wills. He's a very attractive man, Suli. Yours, I hope."

Suli drops her eyes, but I can see a smile toying with the corners of her mouth.

"Alan is my friend," she says, her voice gloriously noncommittal.

"It seems to me he looks at you with something more than brotherly love."

"Perhaps so," Suli allows. "Alan was very moved by your poems."

She tries to change the subject by appealing to my vanity. It works, of course. I'm hungry for feedback, anxious to recapture some of last night's elation. "Was he really? I'm pleased. Then I didn't embarrass you, Suli?"

She looks puzzled. "Embarrass me? I don't understand."

"No, I suppose not. That's all right. It's just that since it was the first time you were going to hear me read, in my own mind, I was reading to you. It helped me get through it, anyway." I laugh, trying to make my words seem less sincere, so Suli won't be put off by them.

"Oh," she says. "Thank you."

"Tell me about Alan. Have you known him long?"

"About four years."

"That's long enough to know a man."

"Yes. Alan is a good man."

I shouldn't ask, but do. "And you love him?"

Suli meets my eyes with a kind of smiling defiance. "Certainly. And he loves me."

"Will you marry, Suli?"

"We can't."

"Why not?" I ask. "If you're worried about your job, you won't lose it. You're welcome to live out."

"It's not that. Alan isn't an importee. He was born here.

He's not a servant. The law prohibits natives, of any race, from marrying with importees."

"Right. I remember now." Damn Jason. That was just one part of a massive bill he drafted several years ago. That clause, about marriages, was a way to keep importees from being naturalized and attaining the full complement of civil rights. It set up the importee police, too, and special courts to handle infractions—in effect, it created a totally separate and unequal legal system for the domestic work force.

I thought the legislation was abominable then, even though it passed easily and won Jason his first major boost up the bureaucratic ladder. Now, for the first time, I see its human implications.

"Is there no way around it, Suli?"

"No good way," she says. "The only way is to go back to my country. And it would take years, and a fortune, to get us both released. And if we were, we would be going home to famine and chaos. Our lives would not be long or prosperous."

"No, I suppose not. Is there no other country you could go to?"

"Not as free people. Russia or Europa might admit us as importees, if this government would let us go. But that's no improvement."

"What about going to another city? Losing yourselves in this country?"

Suli looks directly at me. "Perhaps. We've thought of it. But the chances aren't good. The Ministry likes to make examples of those who try."

"Maybe I could pick Jason's brains. Try to find out how the enemy thinks," I offer, because I don't want to believe that nothing can be done.

"Please don't, Mrs. Harmon. He would guess why you were asking, and that would only make it worse. We've managed for four years."

"But it's wrong, Suli. It's worse than wrong."

She shrugs. "Yes, it's wrong. But it's also how things are."

"At least I can give you more time. They can't stop me from doing that."

"My card says I have liberty on Wednesday nights only. Alan works in the days."

"We'll change your card then. Surely that can be done."

"Perhaps so." She smiles at me ruefully. "We have found, as a rule, it is better not to make oneself too visible to the Ministry. To be visible is to invite harassment."

"If Jason has a humane bone in him, and I'm not sure, mind you, then we'll get it changed. I promise you that."

"Try if you like, Mrs. Harmon. But do not expect to succeed."

"I will try, Suli. It's time I tried." Another idea comes to me. "Wait. If Alan is a citizen, he can go anywhere he likes, right?"

She nods.

"Then he can come here. Every night, if you like."

"Dr. Harmon might object. Mr. Jason surely would."

"Well, not on nights that Jason's around then. But they're infrequent enough. We can plan around that."

"But Dr. Harmon . . . ?"

"If I have influence over nothing else, I should at least be able to bring my own husband around. He's not a monster, you know. He was in love once himself."

Something like pain casts its shadow on Suli's face. "Mrs. Harmon," she begins.

"What, Suli?"

"Well, nothing." She seems to have changed her mind. Instead, she asks, "Will you teach at the Poets' Guild? Mr. Powell seemed eager to have you."

"Yes. I don't know, Suli. I want to, I think. But there are problems."

"Dr. Harmon would not like it?" She puts as a question what we both know to be a certainty.

"No, probably not. But that's not my only concern. I wonder if I'm up to it."

"I know many people who would study with you," Suli says.

"That's reassuring. I will think about it. Right now it seems to be the only show in town."

"I beg your pardon?"

"It's the only place I'm wanted. And that certainly makes it more attractive. More so than sitting in this house and waiting to die, however long *that* takes me." Here I laugh, deliberately.

"No. Do not invite your death to visit you. It comes unbidden soon enough."

"That's very nice, Suli."

"Thank you," she says, and smiles.

12

"Ask him to call his mother then, will you?" Not finding Jason in, I leave a message with his secretary. Perhaps I am putting the cart before the horse. It would be wiser to speak to Marcus first. Jason listens to him more than to me; I should not try to move mountains by myself, but apply politics instead, be wise, wary, and manipulative. Already the gulf between me and my son is so great that my endorsement of one position would probably drive him to the opposite pole, despite the merits of either.

I should proceed more carefully. I will. It's just that I feel so useless, here in my room, that I'm anxious to undertake anything that will give me some sense of purpose. Still, I shouldn't jeopardize my cause to satisfy my ego. If history has lessons, that, surely, is one of them.

I feel good today, I do, in spite of the syringes in my drawer, the red tag hung around my neck. Too good, in fact, to be as I am, without prospects, without places to go. In the first years of my professional career, I worked to escape institutions and to win the freedom to write, at my own pace, in my own home. I won my leisure, and when I could escape it at will, it became all the more precious to me; I thought carefully before relinquishing my self or my time to any cause.

Today, without a task, my time has turned on me. If I write, my poems will not be published. I may never give a reading again. Suli manages my house far better than I could, even if I wanted to. My daughter is dead, and I am estranged from my son. In the old days, I might have had grandchildren to fill the house and my hours with their harmless demands. One among them might have been interested in poetry, or stories; we might have read together.

What do other women do? Plenty of women, plenty, fill days like these for forty years or more—how, I cannot begin to imagine. Maybe they are privy to secrets that elude me, have different needs than mine. I envy the others, too, able to be absorbed in bureaucratic games for countless years, committed to the long, slow climb to longer hours, greater glory, more people to give orders to. Had I been a doctor or a mathematician, and believed in medicine or mathematics, I would be very different now.

But this is useless speculation. What is Eve Harmon to do while waiting to die? There is always the blue chair, waiting, welcoming, ready to whisk me away with magic carpet swiftness into the past, where the suspense of living is still strong and the simple curiosity about how it will all end is sufficient motivation to keep one going through the best and worst of times.

There is John Powell (intriguing thought), somewhere in this city, perhaps still interested in using me to his own good ends. He said he would be in touch, and I am waiting for him to call me. Though I don't like to admit it, the man has infiltrated my consciousness, touched some chord that wants striking again.

Powell. Yes, he has been on my mind. I would like to talk to him again, because talking to him felt good. No, more than good, if I'm honest. It made me feel interesting, and attractive. Damn it, he made me feel like a woman, exercised some invisible female organs that had begun to atrophy. I was, in short, the victim of his charm. And it was nice to be so victimized. At seventy-five, one should perhaps allow oneself to be taken in, or even used. If the rewards are sufficiently pleasant, who says they have to be real?

It's quite impossible to believe that Powell could be interested in me as a woman. And yet, if he is willing, for obscure reasons of his own, to pretend to be, should I deny myself the pleasure that it gives? Where is the harm?

I am foolish to think of him at all. He has a lover, probably beautiful, maybe an importee. Perhaps many lovers. Certainly much business in his life. No need for me. I must not think of him.

Suddenly I am curious about myself, my physical self. A mirror hangs over my dresser, most often avoided as I pass, and I go to stand before it now to see, objectively as possible, what this woman, Eve Harmon, I, am like.

Well, still slim. The planes of my face are still visible, and they are not *bad* planes. The years have softened a certain sharpness in my features, without obliterating them. My eyes are still big, still very blue, and the lines around them, though many and deep, do not distress me. They have not contorted my face, but reinforced it, imprinted my personality upon my flesh. My hair, a reddish brown, did not begin to change till rather late in life, and when it did, the white hair diffused itself with amazing evenness, so that the total effect is one of lightening, and leaves me rather sandy-haired. It is long, because I once promised Marcus I wouldn't cut it short, and I wear it up and off my face, concealing nothing, revealing all.

I lean across the dresser and try to read my eyes, asking them to tell me who I am. Somewhere inside the mirrored face, I see another, as clearly as my own: a little girl, eyes earnest, looking for a vision of the woman she will become. I close my eyes and shake my head twice, to exorcise the ghost.

The buzzer rings, and I go to the desk. "Yes, Suli?"

"You have a visitor."

"Who is it please?"

"Mr. John Powell."

"Oh, Suli. Ask him to wait. In the living room. Offer him something. I'll be down."

Powell is here, in my house, and I'm upstairs in my dressing gown, nervous and excited. I rush to my closet and throw back the door. This is no time for experiments. I must find something that feels right on my body, that makes me feel in harmony. I pick a lavender dress, not new, but friendly, that shows my slimness and has long, loose sleeves. Kicking off my slippers, I replace them with shoes, and though I have never trafficked much in makeup, apply what I have, to pinken my cheeks a little, and put a shine on my lips. My hair is already done in its customary way; I pat a few stray hairs into place. Five minutes, and there is nothing more I can do.

Wait! Earrings. I find gold hoops and put them in my ears, then head for the door, trying to ease my accelerated breathing, to appear calm.

Perfume. I've forgotten it. I hurry back to the dresser and spray myself with a grass and sunshine smell, start out once more.

I really should brush my teeth. I can't remember if I have today. Into the bathroom I go, succeed in dribbling toothpaste down my chin. I wipe it clean. Now I have wiped off the shiny cream from my lips. I restore it.

Ten, eleven minutes have gone by, and my toilet has reached the point of diminishing returns. Nothing I can do now will be of sufficiently good effect to justify a longer wait.

Coming downstairs, I try to compose myself. Near the bottom, I regret my choice of the lavender dress, and must clamp down on the impulse to run back to my room to change it for something else. Who wears dresses like this around the house? Well, perhaps *I* would, if I were a different sort of woman. And now I must pretend that I do, though Suli knows better, and will think me foolish.

I meet her coming out of the living room, and flinch under her smile.

"You look very nice."

"Thanks, Suli."

"What is Mr. Powell having?"

"He said he'd wait for you."

"Come back, then. In a little while."

She moves away. For some reason, I am hesitant to go into the living room, regret, almost, letting on I was at home. Powell might have called first. It was really quite impudent of him to come. I feel a little angry. He has assumed my life's so empty now he would be welcome anytime.

He's right. I sigh, then straighten my shoulders and walk into the living room. Powell sits on the sofa, settled comfortably, his arm spread across the back, legs crossed. In the familiar context of my living room, he seems larger than he did at the Guilds, looks younger. My heart sinks with shame; I've been very foolish indeed. The defensiveness in my own mind extends now to him, as a certain coldness in my greeting.

He stands all the same, and half crosses the room to take my hand. I blush violently, the victim of my own fantasies.

"I really shouldn't have stopped in like this," he begins.

"But I'm rarely in this part of town, and so I did. I know I wasn't invited, but I did, somehow, feel welcome."

"Of course. Sit down." I sit myself, on one end of the sofa, wondering if this will drive him to a chair, but he takes up his place on the sofa as before, apparently without thinking about it.

"And what have I interrupted you in?"

I turn a little to face him. "Thinking, is all."

"A valuable pursuit."

"Not necessarily."

"What were you thinking about?"

The question brings me up. "A number of things. None of earth-shattering significance."

"No?"

"Well, perhaps for me. My world's shrunk so I'm becoming your classic solecist. Though I haven't quite reverted to thinking the sun moves around the earth. Perhaps that will come later."

He smiles. "Then we must expand your universe a little. Have you thought about joining us?"

"I've thought about it, yes."

"And?"

"Decided nothing."

"Well, I've come to push you over the line."

13

"What are you doing?" Marcus asks.

"Who me?" I put my folder down beside me. "I'm reading."

"Mm. You look nice. I've always liked that dress," he says, coming around to the front of the sofa. "New poems?"

"Yes. But not mine."

"Did some aspiring fool send you another third-rate manuscript to look at?"

"This is far from third-rate stuff," I tell him. "Some is quite good. Most of the rest is promising."

"So who is the promising poet? Anyone I know?"

"I really doubt it."

"You're awfully close."

"Do you really want to know? Sit down."

Marcus sighs, shakes off his coat and puts his briefcase down, then takes a chair across the coffee table from me. "Well?"

"Well, these are poems written by members of the Poets' Guild. Good poems."

"Uh huh."

"Some of the freshest talent I've seen in a long time."

Clearly Marcus wonders what I'm getting at; for years I mistook husbandly interest in my career for an interest in poetry, but eventually resigned myself to the untruth of this, and now try not to bore him with long dissertations. "John Powell has asked me to teach some workshops there. He brought me these as supporting evidence for his case."

"Powell came here?" Marcus asks, leaning a little forward in his chair. "When?"

"Oh, today. Late morning, I guess. He stayed for lunch."

"Well," Marcus says. "That must have brightened your day considerably."

"It *was* pleasant, yes."

"When did you invite him?"

"I didn't. He just turned up. It was almost lunchtime, so I asked him to stay."

"It never changes. These sleazy poet types come sniffing around my wife while I'm away at the lab. And she, bless her naive little heart, lets them in and invites them to lunch."

"Marcus!" It is fine for him to impugn other men's motives; if he wants to believe that every man on earth is salivating after me, so much the better. When it comes to a question of my honor, though, I immediately become defensive. "You know that ever since I met you, you've had absolutely no grounds for jealousy."

"I've been jealous," he says, a little defensive himself.

"But without cause. You know damn well that in fifty years, you're the only man I've slept with."

"Really?" Marcus asks. "Is that true?"

He knows it is, of course, or suspects it strongly; assuredly, he's not lost sleep over rivals for many years. But it seems to please him to be reassured every now and then, so I make this little speech. "Really, Marcus. But you know that. If only you were so straightforward."

He laughs. "It pays to keep you guessing, Eve."

"For forty years? Did you sleep with Liz Wilson, or didn't you?"

"Eve. For pity's sake."

"Come on, Marcus. Surely you can tell me now. Neither one of us has even *seen* the woman in thirty-five years."

"Well, all right," Marcus says, picking at the knee of his trousers. "No, I didn't sleep with Liz Wilson."

"Hallelujah!" I whoop, vindicated after so much time. In my heart, it has never seemed to me that Marcus could have dallied with his lab assistant, partly because he is too discreet, partly because our own sex life was so good at that time it would have taken a remarkable man, a satyr, to have kept up a side affair at the same time.

"You needn't gloat," he tells me. His smile is rather sheepish.

"Of course I'll gloat. You've been torturing me with that for decades. This calls for a celebration." Impulsively, I ring for Suli, and when she appears, ask for a bottle of wine and two glasses. Her expression, setting the tray down between us, mixes amusement with a little wonder. I wink at her, when Marcus won't see.

"Well, pour the wine."

"Eve, this is silly," Marcus grumbles.

"Of course," I say. "Open it, *garçon*." I hand him the corkscrew. He looks at the label on the bottle.

"This is good wine, Eve."

"Uhm hmm. What better occasion?"

We listen in silence to the tantalizing pop of the cork. Marcus fills his own glass and takes a sip.

"Very nice."

"You big phony."

"It *is* very nice. I never said I would have known the name without reading the label."

"You're right. I'm sorry. You're only a *little* phony."

"Thanks." He fills my glass, then his own.

I raise mine. "To fidelity. A beautiful and difficult thing."

Our glasses touch, and I look up to meet Marcus' eyes, but he avoids my gaze. I sip, then sigh.

"I'll never make a romantic of you, will I?"

"And I'll never make a scientist of you. Nor a realist, I suspect."

"*Touché.*" Then something turns me serious, just a bit, and I say, "We *have* done well, haven't we, Marcus? All things considered, it's been a good fifty years."

"All things considered," he says drily.

"Oh, Marcus, you know what I mean. We've done better than most people, I think."

"People," he muses, looking into his glass. "People are unreliable at best."

"Well, that's one of the things to be considered."

He laughs. "Most people aren't like you, Eve. You're very loyal. You set yourself high standards."

His praise embarrasses, even frightens me a little. "No higher than yours, Marcus."

"See? That's what I mean. You're always insisting other people are as good as you are."

"Marcus, please. Don't canonize me yet. It makes me feel ancient. Dead, almost. I've got a few transgressions left in me yet. Let me enjoy them."

"Such as?" he asks, smiling paternally, as though he expected to be bored by my sins.

"For instance," I counter, "I imagined John Powell to have the crassest of motives concerning me. And at my age, that doesn't mean sex. It means politics. As it turns out, I think he's really quite sincere."

"Does that mean he wants sex after all?"

"Marcus, you're a master at being exasperating. If you must know, I think he genuinely likes me and admires my work."

"What a delightfully soft touch you are," Marcus says.

"I am not." His paternalism begins to irritate. "Is it so very hard to imagine someone liking me and my poems without having some unspeakable, nefarious purpose behind it?"

"Theoretically, no." Marcus smiles. "I do."

I refill both our glasses, then sip from mine. "That's good." I smile back at him. "Marcus, I'm going to do it. I'm going to teach at the Poets' Guild."

14

Michael is merely sullen. I try to make him angry. "But what does 'strength' mean to you, Michael? What makes you strong? It's awfully arrogant to expect the rest of us to believe you're strong just because you say so."

Michael's dark eyes flash. His voice, when he speaks, is very level, because he exerts enormous control over it. His fingers grip the table's edge tightly.

"My strength is of the endurance kind," he says with dignity. "My strength lies in what I do not do. I do not correct my employer when he is wrong. I do not break his dishes or dent his car because I hate him. I do not hit the IP pig who asks for my card and harasses me in the subway station, to make me miss the train. I do not break the law under extreme provocation. But I do not surrender the integrity of my thoughts to any man." His voice has risen, now falls slightly, and the first hint of self-humor steals over him and shows itself in the beginning of a smile. "Nor to any woman," he adds. "But that is another matter." He pauses, and looks at each of us in turn. "That is my strength," he says.

All are silent for a moment, then I let my own smile break through, and lean across the table slightly to touch Michael's arm.

"That's it, Michael. That's right. And that's what belongs in your poem." I laugh a little, delighted, "If you put it like that, no 'IP pig' would ever make the mistake of thinking you meant to say you lift weights."

He looks down at the sheet in front of him, already marked with transpositions, annotations, and cruel cross-outs. At first he smiles, then laughs a little at himself.

"You're probably right." He sighs, looks at the marked-up poem with skepticism. "It *is* no good."

"Wait," I tell him. "It's a fine poem. Or will be. Not to be laid aside. We've dissected the corpse, now you must resurrect it."

He looks to the others, for support in thinking, I suppose, that I'm a hard and sometimes incomprehensible old bat. Each face around the table sends him back a slightly different message. Everyone is sympathetic, of course, having undergone a similar attack sometime in the last few weeks, but they have learned from the experience, too, and, as they are not my current victims, can be much more objective than he.

"You know, Michael," Tina says, "if you put it in specific terms like that, it would give the whole thing more focus. I can only take so many of those big, heavy symbolic nouns in a row before I start wondering if you really have anything to say."

"Tina's got a point," Mitbu says. "I'd certainly like to see more concrete imagery. It's your poem, man. But it's going to stay that way, unless you get other people into it."

I lean back in my chair, privileged to be a listener. This is just beginning to happen, that my students are relaxed enough to criticize and help each other. Frankly, I'm glad, for more reasons than one. Teaching exhausts me, as much as it exhilarates. I had not really done enough of it before to know how much one must use, not just one's knowledge, but one's whole personality. I am suddenly very tired, and glad that the discussion can progress by itself, without my prodding. It is close to the end of the hour, and this is my last class of the day.

"What should we do for next time?" Tina asks.

As I lean forward to strike a better thinking position, a knife-sharp stab of pain shoots under my left arm. I feel my face contort with it, and don't move my body, waiting for the pain to pass, as it always has before.

"Mrs. Harmon, are you all right?" Tina asks.

"Yes, certainly. I think one of you should think up next week's exercise. Michael, how about you?"

He looks up from his massacred poem and smiles widely at the class. "That's easy," he says. "I give us all the same task I set for myself. Write a poem about hate, without ever using the word 'hate' or any synonym."

I look around weakly. The pain has not passed as I anticipated, but seems to hold me in a vise. "All right?"

They nod and close their notebooks, rise to go. I stay paralyzed in my chair, waiting for relief. Through the open door, I see Tina stop Michael in the hallway with a light touch on the arm, with a question I cannot overhear. Smiles bracket his response. Tina listens hard, then says something back to him. There follows one of those lovely, awkward scenes, the caesuras of human relations, wherein people metamorphose to become something to each other they have not been before. The junction is passed smoothly; I see them leave together, and know they will remain together for a while.

I smile, despite the pain that still haunts my left side. I think it has let up some, is giving way, but I feel weakened by it, and remain sitting.

There is not much traffic in the halls. Most of the students are gone within five minutes, and no one passes the door for a long time. The pain has gone now, but left me shaky and frightened. Each time it comes, it is sharper and stays longer. Seduced by the solitude of the old school building, I lean forward over my crossed arms and let tears come, not, I tell myself, from self-pity, but because teaching makes me nervous and I need the release.

For whatever reason I am crying, it absorbs me, and I do not know John has come into the room until he puts a gentle hand on my head and says, "Come, Eve. Teaching here isn't all *that* bad."

15

While John is in the kitchen, I try to arrange myself with a little more dignity. He has pulled the old green blanket up to my chin; I draw it down a little and put my arms outside, prop myself a little higher on the cushion, even try to pat my hair in place a bit. I feel much better now.

John comes back, walking cautiously with two full cups of tea, and does not look at me until he puts them down on the table by my side. Now he straightens up, with obvious pride and relief.

"Well done," I commend him.

"Not so bad, was it? I didn't spill a drop. Still, I wish you'd have something stronger."

"I never drink before five."

"In ten minutes, I'll pour you a whopper then."

"In ten minutes, I should be on my way. I feel much better." I pick up my tea and take a sip. It's so strong it seems to turn solid on the end of my tongue. "Maybe I'll break my rule after all."

"Is it that bad?" he asks.

I nod.

"Good." He gets up and goes to an old cabinet, takes out a bottle of whisky, and splashes a stiff drink in each of two unmatched glasses. "Specialty of the house," he says, handing me one. "I think I do it rather well."

The whisky does taste good. "My compliments."

He takes a swig from his glass, makes an appreciative noise, then sits down in a tattered armchair across from me. The springs creak audibly under his weight, and he shifts in the chair until he finds a position where they don't torment him too much.

"This is a fine chair, basically," he says. "But it takes some knowing."

"Yes. I can hear it talking back."

He shrugs. "It's old and tired. Like everything else in this hole."

"Occupant excepted."

"Hardly," he says. "I'm seventy-six myself," he says.

"Older than me even. That's a surprise. But it doesn't count. You don't look a day over forty."

"Nor will I ever, damn it. But inside my head, I'm seventy-six."

"I wonder." The man opposite me seems vigorous and strong. He even crosses his legs like a young man, like one who need not think about stiffening joints or muscles less elastic than they once were. Age is of the body, too, a process of learning to calculate and compensate for increasing limitations. "I can't argue that you've got seventy-six years of experience stored away, of course."

He leans forward, striking a new truce with the chair. "It all comes back to the same thing. I envy you, Eve. I didn't know it was going to be like this."

I smile at him, feeling, for the moment, a little motherly. "You won't envy me so much in a year or two, when I'm dead and you're still brewing awful tea."

"That's just it," he says. "How terrible to contemplate an eternity of bad tea."

I laugh. "You're right. I'll be spared that, anyway."

"No, really," he says, seeming to ask to be taken seriously. "I'll never be any better at the things I can't do now. I'll just go on and on, being somewhere between mediocre and ridiculous. And the things I can do, well, it just seems too easy. I suspect that growth requires change."

"But you can change. You do. Everything does."

He resists my point. There *is* a barrier between us, although I think we both want very much to be in sympathy. I cannot pity him his life, or he my death.

"Oh dear," I say.

John gets up and goes to the cabinet to pour himself another drink. "Take sex," he says, turning back to face me, a little flushed. "How can there be any poignance, without change?"

This turn amuses me. "Poor thing," I cluck. "It must be dreadful, always banging the same old young, firm bodies. How boring."

"Well, it *is*," he says defensively. Though we speak in negatives, the topic gives me a little positive charge of energy. I feel silly reclining, and swing my legs down from the sofa, pulling the blanket away. Because I don't know quite what else to do, I pick up my drink and finish it, in one long swallow.

"Oh, you're ready for another." He snatches up my glass. "I'm sorry. I should have asked."

I reach out after the glass. "Wait, John. I shouldn't."

"Of course, you should." He takes it to the cabinet and fills it, fuller than before, then comes to sit on the couch, in the place recently vacated by my feet. Almost, he has the air of a suitor. It strikes me as so incongruous, and so delightful, I have to laugh.

He smiles back nervously. "What's funny? Me, I suppose."

"Well, yes," I tell him. "You, and me too. Being here is funny."

"In my apartment? Why?"

Involuntarily, I blush a little.

"Well?" he says.

I feel compelled to answer. "It's a compromising situation, and yet it's not. The irony amuses me."

"You believe too much in irony," John says. "It's one of your major faults."

"For god's sake, John."

"It is."

"What do you know about my faults?"

He looks at me sideways, a little sulkily. "A lot," he says. "More than you'd imagine."

I resettle myself on the sofa. Everyone enjoys being the topic of conversation, and I am no exception. I let myself be drawn in. "Such as?" I ask. "Tell me about my faults."

He laughs. "Wouldn't you rather hear about your virtues?"

"Not at all. I'm sure my faults are more interesting."

"All right then." He takes another drink. "Perhaps your biggest fault is the extent to which you underestimate yourself."

"Oh, stop it, John. Don't be absurd."

"I really don't understand it, Eve. I even suspect foul

play. You're a lovely woman, but won't believe you're attractive. You're a vital woman, and pretend to be tottering on the brink of senility. You're talented, and won't believe your work's worth anything. It's crazy."

"Realistic," I counter, smiling.

"I don't understand. The Government, your husband, everybody's putting you out to pasture, and you aren't even angry."

"Angry? Why should I be angry? I knew what bargains I was making."

"Did you?"

"Well, some of them, anyway."

"Don't be so damn stoic."

"It's a privilege of age. Besides, it saves energy."

"I'd rather see you mad."

"No you wouldn't. I have a wretched temper. I've only seen it about three times myself. But it's awful."

"Only three times?" he asks in disbelief.

I nod. "Three times too many, too. My knees locked back so tight they trembled, and every one of my muscles did a nice imitation of tetanus. I made myself sick. Really physically ill."

"What did it take, to make you so angry?"

I smile at his curiosity. "We won't go into that."

John sighs. "I wish you'd trust me, Eve."

"I trust you. I'm in your apartment, aren't I?" I try to tease him out of his seriousness, laugh a little. John's melancholy disturbs me, it doesn't fit him well, and makes me nervous. Instead of answering, he looks at me for a very long time, until I have to say, "John, stop it. You're making me nervous. You're worse than all the machines at the Clinics that take pictures of your insides."

He drops his eyes to his glass, and finding it empty, gets up roughly to fill it for a third time.

"Look, John," I say to his back, "I really have to go." I look around for a telecom, then rise to use it, punching up the number for information.

"Yes. Burton Car-Hire Company, please," I tell the operator.

Suddenly, as she begins to read me the number in her nasal tone, John takes the receiver from me and puts it back in the cradle. I spin around to see what he means by it. When I face him, he puts his hands on my shoulders and pulls me toward him, very quickly. His face, blue eyes intent, comes down on mine. As he approaches, my own eyes close, by reflex, and I receive his kiss in my own physiological darkness. It startles me, because it is so unexpected, and because it feels so good.

John's skin is very warm, his cheeks a little rough with beard, but his lips are soft, just moist enough. An old feeling, long forgotten, stirs inside me, somewhere near the center of my being. It is the feeling of a flower opening inside me, stretching out petals and raising its head to the sun. The flower blooms somewhere near where my liver is supposed to be, though I'm sure this practical organ contributes nothing to the sensation. I imagine I can smell the flower's fragrance, yielded up to the light.

When I open my eyes, they look into John's, more than half a foot above. I can think of nothing to say to him. This is preposterous, I say to myself.

He loosens his grip on my shoulders and automatically I move back a little, away from him. His face fills my vision and makes me dizzy. In his expression, I can read only enormous tenderness. Something not organic shifts perceptibly inside me, reordering the elements, disrupting stability, and it drives me back into his arms, my own around him tightly. My head does not reach his shoulder; my face is lost in his blue sweater.

I don't *think* of anything at all, except perhaps how deliciously silent and blank my mind *is* for the moment, how very good it feels to exchange warmth for warmth, sorrow for sorrow, across our skins.

Then John's arms go slack around me for a moment, and I start to step out of them again, the beginnings of embarrassment infiltrating my brain. Before they take hold, though, he dispels them, picking me up unceremoniously, his arms tight around me. There is nothing to do but wrap my arms around his neck.

He carries me to another room and sets me down gently on his bed. For a moment he stands looking down at me, then sits beside me. His room is dim and disorderly, full of the smell I've come to associate with him. Two shirts and a sweater I recognize are heaped on a chair, and a wine bottle, not quite empty, stands on the dresser amid his toilet things. The bed, surprisingly, is made, but towels and clothing hang rakishly from the bedposts. Looking up, I see blotted stains on the ceiling, a maze of cracks in the old plaster.

"Oh, John," I say, and it sounds more reproachful than I meant it to.

He stretches out one arm and leans on it, leaving a triangular space between it and his body, through which I see his half-closed dresser drawers.

"Are you angry now?" he asks, looking hard into my face.

I examine my feelings before answering. "Oddly, no."

Now he puts his hand over mine, and strokes my forehead with the other, pushing back a few strands of hair that have managed to shake free. His tenderness is overwhelming. I have felt such tenderness inside myself, sometimes, with such intensity, holding my babies or, long ago, watching my husband as he slept, but never have I seen it manifested in another. Not toward me, anyway. It makes me feel safe, wonderfully secure, and my body relaxes past the point of what I know as relaxation, into a delicious, sleepy warmth. I try, once or twice, to shake myself out of it, then give up. It is entirely too pleasant to fight.

My voice, in this state, is soft and husky. "I *would* like to know what's going on, John."

He smiles at me, a lovely, gentle smile. "I want you," he says.

My eyes open a little wider and, though wary, tell him I feel the same.

16

"Call him then, if you must," John says, wriggling his arm from under me. "There. You can put on one of my shirts." He points at the chair.

Slowly I sit up, trying to hold myself erect, even though it's quite dark in the room, so John will not be disappointed in the body he's just partaken of. Quickly I cover myself with his shirt, down to the thighs, anyway, and reflect, as I leave the room, that my legs have always been good, and still are, with no bulging blue veins, no edema swelling the ankles.

In the fast-fading light of the living room, I call my home, glad it is Suli who answers.

"Mrs. Harmon, I've been worried about you."

"Don't, Suli." I hear the inappropriate lightness in my own voice, and try to tone it down. "I'm much better now. I had an attack of something or other at the Guilds. Quite unpleasant. I was afraid I couldn't make it home, so Mr. Powell brought me to his apartment, which is nearby."

There is alarm in Suli's voice. "Are you all right? Shall I come for you?"

"No, no. I really am pulling out of it. Just need to rest a bit more, I think. Then I'll come home. Is Marcus there?"

"Dr. Harmon called from the lab to say he wouldn't be home until rather late."

I smile at this stroke of luck.

"It seems that one of the experiments is in a crucial phase. He doesn't want to leave it. They'll send out for supper."

"Very well, Suli. Did you say what time he expected to be home?"

"Not before ten, Mrs. Harmon."

"I see. I won't hurry then. I'll wait till I really do feel square enough to travel. Thanks."

"Mrs. Harmon, wait. Let me call a car and come get you."

"Nonsense, Suli. It's not necessary. I'm sure Mr. Powell will bring me if I'm not well enough to travel by myself."

"Yes," Suli says. "Under the circumstances, I'm glad you're with Mr. Powell."

"Right, Suli. So am I. He's very kind," I say, glad she doesn't know quite how kind. "Till later, then. Don't worry."

We say goodbye. As John requested, I bring the whisky bottle back with me. When I enter the room, he says, "Turn on the light, if you will. The switch is by the door."

I shrivel inwardly at the thought. I have been regarding the darkness as an ally, something to help erase the startling physical discrepancy between our bodies. Still, light on, I will be able to look at John. I throw the switch.

"Hello," John says. A pillow is bunched up underneath his head, the sheets and blankets pulled up to his armpits. He pats the bed beside him. "Come, join me."

I move toward the empty side of the bed, wondering a bit that I do so, but proceeding nonetheless; the strange-but-plausible aura of a dream envelops me. As I turn back blankets and sheets, I uncover John's body, not wholly by accident, and take it in—his broad shoulders, nipples dark on a firm, hairless chest, a cherubic pillow of curly hair for his reposing genitals, and the beginning of long, sturdy thighs beyond. His body is pleasing, but very strange, being unlike Marcus' body, which is the only man's body I have seen naked for years.

He reaches up for the bottle. "If you must examine the merchandise, at least be decent enough to give me a drink to placate my modesty." He unscrews the cap and drinks. "That's better. If you keep staring at him like that"—he looks downward at his groin—"I won't be responsible for the results."

I sit on the edge of the bed and swing my legs under the covers, pulling them chastely up to my navel.

"And take off that silly shirt."

I don't move.

"Come on. It smells of me. How appealing is that?"

"I think I'm more comfortable with it on, John."

"For god's sake, Eve. I want to see your body, too, you know."

"But I'm *old,* John."

He rolls over on his side and begins to open the buttons I've so carefully closed, then draws the shirt away from me.

"Up now. Let's get it off."

Miserable, embarrassed, dreading the sight of myself, I rise up and feel the last vestiges of protective covering being pulled away. I lie back down and try to cover myself with the sheet, but John prevents me. When he puts a hand on my left breast, I start involuntarily.

"Relax," he tells me. "Look at yourself. You're fine. Plenty of women would be happy to look like you."

He passes me the bottle, and I take a wild swallow. The liquor burns the back of my throat and leaves a ribbon of warmth all the way down to my stomach.

Shyly, I *do* look at myself, expecting to be mortified. My skin no longer has the firm translucence of youth, but it is still smooth to the touch, and fits snugly around my bones. At last I find some virtue in my small breasts. Enhanced by motherhood, they haven't sagged too much, and hold their own against gravity. I am not thirty-five, but I'm not ugly, either. John's willingness to accept me as I am helps me accept myself; I am suddenly grateful to him for that.

"Wait a minute," he says. "I liked it better when you were looking at me."

I laugh. "Me, too. You're lovely, John."

"Enjoy, then," he says, pulling me down beside him, one arm under and around me. I nestle in, sending one hand to explore the planes of him, to enjoy the surface softness of his firm flesh.

"If you'll direct your attention a bit more," John says, "you might be pleasantly surprised."

"You mean there are seconds, John? That *would* be nice."

I take him in my hand, soft and limp at first, and play with him a little, until with coaxing he becomes increasingly long and hard. "How marvelous." I laugh, delighted.

"It's nothing, my dear. Just a little trick I picked up somewhere along the line."

He rolls over, half covering me, and begins to stroke my body with his hand. This time I lie back into the pillows, resolving to savor every sensation, every touch of his hand. Somehow I am afraid this will be the last time I feel these things, did not expect even this, this glorious reprieve.

Finding me moist, John laughs. "You like it," he says. Then, "Why didn't I meet you long ago, Eve? We'd both be better off."

A vision of Marcus stirs behind my eyes. I have to subdue it forcibly, to postpone the guilt that will doubtless be upon me soon enough. "Don't, John," I tell him. "None of that. It'll spoil everything."

"It's true," he says. "I would have treated you better than your famous scientist. I'm not sure what it is, but he's done something terrible to you, Eve."

"Or I've done it to myself. Did you ever consider that?"

"Only momentarily."

I sigh. "I wonder."

"It's all my fault, anyway. I used to hang around with Everett MacDougall a bit, years ago. Never liked the man, but I was young and foolish. He invited me to come with him to a reading one night. A young woman, said to be very promising, and not bad-looking, either. Everett was licking his chops."

"You didn't come."

"No. I didn't have much use for the whole Ministry of Culture crowd by then, let alone their notion of a promising woman poet. I can't tell you how awful it sounded."

"You snob."

"Well, I'm suffering for it now. What about it, Eve? Might I have had you, if I'd come that night?"

"I don't know," I say, remembering. "I met Marcus that night, for the first time."

Now John rolls over fully on top of me and pins my wrists, very gently, above my head. "Enough," he says. "No discussing another man in my bed. That's a house rule."

As I look up at John, I feel another part of him, seeking blindly, then by inspired chance, finding entrance in another quarter, far below our eyes.

17

No guilt at all, not even the tiniest speck of it, catches up to me while I am still with John. It seems to be another world, one with its own rules, its own code of honor and loyalty, that does not condemn our being together. On the way home, though, in the hire-car, it begins to come on.

It is past eight o'clock now, and dark in the streets. The driver is not talkative, but leaves me to my own seesawing thoughts. When I think about John, a smile crops up, unbidden, on my lips. It is so improbable, and so delightful, that we are lovers now. A girlish impulse stirs in me: I would like to talk to somebody else, another woman, about John. This is partly because he fills my mind, and a little, I suppose, because I would like the satisfaction of having someone besides me know that an attractive man finds me attractive. I used to privately condemn those friends who were voluble about their affairs; if you're going to do it, do it, I thought, but keep your mouth shut after. Now for the first time, I begin to understand their eternal need to talk about their sexual adventures.

I wish now I had not asked Marcus about his voluptuous assistant of forty years ago. If I could still suspect, as I did for so long, that Marcus had transgressed with her, I could at least feel as though I'd evened a long outstanding score. Maybe there was someone else; I wonder, hoping for the moment that there was. Fifty years is a very long time to be faithful.

Maybe there is even someone now, and not enough Marcus to satisfy us both. Certainly he is out late often enough. I try to think who it could be.

Suddenly the driver accelerates wildly, swerves up the middle of the street. I grasp the seat to hold myself erect.

"Damn!" he says. "I missed it."

"What did you miss? A turn?"

He swivels his head around to look at me and I see, briefly, a terrible gleam in the man's eye. "No turn, lady. A rat. The devil ran right out in front of me. I like to get 'em."

"Oh," I say weakly.

"Well, maybe I'll get another shot. Once it's dark out, they're all over the place, this part of town. Bold as you please."

I peer out into the dark street, expecting to see hundreds of gleaming eyes peer back. But there is nothing for the moment, and I will surely know it if the driver spots another. I don't like to think of John living among the rats. Already, I'm being proprietary. Well, he wouldn't grudge me my concern; I've earned the right. I smile to myself. Mostly, it seems, I am pleased.

My elation is easy to maintain through the Government complex, with its savage architecture, doing violence to the city skyline. These buildings are easy to dislike as buildings, and as symbols, easy to detest.

Now, though, we are coming to the gracious part of town, to the houses that shelter one family only, to the neat little yards, maintained at fantastic expense, now that water is in such short supply. These are the homes of the cardholders, of the master class. Our lives are made too easy, our talents overrated, and our spheres of vision constricted to a single ray. Here I have lived with Marcus, most of our married life.

As we drive closer and closer to my home, a kind of panic seizes me, and I wish I could erase the previous few hours from my life. Surely the change will show in me. As soon as Marcus sees me, he will know. Suli, too, probably. I know this cannot be true, yet become sure that it is. Maybe, I tell myself, if I never sleep with John again, no one will be able to tell. Wildly, I promise myself to renounce him, then, imagining his face as he bid me good night, want to be with him again, right now.

At last the car pulls up in front of our familiar door. Scanning the second story, I find no light in Marcus' room. I use my key. Almost immediately, Suli appears in the hallway. She seems relieved to see me.

"It's nine o'clock. I was very worried."

An irresponsible grin tugs at my face. I turn around. "See? All in one piece, and no harm done."

"I hope you haven't got the flu that's going around," she says, studying me.

"No. I'm sure it's not that. Something they mentioned to me at the Bureau of Geriatrics when I was there, I think."

Suli looks at me sharply, puzzled by my undeniable good humor in the face of disease, so puzzled, in fact, it assures me she hasn't guessed my secret and does not suspect I have one.

"Well, Suli, are you satisfied? May I go to my room now?"

Her face remains clouded.

"Come on, cheer up," I tell her, feeling far younger than seventy-five, younger even than she is. Then, when her troubled look persists, a little worry, for her, penetrates my euphoria. "What is it, Suli? Is something wrong?"

She looks at her feet; I try to think myself into her life. "Is it Alan?" I ask. "Have you had a fight with him?" There's no denying it, romance is on my mind.

"Alan is here," she says in a low voice. "I meant to ask you. But you weren't home. I didn't think you'd object."

"You're right. I don't. But what's the matter then?"

Suli seems almost reluctant to speak, and does so slowly. "Will you come to my room, Mrs. Harmon? There is something we ought to discuss."

I'm surprised by the request; Suli has never invited me into her room before. I follow her, blithering. "Have you found a solution to your problem? An escape plan? May I be an accessory after the fact? I'd be happy to oblige."

We pass through the kitchen and on to the servant's apartment on the other side—a large bed-sitting room, with its own bath. Suli says nothing. We find Alan Wills seated on a small sofa. He gets up when we enter and offers me his seat. I decline it.

"Oh, no. That's just right for two. You two. Go ahead. I'll just sit"—I turn around, looking for a place—"here, on the bed. If you don't mind, Suli."

"Anywhere you like, please, Mrs. Harmon."

I settle on the bed, my spirits high, and lean toward

them. "Now, what's all the mystery?" I ask, then interrupt myself to say, "You do make a fine couple. Very handsome."

Suli smiles indulgently at me, then looks to Wills.

"Alan, please," she says.

Wills looks directly, gravely at me. "Mrs. Harmon, Suli found something about six weeks ago, and it's caused her a lot of worry. She couldn't decide whether she ought to show it to you, or not. When she finally explained the situation to me, I advised her to come to you."

He pauses, and I nod at him.

"She was afraid to, though. She didn't want to hurt you or cause you unnecessary distress."

I feel some of my elation shrink and harden into a small stone that drops down deep inside me. "What is it, Suli? What couldn't you show me?"

She looks imploringly at Wills. He nods, and Suli takes a Mylar sheet out of her pocket, unfolds it and hands it to me.

As I take it from her, I look into their faces. They are unsmiling, very grave, and I think I can read pity in their eyes. Despite their kindness, or perhaps because of it, I suddenly feel very much alone.

The paper has a doctor's name imprinted on it, a few lines of typing beneath. It is addressed to Marcus.

"You are advised that the concluding portion of your IMM VI treatment is scheduled to be administered at 8:30 p.m., December 28th. As before, you are requested not to take any solid food for the twelve hours preceding the treatment." The signature is an undecipherable scrawl.

For a while I stare dumbly at the note. Somehow, I am not terribly surprised; it is as though something I have known for a long time has been confirmed at last, and I need not question my perceptions anymore. In that sense, it is a relief.

Suli and Wills stare at me, compassionate but silent. I think again how good they look together, like an extravagant and lifelike sculpture on the old settee. Their unity seems to underline the fact I am alone, and I feel some pressure to perform for them. The show must go on.

"Well," I say, "that settles it, doesn't it?" I close my fist around the note, crumpling it, then deposit it in the waste-basket beside Suli's bed. It makes a slight thud, hitting bottom. "Empty," I comment absently.

This silence is quite awful. The best thing I can do is to extricate myself, as soon as possible, but I'm strangely lethargic, my limbs are heavy. Perhaps a drink would help. I ask Suli to bring me one, apologizing as I do.

"Bring glasses for both of you, too," I call after her. When she is gone, I feel Wills' gaze on me, though I don't meet it.

"I'm sorry, Mrs. Harmon," he says in his deep, smooth voice. "It must be a shock. Maybe I was wrong to advise Suli to show you the note."

I look up at him. "No. You were right. I can imagine how upset Suli must have been." I pause. "She's very loyal, you know."

He nods vigorously, and I sense how uneasy he is. "Oddly enough, I think I knew. I must have suspected, anyway. Because this doesn't come as a surprise, exactly. It's almost a relief." I stop for a moment. "I suppose I should be happy for Marcus."

Wills laughs, a derisive snort.

"No, I mean that. Shouldn't I? If you really love someone, then you *want* them to live, right?"

I look across at Wills, wishing he would turn oracular and spout me some answers. I need someone to tell me what I'm supposed to feel.

Suli comes back with a bottle and just one glass. Wanting to be hospitable, I drink from the bottle, then offer it to them. Suli shakes her head, but Wills takes it and drinks. Suli sits on the very edge of the loveseat, watching me closely. She looks very unhappy, and I want to make her understand.

"Thank you, Suli," I say at last. "You were right to tell me. I understand why you had to. And it's all right. It really is. I'm all right."

Her gaze finally wavers. "I'm sorry, Mrs. Harmon," she says. "I'm very sorry."

The house settles, or a car passes in the street—I'm not quite sure what the noise is that makes me start, but I realize that I am not ready to meet Marcus now. Suli's digichron reads nine-fifty; I have only ten minutes to get to my room and feign sleep. I stand up and put my hand on her shoulder.

"It's all right, Suli," I repeat. "I'm going to bed now. Thank you both."

I make my way through the kitchen, the dining room and hall, bumping into furniture unexpected in the dark.

In my own room, I undress quickly, then sit on the edge of my bed. The telecom on my desk draws me toward it; I want to talk to John Powell. Deciding to chance it, I pick up the receiver, then punch up Powell's code. The connection is still bleeping through when I hear Marcus' car in the drive. The phone rings just once in the apartment I've just left before I disconnect the telecom. As I hear the front door swing open, I turn out my light and burrow deep into the bedclothes, willing my body to relax and be still.

Seconds later, I hear Marcus' steps in the hall outside my room.

18

There are hands on me, cold, cold hands, shaking me like the last leaf in an icy wind.

"No. No. Please. Leave me alone!" I try to form the words, to speak them, but my tongue is somehow stuck to the roof of my mouth, and speech is impossible.

"Eve. Eve." Someone calls my name, far away. I think it is Marcus, and I want to run to him, where I will be safe, but my legs have turned to wood. They will not move.

"Eve," he calls me.

The shaking does not stop, but I surface from sleep to see Marcus beside me, his face pale, with deep, sleepless smudges under his eyes.

"Oh, Marcus. Thank god. I've been having a nightmare."

"I know," he says gently. "I'm sorry to wake you, just when you'd finally settled in. But I thought I should. It's all over, Eve. She's dead."

I peer up at him, my eyes still cloudy with webs of nightmare, burning now.

"When?" I ask him.

"Now. Just a few minutes ago."

I try to sit up, but my body is heavy and falls back into the pillows.

"Easy," Marcus says.

I try again, make it this time, and swing slowly around to sit on the edge of the bed in my nightgown. Normally, I wake easily, being a light sleeper, but it was three o'clock when Marcus relieved me. I see it's now a little past six-thirty in the morning.

"Was she conscious?"

"No. I don't think so, anyway. She opened her eyes, very

briefly, just before the end. I thought—well, I thought it was a good sign. I got up and went over to her, spoke to her, hoping she'd recognize me." Marcus stops. His voice is shaky. I reach out and take his hand, draw it to me, and lay it for a moment against my cheek.

He goes on. "I doubt she did. We'll never know. Her eyes were very bright, seemed alert, except she didn't blink them. She was looking right at me, yet she wasn't. It was strange. Then she smiled a little, or started to, anyway. And then she just . . ." He pauses. "It's hard to explain how I knew she was dead. She stirred a little, or maybe I only imagined it. And then changed somehow, I can't describe it, almost imperceptibly, but I knew she was dead."

"Are you sure, Marcus? Maybe she just fell back into the coma." I get to my feet, grab my robe and wrap it around me.

"No, Eve," he says quietly. "I checked. Breathing's stopped. No pulse. She's gone."

My slippers are next to the bed; I shove my feet into them and walk toward the door.

"Where are you going?" Marcus asks, plaintive.

"To say goodbye, I guess."

"It can't help her any, Eve."

I turn at the door. "No. But it might help me. Okay?"

Suddenly I seem to see my husband for the first time. He looks terrible, drained, and I suspect that it's not only lack of sleep that makes his eyes so red and swollen. Till now, I've thought only of myself, not him. But he was there when it happened.

I go to him, put my arms around him and hold him tight. He leans into me, and we rock gently together, back and forth, neither of us cast as parent or as child, but both assuming both roles, giving comfort, and taking it.

After a while, he says, "I think I'll go down to the kitchen and make some tea. Shall I bring you some?"

"Please. I shouldn't be long."

We draw apart. Marcus goes to the kitchen, and I down the hall to stand outside the room that has been my mother's for several years. I don't want to turn the knob. So many times, I've hesitated outside this door and asked myself, "Will she know me today? Is she better? Is she worse?" For a little while, she was completely lucid, and I liked coming to her, to tell her what was happening in my life, how the day was passing, what there was to look forward to at supper.

I hear Marcus, rattling pans in the kitchen below, and turn the knob. Once the catch slips, the door swings open several inches by itself, then I push it back and step inside. With relief, I see that nothing here is really different now. The furniture is in its place, the photograph of my father still beside the bed, next to the water pitcher. An empty coffee cup and open magazine bear witness to Marcus' vigil. I close the door quietly behind me.

Even Mother looks the same, as though she were deeply asleep, and her sleep untroubled. The faint suggestion of a smile still hangs about her lips, and her lips are still rather thin, like my own. Only the stillness is different now, complete, unbroken. When she was comatose, and I sat with her, I often thought how quiet it was in the room, how far removed it seemed from the rest of the house, the rest of the world.

I realize now there *were* sounds, too subtle to be heard, or too easy to take for granted: the sound of breathing, of cells metabolizing, the minute sounds of life. They are gone now. In their absence, I recognize them for the first time and know that now I am alone in this room, as I was not alone before.

Slowly, made quiet by the quiet of the room, I approach my mother's bed. My senses seem ready to betray me; my hope persists, and I will her to open her eyes and look at me, will her to complete the smile beginning on her lips. My nerves expect it to happen; my mind tells me it will not. How softly, how silently I walk, closer and closer, expecting something to happen that will terrify me, waiting for my mother, against all odds, to show some sign of life. I watch her closely, carefully. I do not take my eyes from her.

Yet nothing happens. I am at the bedside now. Nothing happens. Her hand lays on the blanket. Normal. Usual. I know my mother's hand, and the gold ring on her finger, her wedding ring. I reach out, curious, to take her hand in mine. It is warm. I thought the flesh of the dead was supposed to be cold, but my mother's hand is warm. I take this for hopeful evidence, and feel my heart accelerate. Her hand is still warm. Perhaps Marcus is wrong after all.

"Mother," I whisper, trying to rouse her. "Mother, it's me, Eve."

I listen intently for some response, listen so hard I can hear molecules bounce off my eardrums.

"Mother. Mother." I call to her again, louder this time.

I watch her with painstaking care, not blinking until my eyelids burn so they shut of their own accord. My senses take in evidence: the hand is strangely inert, heavier than it ought to be, and firmer, somehow. Yes, quite firm, and the skin has an odd texture, as though it is not skin at all, but some amazingly lifelike plastic. But my hope combats this evidence; my brain refuses to compute it. I focus on one fact only—that her hand is warm—because it is the only shred of evidence that underwrites my hope.

As I hold the hand and wait and wait, it seems to change slightly. It seems to become a little firmer still, and the warmth, much as I hate to acknowledge it, grows slightly less as the minutes move away. But does it really? How can I trust my senses now? Yet Marcus says she is dead, and Marcus is a scientist, a biochemist. Marcus knows.

He must be right. Yes, Marcus has to be right. My mother is dead. It strikes me now that the most horrible thing about death is how closely it simulates life, how it fools my senses, that rage against it so. So this is death.

I put out one finger to touch my mother's cheek, then cannot bear to do it. Instead, I put my hand gently on her hair. Her hair, I think, will feel the same. It does. I stroke my mother's hair.

My senses suddenly give up their disbelief. Suddenly it is incontestably clear to me: my mother is dead. It becomes reality and supersedes all else, settles over my body and my brain.

Sorrow rises up from my depths as naturally and inexorably as a geyser springs up out of the earth. It is neither separate from me, nor contained by me; it *becomes* me, no more reversible than menstruation, or the movement of the stars.

I sob and moan, make animal sounds. Tears stream from

my eyes, hot and steady; saliva fills my mouth as I try to breathe and my nose fills with mucus that drips down the back of my throat and makes it even harder to seize the air. I am wet all over, wet as in the womb, wet as if my precarious human form had vaporized and left only water, the primal ingredient.

Somehow I understand that this must happen to me, and I must give myself up to it. My grief is so natural and irresistible that I *must* trust it, and trust it further, to stop when the time has come to stop.

I kneel beside my mother's bed and let it come, this physical grief. Higher orders of consciousness disintegrate; my mind is empty and animal. It forms no thoughts. My body absorbs the shock of bereavement; my *body* grieves.

Slowly, I become aware that I am alone in this room, and weeping for myself.

The tears do stop, finally, of their own accord, and are followed by a strange kind of peace, a feeling of being whole, and clean. Yes, they do seem to be over. For a moment, I wait on my knees, trying to make sure this is not a false ending, then pull myself to my feet. The room feels different now. I feel different. I look at my dead mother and am glad for her smile. I straighten the bedcovers a little, over her corpse.

The first great pressure has broken and flowed out; now I am calm, empty inside. It is time to leave the room. At the door, I turn back once more and whisper, "I love you, Mother. I really love you." The words throw some visceral switch, and more tears come that I cannot help but shed. These, too, find their own proper end and finally have done with me.

I find Marcus in our bedroom.

"Are you all right?" he asks. "Here's your tea."

I take it and nod thanks, sit down across from him. The tea is remarkably soothing, and I taste it minutely. We sit in silence for a while, until it occurs to me that we must make arrangements for the body, must arrange for a memorial service. Suddenly there is a great deal to do.

"We have to arrange for cremation," I tell Marcus. "And some kind of service. And where's her will? I think she left some kind of instructions, about what we're supposed to do." I put down my cup and stand. "Let's see. . . ."

"Eve," Marcus says gently, "sit down. It's only seven-thirty. We can't do anything before nine at the earliest."

"Oh. You're right, of course. I hadn't thought. What shall we do in the meantime?"

"The best thing to do is to get some sleep, so you'll be able to handle the rest later. Come to bed with me, Eve."

Obediently, I follow him to the bed and climb in beside him, pressing tight against his warmth, listening to the little sounds his stomach makes, to the rhythm of his heart. We do not speak, and sleep approaches me.

Just before it overtakes me utterly, I say, "Marcus?"

"What is it, Eve?" He pats my stomach gently.

"Marcus, if we have children and don't take the treatments, that's what will happen to us. Right? We'll be like that."

He waits a moment to answer. "Yes, that's right. It's not so bad, is it?"

I think about it. "No," I tell him. "No, I guess it's not."

"Sleep now, Eve," Marcus says, and we do.

Later I wake up thinking, "Mother is dead and I have a lot of things to do." Anxious to begin, I struggle to sit up, then find I am already sitting. At first I am afraid, to find myself in strange surroundings, but slowly I come to recognize my room, and my blue chair. It is decades later, a Saturday, and I have been asleep.

Slowly, my mind catches up to the present.

19

Saturdays. They are strange days for me. Either I love them, or I hate them; always, they seem difficult. Being weekend days, free days, they are supposed to be pleasant, and I feel an unreasonable pressure to enjoy them that makes it particularly difficult to do so. As a child, I loved school, and since there was no school on Saturday, I regarded it as a necessary evil, a hiatus sort of day I drifted through like a lost soul. Some of this Saturday melancholy clings to me still.

If we slept late and made love on Saturdays, in later years, I had a vague persistent guilt about wasting time while the rest of the world continued on its course. If we filled the day with errands and activities, I missed our lovemaking and felt a little cheated. In the last ten years or so, Saturday has become another working day for Marcus, another day alone for me.

He has already left for the lab when I go downstairs to breakfast, even though it is still early when I do. At first I sit in the dining room with my coffee, but it is too big a room to be alone in, and I am tired of being alone. Ultimately, I pick up my cup and carry it to the kitchen where Suli is busy with the week's baking. She is kneading dough energetically at the little kitchen table.

"Do you mind if I eat out here?" I ask her. "Will I be in your way?"

"No. Sit, please," she tells me. There is a film of sweat on her forehead from the exertion of kneading. Watching her, I see it is no easy task. I never tried it myself.

In a few minutes she puts the dough back in a large bowl and covers it with a cloth, then serves me the rest of my breakfast. I pick at the shirred eggs, nibble at the crust of my toast. Only for the coffee do I have some appetite. I wish I had slept much later.

It was a hard night. I had trouble sleeping, and it was agony to lie quiet while my mind squirmed, waiting for Marcus to settle in. Then at last I could get up and stalk around, exhausted but far from sleep, ending, finally, in the blue chair where I dozed off at last. There is still a great deal of today to be lived through.

"I haven't seen Marcus, you know," I tell Suli. "Not since you showed me the note."

"No? I suppose it will be hard for you."

"Yes, I suppose it will."

"Will you tell him that you know?" She gives voice to the question that's been revolving in my mind, without finding an answer.

"I don't know, Suli. We've always valued truth and trust so much." I laugh grimly. "At least, I have. I would have thought it was impossible to live with someone, day in and day out, with lies between you."

I pause and stir my coffee absently, making a dark whirlpool in the middle of my cup.

"Yet Marcus has been lying to me for god knows how long. It must be an awful strain. No wonder things have been awkward."

Suli pursues her normal routine, eyes always coming back to me, between small tasks, to show me she is listening. With clean, economical motions, she clears away her mixing bowls and kneading board, brings out her loaf pans and greases them.

"In one way, it might be a relief to him, to know I knew."

Between sink and cupboard, she makes a noncommittal noise.

"On the other hand, it might make him feel worse. If he didn't feel awfully guilty, he would have told me himself, wouldn't he? I'm not sure it's in my power to forgive him."

Suli looks up. "No, perhaps not. Some things are unforgivable."

Now I look up at her. I have been trying to settle this issue myself, with no success. A chorus in my brain repeats her word, *unforgivable,* while another tries to drown it out with reasons and explanations, with charity.

"Is it, Suli? I don't know. I can't decide. I can certainly understand the temptation. How can I be sure I wouldn't have done exactly the same thing, given the chance?"

"You wouldn't have," Suli says with a rather awful air of finality.

"I'm not so sure," I argue, as much with myself as with her. "Suppose I was in love with someone else? Or suppose my work was so important, and so complicated, that no one else could carry it on? The point is, I don't know. I don't know what's going on in his mind, or in his life."

I sigh a little, and the coffee, when I drink it, tastes very bitter. "At least now I know why I don't know."

Here the telecom rings and I feel my heart accelerate as Suli goes to answer it. I hope it is, I want it to be, John Powell. Suli calls me to the telecom, and Marcus' voice comes back at me.

"Eve? Good morning. Sorry I missed you last night. Things were cooking here, and I didn't want to leave the stove untended."

"Oh, that's all right," I manage to say.

"Listen, I'm calling because Don Weeker and his wife are giving a party tonight, and we're invited. I'd like to go. Don's a good man, and he's worked untold hours on this project of mine. Okay?"

I say nothing, imagining the party.

"Eve? Is that all right?"

"Oh, sure. Fine. What time?"

"Starts at eight. I'll try to be home around six, to eat and clean up. Will there be water for a bath?"

"I'll check. I'll try to save some for you," I say automatically.

"Good. Thanks. I have to go now. See you about six."

"Goodbye," I say to the dead line.

With the telecom at hand, it is very tempting to call John. My desire to speak with him is almost overwhelming, yet doubts prevent me. We made no arrangements, no pledges. For all I know, he was seeing someone else last night, after I was gone. Or tonight. Maybe tonight. If I call his apartment, a woman may answer, wearing one of his shirts, a little drunk on his whisky, his lovemaking. And if she does, she will not be old, like me, but young and beautiful. I have no way of knowing what John's entanglements may be. In fact, I know almost as little about him as about my husband.

Almost as if she could read my mind, Suli says, "How is Mr. Powell? I'm glad he was there to help you yesterday."

"So am I," I tell her. I return to my place at the table. Then, without premeditation, I blurt out, "Suli, John and I became lovers last night."

The silence that follows stings my ears, and I am ashamed of my weakness in speaking, but when I look up at last, Suli's smile warms me. I dare not ask her what she thinks.

"I'm glad for you," she says. "It's strange. Alan said something, that he thought Mr. Powell was very fond of you. He said he hoped that something would happen between you. I didn't think it was likely, to be honest," she says, apologetic. "Women, sometimes, are less generous than men."

"I didn't think it was likely, either, Suli. It's still hard to believe. You don't disapprove then?"

She smiles at me, almost maternally. "It doesn't matter if I approve, does it?" she says. "It's your affair."

"Nice pun."

"What? Oh, of course."

"Yes, I guess it *is* my affair. You're fast becoming the repository of all the Harmon family secrets, aren't you? I hope you don't mind."

"I regret those things that cause you pain, Mrs. Harmon. And I'm glad for what eases it. But there's not much I can do, either way."

"You do a great deal for me, Suli," I say, with a rush of warmth. "Do you realize you probably know me better than anybody else, right now?" I regret saying this immediately, seeing that Suli looks down, embarrassed, and fidgets with some silverware. Soon though, she looks up and says, "Well, let's hope that soon, Mr. Powell will surpass me in that."

The telecom buzzes again, my heart leaps again, and again I am disappointed. This time it is my son, returning my call. I question him about liberty for domestics; he answers grudgingly; we spar. At last I disconnect, having learned what I wanted to know.

Suli has listened attentively to our conversation, and looks questioningly at me when I am done.

"We can get you three nights off a week. All it takes is a trip downtown. You'll still be subject to their stupid curfews, of course. But it should be an improvement. I'll see to it next week."

"Thank you, Mrs. Harmon. I hope you won't regret it."

"It's all perfectly aboveboard, Suli. Jason thinks it's bad policy, of course, but that doesn't make it illegal."

She rolls the bread dough into loaves and settles the loaves neatly in their pans.

"By the way, Marcus and I are going out tonight. At eight. Alan is welcome to come, if you'd like to have him here."

She thanks me again. I wish she did not always have to be thanking me. Slowly I begin to leave the kitchen, then circle back.

"So you think it's all right, Suli? About John Powell?"

She finishes putting the loaves in the oven and stands before the digichron, watching closely. It takes only seconds to bake in these sound-wave ovens. She removes the loaves before she replies.

"It's strange. Hard for me to imagine." She shrugs. "But Dr. Harmon has treated you badly. You deserve some happiness. I hope that Powell is a good man. I would like to think he's sincere. I hope you, too, will be careful."

"Yes. Certainly," I say. Then, "Careful of what? I don't see how John could hurt me, or I him. He's promised nothing, and I have nothing to demand."

"Yes," Suli says. "Promises are the dangerous thing. Without them, there can be no betrayal."

"You're wise, Suli, for a youngster. I wish I'd known that fifty years ago."

20

There is a poem in me, but the recalcitrant bastard is biding its time. All afternoon I've been stalking it, chasing it around inside my brain, trying to lance it with my stylus and make it come spilling out. I persist in believing it's a good poem, though the fragments I've managed to array before me are disappointingly imprecise and prosy, nothing at all like the effortless eloquence I suppose this unwritten poem to possess.

Just what it's about, I'm not yet sure. My poems grow out of my life, usually, and my recent life is certainly fertile ground for poetry. New lovers almost always cause new poems, and betrayals often hurt one into poems. Changes of any kind are promising, because they bring new input to bear on old convictions. The eternal trinity is there—love, death and betrayal—but the new poem has not yet arrived. There is so much to synthesize, so much truth to be simplified, so it seems more probable and less like fiction, that it requires time to sort itself out.

Times like these, digging for the ideas, I lose control of the forms. Words get rude and unruly, refuse to fit together right and sit lumpy on the page, inert and graceless. First it has to come together someplace below my conscious mind, images have to mate with other images in order to produce the real and hybrid truth.

Once it comes, though, I'm convinced everyone and everything will be sorted out nicely. If the relationships seem strange, then it will be because the poem happens according to the logic of the heart, and not the mind. I expect to learn a lot from this poem, when it comes.

Here, suddenly, is Marcus; I don't hear him come in, absorbed as I was in cursing the ill-fitting pieces of my jigsaw poem.

He smiles at me, and I find I mistrust his smile, and would like to relieve him of it with some harsh word. Advancing, he puts a hand on the back of my chair, his fingertips just touching my shoulder. I recoil involuntarily. He looks at the untidy mountain of Mylar sheets on my desk, some crumpled, some marred by big X's and savage crossings-out, some with no more than a line or two on them.

"You're having a frustrating day," he says brightly.

"Damn right."

"Well, it'll come."

"Sure."

"Maybe the party will help. It'll do you good to get out and see people."

"Maybe so."

I'm having trouble talking to Marcus; quite honestly, since I prevent myself from saying what's really on my mind, I haven't much to say. He makes his own diagnosis, though, to fit his own disease.

"Eve, I know I've been gone more than here lately. And it's come at a bad time for you, I suppose. But when this set of experiments is done, I'll be able to take some time. We can go somewhere, if you like."

I smile at him and keep my own counsel.

"Really, it's been absolutely necessary for me to spend the time at the lab. No one else could do it. Otherwise, I would have been home early, every night." He pats my cheek; I find myself indifferent to his touch. "I'll make it up to you, Eve. Soon, too. Think about where you'd like to go."

"All right."

My unresponsiveness finally reaches him.

"Have I done something? Are you angry with me?"

"Should I be?"

He looks a little startled. "Of course not. No. I can understand, about being away so much, if it's that. But I will make it up to you. You'll see."

"I look forward to seeing," I tell him.

Marcus looks at me sharply. "Eve, something's wrong. What is it?"

But I shake my head. "There's water for your bath. You can just make it before dinner, if you start now."

"Okay," he says. "Have it your way. Maybe you'll like me better clean."

We take Marcus' car to the party. He's in fine spirits, humming to himself, well dressed and looking rested.

"You know Don. Have you met his wife, Ilse?"

"I'm not sure."

"Nice woman. And you'll meet Miss Mitchum, my assistant. I'm not sure who else is invited, but there should be some people there that you know."

"Good."

"They plan on dancing, too."

"Uhmm."

"You're awfully quiet."

"Saving myself for the party, I guess."

"Well, we can't talk shop with you wives there, since the project's secret."

"That's a relief. I was afraid you might have worked up a special code or something."

He laughs, more than is merited. "Didn't have time. Not a bad idea, though."

It is only a short drive to the Weekers'. The parties of Marcus' colleagues have terrified me for years. None of them have children, and while they have accepted Marcus' evident age, mine always comes as a shock, and invariably they make things worse by trying to conceal it.

Tonight, getting out of the car, I'm scarcely nervous at all. It doesn't seem to matter anymore if I requite myself well for Marcus' sake. What he's done has dulled any reflection I might have on him. I don't care if his friends like me, or if he is proud of me. The party, I expect, will be boring as usual, the women dull and their scientific husbands patronizing.

How many times have I been asked politely, with no interest in the answer, "What kind of poetry do you write?" Sometime before I die, I shall answer "limericks," and let them think what they will.

Don Weeker is still ungainly tall and his wife, I find, is uncommonly short, set by now into the mold that makes some women thick in profile and frontally round. There is some satisfaction in knowing that, for eternity, Ilse Weeker will resemble an overstuffed laundry bag when, on meeting me, she frankly stares at my wrinkles and my white hairs, and begins our acquaintance by saying, "Mrs. Harmon. I hear you write poetry."

Don Weeker shakes hands heartily, doing his best imitation of a gracious host. Before I become flattered, I remind myself that I *am* the boss's wife. Marcus goes on to join the other guests, while I do a few more rounds with Weeker in the vestibule.

"I shouldn't hoard you," he says, meaning "There, my duty's done," and escorts me by the elbow into the living room, leaving me parked beside a tall, thin lamp. For some minutes I stand there, hoping someone will spare me the effort of hunting down someone to talk at. One advantage of my age is that I no longer dread being unpaired at cocktail parties, but can amuse myself quite well for long intervals, frankly watching others.

Weeker pops up at my side. "Where is that husband of yours? You should have a drink by now. What'll it be?"

I ask for gin, and he trots off.

Whatever else he may be, Marcus is not rude; it's unlike him to cut adrift so early in the evening. I look around for him, among strange and half-familiar faces, and find him at last in an out-of-the-way corner, behind the buffet. He is leaning over slightly, in order to hear better, as a woman speaks to him. Somehow I know her voice is very soft, perhaps deliberately. Marcus smiles at her, and I watch their eyes meet. My blood runs cold.

Weeker returns with my drink. I take a stiff pull before thanking him. "Just right. And not a moment too soon."

"You should get on the old man."

"I certainly will."

"Excuse me. I think Ilse needs me for something."

"Of course. Thanks again."

They're still together, after this exchange, outside the traffic pattern of the party. She holds a plate covered with various comestibles, and now proffers it to Marcus. He leans closer to inspect the hors d'oeuvres and, in taking one, contrives to let his hand touch hers.

A moment later he looks up and intercepts my gaze. He smiles bravely and waves, then motions me to join them. Walking as smoothly and elegantly as I can, I cross the room to meet my husband's mistress.

We play our parts, and I do very well, I think, without rehearsal. Marcus, I see, doesn't know that I've guessed their little secret. Julie Mitchum, on the other hand, knows, and knows further that the advantage is all hers. I spend a few minutes hating her blond hair, her strangely pale eyes and flat, broad face. She is an attractive woman, I'll say that for Marcus, though not, I think, as attractive as I was at a similar age. My intuition tells me she really *is* rather young, Suli's age or less, and not simply well preserved by the treatments. An older woman would have more humility, perhaps more compassion, too. Her sole virtue seems to me to be that she does not pretend to be interested in poetry.

After Marcus pronounces her the best assistant he's ever had, I make myself think of John Powell a minute before I speak. The best way to throw her off balance, I suspect, is to kill her with kindness, and to do that, I must first think of my own lover, rather explicitly. I am very glad I have one; it helps me stifle the temptation to lash out at her, with either my nails or my words.

"I'm so glad Marcus has good help. He must be a difficult man to work for, being so dedicated. But he seems quite satisfied with you." I turn to Marcus. "You haven't spoken so highly of anyone since Liz Wilson left you." I give him an innocent smile. He is just naive enough to believe I've made an unfortunate blunder, and laughs nervously.

"How long have you been at the lab, Miss Mitchum? It is 'Miss,' isn't it?"

"Yes," she says, a bit sullen. "I've been there over a year."

"Well, with a girl as pretty as you, my dear, that shouldn't last for long. I'm sure all kinds of young men would be delighted to change that." I come down a little heavy on the "young," hoping Marcus catches it, preferably below the belt.

When I was a young woman, I detested the old busybodies who stupidly assumed that every young woman would trade an arm or a leg, at least, to procure a husband. They've died out now, of course, and there's no one to replace them, though I think I play the part rather well.

A sudden insight comes to me; perhaps statements like that have always been ironic, intended to infuriate.

It has its effect on Miss Mitchum. "I wouldn't know," she says coldly.

Marcus shifts from one foot to the other, barely able to maintain his grin.

"Or perhaps you're determined not to marry. I can see your point, of course. A lifetime is much shorter than an eternity. Though"—here I take Marcus' arm and squeeze it—"I've had very few regrets myself. It's been a good fifty years."

Julie Mitchum is beginning to wonder if I'm stupider than she thought. Marcus twitches slightly in my grip. I carry on. "At least I can look forward to some respite from your massacre of toothpaste tubes, my love, and other small perturbations."

He laughs weakly.

"Have you any family in the city, Miss Mitchum? Do you live at home?"

"My family is gone," she says. "I live in an apartment."

"I see. That must be lonely. You'll have to come to dinner with us sometime. Suli's a fine cook. We'll have to invite Jason, Marcus."

"That would be very nice, I'm sure," she mutters.

"We must see to it, Marcus. Help me remember."

He nods, looking a bit green.

"Hey, are you all right?" I ask. "You don't look well at all. It's not that old ulcer acting up again, is it? Or your prostate?"

"Eve!"

"What, dear?"

"Nothing. Are you ready for another drink? You, Julie?"

"It looks as though I am." I examine my glass. "But I'll get it for myself, thanks. I'm afraid I'm interrupting you two, talking shop. All these top secrets are awfully inconvenient."

I sail away, acutely aware of them behind me. As I stand at the bar, I see Marcus take both of her hands in both of his, just for a moment. He releases them, and they move apart. First disappointed in Marcus' honor, now I am disappointed in his taste, as well. My rival is nothing, except young.

Despair and anger mix as thoroughly inside me as the gin and tonic do in my glass. I drink my drink quickly, for sustenance, then try to pick out the most attractive man in the room, excepting my husband. The selection is not impressive, but finally I spot a man by himself on the end of the sofa, looking perfectly content to be alone. This I take for a good sign; if the man likes his own company, it must be tolerable. I go and sit beside him.

"Ah, that feels good. Besides being hard on the liver, cocktail parties do put a burden on one's feet."

He turns to smile at me, and I put out my hand.

"Eve Harmon."

"Ralph Johnson. Ilse's brother."

"Not a scientist then?"

"No."

"Good. I *do* know how to pick my men. What is your line?"

"Ballet, actually. My company's here on tour. I'm staying with Ilse and Don. There was no performance tonight to save me. We open tomorrow."

"That's marvelous. Do you perform under your own name?"

"Yes. But it's always in small print on the back of the program. I'm in the line, mostly. You know the scenes where they have half a dozen men dancing with half a dozen women? Shepherds and stuff. I'm one of them."

"Well, you have to start somewhere."

"I suspect I'll always be a shepherd. I don't have a star's temperament. Not enough drive."

"Content, then."

"Oh, yes. I'd like to choreograph someday. I'm sure I'd be much better at that. Nobody knows that yet but me, though."

"And me."

"Well, if you're willing to take it on faith."

"Why not?"

He smiles. "All right, believe in me. At your own risk."

"I shall, then. It will give me something to do. You have your first fan."

He looks embarrassed. "Not quite the first. Now there are two."

"Another lady, I presume?"

"Well, yes. Amalia's a ballerina. She's bursting with talent."

"I begin to see. And you're going to write dazzling ballets, to show her off."

He colors deeply. "I suppose that is one of my fantasies, yes."

"And does she share it?"

"Oh, yes. We're getting married, in fact."

"Congratulations. Is she here tonight? I'd like to meet her."

"No, she's not. Don and Ilse don't know yet. Amalia's black, you see. Native born and all; it's legal, thank god. No problem there. But . . ."

"Yes. I understand. I have a rather prominent bigot in my own family. In the Ministry of Domestic Labor."

"*Those* bastards," he says, then looks apologetic.

"It's quite all right," I assure him. "I know the word."

"It's all their fault, the way I see it. Racism here had almost died out until they started up with this importation business."

I ponder it. "You know, I think you may be right."

"Being native doesn't help much," he says. "Because you're still visible. I can't tell you how often Amalia gets stopped by the IPs and has to show her card. They don't apologize, either, just get sullen because they can't push her around." He reaches for his glass and finds it empty, save for some rapidly shrinking ice cubes. He finds mine in the same state and takes it from me.

While he's gone, a few of Marcus' colleagues circle by to pay hasty respects, afraid, I assume, that I remember them and am one to tally snubs and then report them. In truth, I recognize few of them; there is no one I would miss speaking to, and no one who wants, really, to speak to me.

We play the charade nonetheless, and I am relieved when Ralph Johnson returns. All the time he is gone, I restrain myself from looking around for Marcus, though I can't mistake his voice, rising occasionally above the hum of the crowd.

Then from another room, I hear music of sorts, the synthetic kind, performed by computers, that has so much appeal for scientific types.

Weeker, a little drunk, wanders around the living room clapping his hands and nudging his guests. "Time to dance. Come on, man. Let's get it started. Dancing in the dining room, everybody." Finally he staggers into his rotund wife and they lead the way together. The level of chatter diminishes a little, glasses are laid aside, and about half the assemblage follows the Weekers into the dining room to trip the light fantastic.

In this transition, I catch sight of Marcus, making diagrams in the air with his free hand, deep in conversation with another man.

"I hope your troupe dances to a proper orchestra."

"Oh yes. None of this canned stuff. You can tell the difference, can't you? So many people can't."

"The computer doesn't have idiosyncrasies. And of course, it doesn't understand the music. Doesn't feel it. There's no difference between a jig and a requiem, as far as it's concerned."

The first number ends; another begins. The Weekers are back in the living room, urging the lingerers to dance. Not meaning to, I see la Mitchum sidle up to Marcus and lure him toward the dining room. He lets himself be led, casting a worried glance around, presumably for me. A little conversational gaggle in front of the sofa keeps me hidden, and he goes on.

Johnson bolts the last of his drink. "Shall we dance, anyway? You *do* dance?"

"After a fashion. Nothing fancy. You'll find me a dull partner, compared to what you're used to."

"Oh, don't apologize," he says. "I hate that. Everyone can dance, I think, if they just listen to the music."

"That's reassuring."

He gets up and offers me his hand. I polish off the last of my drink, too. "It helps me listen to the music," I tell him.

We're well matched for dancing. Johnson is only a few inches taller than I, so my neck isn't strained, and I can see the other dancers over his shoulder. Mercifully, he leads well, and his own well-tuned body supplies a human rhythm the music lacks. I fall in with him easily, because he is good and helps me to. We dance smoothly for some minutes.

"Shall we try some variations?" he asks.

"Well, I'm game. Can't promise anything."

"Out you go, then," he says, releasing one hand and spinning me away, then expertly drawing me back, with no disastrous consequences. The next time he releases me completely, and I find that I've become so well trained to his rhythm that it stays with me as I dance alone. When we reunite, we are still in harmony. He executes a series of graceful turns and counterturns, giving me just enough subtle advance warning with the pressure of his hands so that I follow easily, with no lag.

The other couples clear back a bit, to give us space. When the music stops, a number of them applaud us, Marcus among them. At his side, Julie Mitchum pouts a little. He excuses himself, touching her arm lightly, a bit absently, I think, and comes toward us.

"That was well done," he says. "I never knew my wife was such a dancer."

"I'm not," I tell him. "My partner's a professional. Ralph Johnson—my husband, Marcus Harmon."

"Harmon," Ralph says. "Oh, you're Don's boss. I've heard him speak of you." He turns to me. "I didn't make the connection. Sorry. In fact, I think I sort of overlooked the last name when you introduced yourself."

"That's all right. It's much nicer to be myself than the boss's wife. No offense to the boss."

"None taken," Marcus says. "And now, if you can suffer my stumbling, I'll claim you for a last dance. Then we should go home. It's been a grueling week."

"So it has." I turn to Johnson. "I've enjoyed being with you. Good luck on your opening. Break a leg. Or does one say that to dancers?"

"Best not," he tells me. "Wait a minute." He opens his coat and explores an inside pocket. "Here. Two tickets for Monday night. Hope you can come. I'm the one in the purple tights."

"I'll try. Thank you."

Marcus takes my arm and draws me to him. The peculiar precision of the computer-generated music suits him; he moves smoothly with it, and well. The familiar feeling of being in his arms, so long my solace and delight, makes me relax into him, despite the treasons between us. If I shut my eyes, if I empty my mind, I can almost imagine they aren't there. I think he must experience something similar, because he holds me close and warmly, humming a little above my ear. We circle lazily, comfortably, until the piece is done.

Then he lets me go, and takes my hand. "Come on. It's time to head home."

We find the Weekers and thank them, as we must, for a wonderful evening.

Once in the car, Marcus says, "Well, that's done. Actually, I rather enjoyed myself."

"Yes. So I saw."

"What does that mean? You certainly made yourself scarce all evening."

"I'm not one to interrupt a tryst."

"What *are* you talking about, Eve? Julie Mitchum, I suppose."

"Don't you think it's a little indiscreet, Marcus, to hold hands in front of your staff? Or do they know all about it?"

"Eve. For god's sake."

"Well, am I the last to know?"

"There's nothing to know. Julie's a sweet child, that's all. She's nothing to me."

My temper flares. "Well, you're half right, anyway. She's nothing. Nothing but a self-serving little bitch, as nearly as I could tell."

"You didn't exactly give her a chance, did you? I don't know what you were trying to pull, Eve, with all that atrocious batty dowager palaver. I must say, you embarrassed me."

"No!" I say with mock concern. "So sorry, Marcus. As if you needed my help. When you can embarrass yourself so well, salivating over that pouty little piece of trash."

"I won't have you saying things like that about her."

"My, my. I hope you're so gallant in *my* defense when she speaks ill of me."

"Why should she do that? She doesn't even know you. And, I suspect, could care less."

"I suppose you're right, Marcus. Though she might get quite impatient and nasty if I don't exit on schedule."

"What on earth do you mean?" The anger in Marcus'

voice is suddenly replaced by uneasiness. It is tempting to throw my knowledge in his face, but I check myself, dodge a little, and strike again.

"Remind me to call a lawyer Monday morning," I say. "I don't want sweet Julie to enjoy *my* half of our estate, as well. I wouldn't rest peacefully thinking she was dressing herself on what little money *I've* made."

We are close to home; Marcus, in his agitation, almost passes our drive, then has to swerve sharply to catch it before it's too late. The tires give a squeal of protest. He rams on the brake and stops the car short, then turns it off. Lights extinguished, we sit in the dark.

"Eve, I don't understand you. After fifty years of marriage, how can you say things like that? How can you think them?"

He has no right to turn self-righteous on me. I am very angry now.

"Damn it, Marcus, marriage isn't an artifact, for god's sake. It's a living thing. Even if it's almost over."

Marcus is angry too. I can hear the tension in his voice. "That's very poetic. But what does it mean?"

"A lot," I say, almost shouting. "It means it grows, and changes. It means it can get sick. It has needs. It needs work, and honesty, and trust, and love. You can murder it, too, Marcus." I pause for a moment to catch my breath. "It also means," I say miserably, "that I'm going to die of cancer. You don't have long to wait before you can settle in with your flat-faced little mistress. Just be patient."

I break into tears. They start slowly, but soon turn into big, strangling sobs. I lean forward against the dash, shaking, and cry prodigiously.

It is a long time before Marcus touches me, and then his hand feels tentative on my shoulder.

"Leave me alone," I pant. "Go call your mistress. Go on. It'll make her happy. I have cancer. Tell her. Tell her, Marcus. Think of it as an engagement present. Aren't you happy?"

He stays beside me in the dark, lets me cry. I wish he would go away. If we talk more, I won't be able to hold anything back, and I am afraid of dealing the death blow to our marriage. Maybe it would be a mercy, but it seems too late to change the ground rules now. If only pretense is left, then I will cling to pretense, because it is familiar.

Gradually, my energy is spent in crying, and my sobs grow softer, then stop, leaving me damp and sniffling.

At length, Marcus touches me again, that light, uncertain touch. "Eve, the Bureau of Geriatrics sent me a copy of their report. I know, Eve. I've known as long as you have."

I turn to him, astonished. "You *knew?*"

His shadow nods in the darkness.

"Why didn't you tell me?" I ask.

He takes a long, audible breath. "Part cowardice, I guess," he says. "I've been telling myself I was waiting until this phase of the project was done. I don't like to think about it, Eve. It's too horrible." He is quiet for a minute. "Partly, too, because I've been trying to figure out if there's any way to get you treatments illegally, and I didn't want to raise your hopes unrealistically. And"—he sighs again—"partly because I've had some thinking to do myself."

"Oh, Marcus."

"Why didn't *you* tell me?" he asks.

It takes me a long time to answer. "I don't know," I say finally, "I was afraid to. I could make up all kinds of noble reasons, but I'm not sure they're true." I'm trying hard to be honest. "I think maybe it didn't seem official if you didn't know. I could pretend it wasn't really going to happen, I guess."

"Have you been bothered by pain yet?" he asks gently, like a good doctor.

I nod. "Sometimes. It's been brief flashes mostly. Quite bearable, because it didn't last long. Friday was bad. I was at the Guilds. It hit me and didn't let up like before. John Powell found me and took me home with him for a while, until I was better."

"I'm sorry, Eve. I would have come for you, if you'd called."

"I didn't know that. Suli offered, but I waited until I felt well enough to get a car."

"Well," Marcus says, "exhaustion won't help. We'd better go in now."

He gets out of the car. Because I don't move, he comes around to open my door.

"Thanks," I say weakly.

I follow him up the walk and into the house. In the hall I ask him, "Is there any chance of getting the treatments?"

Our eyes meet, one of the first times all evening.

"Not without getting caught," he says. "Not even for me."

The momentary hope dies. I sigh. We head together up the stairs. Marcus' arm behind my waist offers gentle support. At the head of the stairs he pulls me to his side.

"You want me to sleep with you tonight? Would that help?"

I'm torn. One part of me gravitates toward him, seeks the comfort of a body next to mine. Another reminds me that the truth is still only partly told, and nothing has been resolved. Still, we've made a start, and much of my rancor is gone. I *want* to love the man, as simply and trustingly as ever I did.

I wait so long to answer he settles it for me.

"Actually," he says, "you'd probably be better off alone. I may not go to sleep for a while. My mind's racing."

By now I am almost wholly subdued, and willing to be led. "All right, Marcus. If you think so," I say meekly, and go to my room.

21

Bliss. Ecstasy. The sun everywhere, warming my skin and seeping beneath it to untie the knots in my nerves, to massage my tight muscles with its golden fingers. Eyes closed, and a show of red lights projected on the backs of the lids, a very private theatre. Perhaps it is the dance of my own blood that I watch. I'm not sure and it doesn't matter. The swift red shapes amuse me; my mind is peaceful watching them.

I am even getting used to the sandfleas by now, that leap onto my arms and legs, and no longer disturb myself to brush them off (they will go presently, of their own accord), or to scratch the tickling places they leave behind. Every now and then, the sea exhales a breath of wind, and it passes over my body, raising up the fine, soft hairs that cover my skin, interrupting the steady heat of the sun just in time and just long enough to keep me from perspiring.

And the sea's voice, that I knew so intimately in all its moods as a child, speaks to me without pause from the shoreline below. Today it is a steady mumble, without much emphasis because it is, not calm exactly, but very regular.

I can hear the place where, farther down the beach, the sea holds congress with the rocks. There it raises its voice, waxes erratic and voluble, punctuates its monologue with great bursts of spray, symphonic really, making one sound as it approaches the rocks, another as it strikes, yet a third as it smashes into a cloud of droplets, another as the droplets jet through the air, and still another as they fall back, with a gentle hiss, onto the face of the water. Always, underlying these, taking the bass part, I hear the low moans of the undertow as the sea draws back its broken edges and makes ready to advance again.

This is peace. The children are off somewhere; I hope they learn to love it as much as I do. One special part of me, the mother-lobe, stays alert for their voices, for any sound of danger. All the rest of me melts into sun and sand. I am grateful for the respite from their questions, their small, continual demands, and I will be equally glad to see them when they come back again. May their adventures prosper! I'm glad to be home base.

If only Marcus were here beside me, the day would be perfect. His absence is its only flaw. But he's coming on Friday, to join us for a week. Only two more days. Two. They will be long days, of course, as the last two weeks have been made up of long, long days. Some people do this every summer, all summer long. I can't understand it, unless they love each other less than we do.

Sleep is stealing upon me; I can feel it coming. Well, no harm. Days like this were meant to be lived between long, lazy naps.

When I awake, I am fully awake all at once, my invisible mother's antennae pivoting like radar receivers. The only sound I hear is the sound of the sea. The wind has risen out of it; perhaps it was the new chill that woke me. I do not like the silence that prevails beneath the sound of the waves. The children have been gone too long. I stand, the dry sand falling from my legs, and grab my shirt. I cannot see the children from where I stand. My shirt is no buffer against the chill that overtakes me.

"Jason! Maria!" I shout their names in all directions; the wind carries them away. The sky is astoundingly blue, and the sea, reflecting it, opaque and shimmering. Suddenly I am unaccountably afraid, and run up the beach in the direction my children walked when last I saw them. The give of the sand makes running hard; I push it back with my feet. By the time I reach the near side of the rocks I am panting. A sweat starts to rise on my body, immediately cooled by the wind, and makes me shiver. At the base of the rocks, I call for them again, then listen hard.

No answer.

I turn and look the other way, hoping to find them tripping toward me.

They are not there.

The tide is quite high now, and I have to wade to get around to the other side of the rocks. The sun is in my eyes as I look up at them, black against the incredible blueness of the sky. When I shield my eyes with my hand, I see a strange pinnacle, a boy-shaped pinnacle. It does not move.

"Jason!" I scream. "Jason!"

Slowly the figure turns its face toward me. I scramble up the rocks, trip once and cut my leg, not deeply, on a ridge of stone.

At last I stand, somewhat precariously, before my son. "Jason, where have you been?"

He does not look at me, but somewhere beyond me, out to sea. Involuntarily, I follow his gaze. A gull, wings full spread, makes a slow sideways swoop down the back side of a blast of wind. My foot slips a little, and I totter slightly, trying to catch my balance.

"Where's Maria?" I ask him.

He says nothing.

"Jason! Where is she? Where's your little sister?"

My son sits like a statue and does not respond.

I take him roughly by the shoulder; my grip bites into his fragile bones. "Where is Maria?"

He looks up, not at me, into the sky.

"Gone," he says, and drops his head.

"Gone where? Is this a game? I don't like it. You help me find your sister, right now, or I'll whip you, Jason. I swear I will." I shake him again, harder. "Where is she?"

Slowly he lifts his arm and points. "Down there."

Beyond us, toward the sea, the rocks drop off sharply. They make a ragged circle, about 220 degrees, enclosing a small tidal pool. As I stare down into it, I see the low crowns of jagged rocks rising above the tide. Between them, there is a small form floating, face down. It wears Maria's green and white bathing suit.

I scream. A wave of nausea follows the scream up my throat.

"How long has she been there?" I ask, afraid of the answer.

"A long time," he says flatly, staring at the sea once more.

"Oh my god. My baby. My baby." I start down the rocks calling her name, praying disjointedly, "Don't let it be too late. Please, please, please. Don't let it be too late."

The rocks yield before my haste; I seem to descend with superhuman speed. Every atom of my being concentrates on getting there, to the bottom, to my baby, to my broken child.

A door opens; I hear it. But where? Soon Marcus stands before me.

"Are you all right? It's not the pain?"

I shake my head to clear it, then stand up quickly. "No, I feel fine. Just thinking. There's a poem on the way."

"Same one?"

"Uh huh."

Marcus helps himself to my blue chair; I can't help wondering if the past will overtake him, too. I stretch my legs a bit, then settle in my desk chair, facing him.

"I want to apologize, Eve. I was pretty rough on you last night. It wasn't deserved. And we should have talked much sooner, about the other."

"Well," I tell him. "Let he, or she, who is without sin hurl the first vase."

"Don't be nice," he says. "It's my fault."

"I have my transgressions, too. We haven't confessed each other for a long time."

"No. Perhaps it's time we did. I was thinking about it last night."

"So was I."

"How about getting away somewhere for a few days? Someplace comfortable, with no interruptions."

"That's probably an excellent idea."

"Only probably?"

"Well, I'm not committing myself before I know you can get away."

"Things should be in pretty good shape by the end of the week."

"Okay. Let me know for sure. Maybe I could get John to take my classes."

"Ah, the redoubtable Mr. Powell. Always ready to come to the rescue, eh?"

"John's fast becoming a good friend. Where shall we go?"

"Don Weeker has a little house at the beach. Right on the water. Heated, too. He says we're free to use it anytime."

I shudder. "No, Marcus. Please."

"All right. I'm sorry. I thought you might be over it by now. You used to love the ocean so. . . ."

I shake my head again, emphatically.

"Someplace else, then. I'll get a map."

He gets a map from his room and returns to spread it before him on my bed. He spots a mountain town we used to visit, years ago, suggests it to me. The idea galvanizes; we agree. Then he looks up at me.

"You do want to go, don't you? Maybe you'd rather not."

"Oh, no. I'd like to very much." I get up and come to stand beside him, trying to shake off my numbness and show some enthusiasm for the plan. We lean over the map; he points out the town, and I nod vigorously.

"We'll have a fine time, Eve. It's past overdue. If the weather's bad, we'll simply stay in our room." He laughs. "It's time we stole away together, woman. It's been far too long." His arm draws tighter around my waist. "It's my fault, I know. I've let my priorities get all scrambled up by this project. You know how the Government works. They convince you you're nothing short of indispensable, in order to exploit you better."

"Well, it works. Voluntary servitude. It's very clever, really."

"Insidious is what it is," he says. "And I've let it happen. I hope it hasn't hurt you very much."

"You know me." I laugh, a little unconvincingly. "I'm tough."

"That's right," he says. "That's my girl. I'll make it up to you. It'll be like old times."

Now he pulls me down beside him on the bed, leans

forward to kiss my forehead. This simple gesture warms me all over, emboldens me to kiss his cheek, in the soft place just below his eye, before the whiskers start. These touchings, these small delights, were once so plentiful they were commonplace facts of the life we shared. When I remember our first years together, they seem wrapped in a cloud of warmth from the constant touching, the physical closeness between us.

Now they are almost painful to my hungry nerves, precisely because they feel so good, so very sweet. Now when Marcus touches me, it reminds me how seldom he's done so these last years, and my hunger awakes only to be blunted by the fear of another withdrawal. Still, I touch him back, glad to be free to do so, even for a little while. I play with his hair as it falls across his forehead; I rest my cheek against his shoulder; finally, made brave by his tolerance, I nuzzle down between his chin and shoulder to kiss his warm, inaccessible neck.

He laughs a little self-consciously, and hugs me tight, preventing, for the moment, any more of my small affectionate forays into territory too long forbidden. I wriggle in his arms, to free myself again, and find I, too, am laughing, with a childish delight in the pleasure of touching each other once again.

Now Marcus takes the offensive, planting small, nibbling kisses around my chin and lips and neck, a little randomly but with great spirit. The familiar tickle of his moustache, long missed, makes me giggle and chirp happily, half trying to escape the sensation, all the while loving it. A shaft of winter sun pierces the window above my desk and spreads itself like a silver blanket across our knees. Our hands and arms move in and out of the sunlight, flashing silver.

Gaining confidence, I tickle Marcus' vulnerable ribs to invite retaliation. He catches both my wrists and holds them tight, then pushes me over backwards on the bed. The map crackles. He pulls me up a little and draws the map away, dropping it to safety on the floor, then pushes me back down and puts his weight on me. He grins down into my answering smile.

"Uhm. That feels good," I say.

"It does." He settles a bit; I feel his muscles relax. "It really does. I'd forgotten how good." His voice turns softer, serious now, and my mood follows his.

"It's the simplest thing on earth. And the most complicated. Why do people make it so hard?"

"I don't know," Marcus says. "Fear. Stupidity. Pride."

I have a great sense of physical well-being, the same kind of satisfaction that a shower after exercise, a bed after exhaustion, a meal after hunger brings.

"Let's not be stupid, or afraid, or proud anymore, Marcus." I want to say "I need you," but am still, after all, a little too shy.

"Let's not," he says. "Let's not forget to enjoy each other."

His cheek is against mine, his face against the spread. We can't see each other, and neither refers to time, short, precious and suddenly finite, but the thought envelops us both and makes us cling, blindly, to each other.

I join my hands behind Marcus' back. I love this man. I have loved him for half a century. We've done well. I love him still. My brain repeats a small, reassuring litany, over and over and over again, until it doesn't make sense anymore. Other thoughts crowd up to challenge it—the pouty young blonde, the treatments, much that is still unclear—but these cannot break the satisfying pattern of positive thoughts. I am willing to forgive a great deal right now, and to ignore more. The feel of Marcus' body on mine dispels both pride and anger; to die this peacefully, I would forgive a multitude of sins against me.

When the telecom sounds in some distant quarter of the house, we do not move but snuggle closer and lie quietly. Then Suli's voice on the intercom calls for Marcus.

"Ugh," he grunts, rolling off me, "I suppose I have to answer. It might be the lab."

"Don't go away," I tell him. "Take it here."

He picks up my telecom and sits on the edge of the bed. I sit up, too, so close to him that our thighs touch, close enough to hear the tones of a woman's voice at the other end, though I can't make out her words.

"That's right. I told you I wouldn't be in today."

A pause, while the unintelligible woman's voice rises,

spitting words in sharp staccato. Absurdly I imagine an
insect at the other end of the connection, rubbing legs
together furiously to make these noises.

"That's impossible. I'm sorry. No, I can't discuss it
now. . . . I'm afraid not. . . . I asked you not to call me
at home. . . . All right. Goodbye."

With each exchange it becomes harder to ignore the
fact that Marcus' caller is Julie Mitchum, that she has, and
exerts, some influence on my husband. His voice is not
quite angry, but ruthlessly controlled, as though it is
costing him much to remain calm. Much of my mellow-
ness deserts me; much of the wronged, hurt feeling comes
back again. I am no longer so willing to forgive.

"Don Weeker," Marcus lies. "He's at the lab. But they
don't really need me. A six-day week is quite enough."

"Oh, quite."

"I mean, I've been there too much. They'll never learn
to exercise their own judgment if I'm always there to hold
their hands." Marcus puts his hand on my thigh.

"That's right," I say. "You hold hands with your staff
far too much."

"That again?" Marcus says. "Your jealousy is flattering,
of course, but terribly misplaced." He pats my thigh.

I pick up his hand and put it in his own lap, then stand
up. "Marcus, that wasn't Don Weeker. It was a woman."

My husband looks at his hands for a long time, turning
them, picking at the nails. He will not meet my eyes and
I, suddenly, have no intention of making things easy for
him.

"You're right," he says finally, his voice very soft. "That
was Julie. She wants me to meet her somewhere."

I turn my back to him and study the swirling play of
dust inside the sunshine. "I see. And are you going to
meet her, Marcus?"

"No. Of course not."

Now I turn to face him again. "Is she in love with you,
Marcus?"

By his face, I see this is not the question he expected.

"Well, is she?"

His gaze moves downward, to his feet. "I don't know."
He pauses, then, "She says she is. It's nothing more than

a crush at most. She's very young. I don't think she knows what love is. But it doesn't matter. I've told her I'm not going to see her again."

I take a deep breath. "That amounts to an admission that you *have* been seeing her."

He nods miserably, then speaks, very quickly. "I've seen her a few times. Dinner, a few drinks. That's all. Really. We've talked about the other, once or twice, but decided it was a bad idea, all the way around." He drops his eyes. "I had her transferred to Frank Kaplan's staff. She just found out about it. That's why she called."

"You didn't tell her first?"

"No. I thought it would be easier to deal with an accomplished fact."

"Marcus, Marcus. I'm ashamed of you. I thought I'd raised you better than that."

He looks up at me now, pained by what he takes for attempted humor.

"No, I mean it, Marcus. I thought if you'd learned nothing from me in fifty years, you'd have absorbed the fact that women are people. We have feelings."

His look of hangdog remorse will not subvert my sermon. On the whole, it feels good to be self-righteous.

"Not only have you treated me badly, Marcus. But you're not even conducting your *affair* with honor."

"The affair's over, Eve. It wasn't one to begin with; I told you that. Whatever it was, it's over. I'm not going to damage our marriage anymore."

Suddenly I'm very tired. "You'll damage it a great deal unless you end this thing decently, Marcus. You ought to talk to the woman. You owe it to her."

Marcus looks puzzled. "I don't understand you, Eve. Judging by last night, I thought you didn't like Julie."

"I don't like Julie. I think she's a worthless little bitch. But I don't like people taking the easy way out. Emotional cowardice is very unappealing to me. Close it out right, if that's what you're going to do."

"For god's sake, Eve."

"For god's sake, Marcus. Are we *all* your playthings?"

"It wasn't like that, Eve. I'm not that much of a bastard."

"I don't think I want to hear what your affair was like right now, Marcus."

"Eve."

"Shut up, Marcus. Save it for our second honeymoon. We'll talk about it then."

The intercom buzzes, making us both jump.

"Telephone for you, Mrs. Harmon."

"Who is it, Suli?"

She hesitates a moment. "Mr. John Powell."

I keep my voice very steady. "Please tell him I'm not at home."

"Yes, ma'am." The intercom goes dead.

When I look up, Marcus' eyes meet mine and hold them. We stare at each other across the rubble of bright old dreams.

22

"I wish her teeth would drop out of her gums, and her hair out of her skull. I want her arms and legs to swell until they're fat and useless. I wish her tongue would split in two and her eyes be locked in unending night," Michael reads. "Jesus. That's pretty strong."

"It sounds like a curse," Tina says.

"It is." Belinda doesn't look at them. Her voice is quiet, emotionless, a striking contrast to the voice of her poem.

"Who is it that you hate so much?" Mitbu asks.

"That's not the point, Mitbu," I interpose. "We're not here to get personal. Does it work as a poem?"

"How can I tell, unless I know who it's about?" Mitbu argues.

I start to protest again, but Belinda raises her head. "It's all right, Mrs. Harmon. The assignment was to write a poem about hate. There's only one person I hate, so I thought of her and wrote the poem."

"But who is she?" Tina asks. "Your employer?"

"The woman who took away my man." Suddenly, Belinda smiles. "You know, the poem helped me. There was a time I would have killed the woman, I think. I wanted to. There's been hate in me for a long time. The poem helped get rid of some of it."

I leap to play the teacher. "That's right, Belinda. Poetry is often therapeutic, in its way. It helps us objectify our problems. Sometimes you even discover the problem isn't what you thought it was, but something entirely different."

Belinda nods vigorously, her large ovoid earrings dancing. "That's true," she says. "Now I realize I want to kill *him* instead."

"It's always the man's fault. One should never trust

them." Tina's eyes flash at Michael; he grins back. I intercept the gaze and both drop their eyes, embarrassed, but also, I think, quite pleased.

"How about you, Michael? You opened this can of worms."

"I think," he says judiciously, "the woman is most often at fault. We men are so susceptible to their wiles."

"I didn't want your opinion, Michael. I wanted to hear your poem."

"I didn't write one," he says. "Last week, I hated. This week the world seems all right." He shrugs. "You said yourself it's better not to sham emotion."

"Tina, how about you?"

She pokes shyly through her notebook. "Well, I wrote a poem. But it's not about hate."

"Do you want to read it?"

"I think so. Yes." She pulls it out of her notebook and holds it in front of her with both hands. "It doesn't have a title," she says.

I nod. "That's all right."

Tina clears her throat, looks up at Michael, then down again at the page. "My love," she reads, in a tiny voice, "Your marble legs . . ." She stops. "Mrs. Harmon, could I ask you to read it, please? I don't think I can do it right."

She hands me the page. I, in turn, clear my throat and sail into the poem, finding, by the second line, that it is heavy stuff. "Excuse me." I start again. A blush rises on my own neck as I unwind images from Tina's spool. They are pungent, erotic, wholly right. "Then in the interval I sing him special songs, to make him strong once more."

The poem is met with silence, everyone, like me, I imagine, drifting through intimate memories.

"Well, what do you think of it?" Tina asks at last.

"A good experience and a fine poem," I tell her. "Excellent on both counts."

Michael laughs loudly. There are the first signs of tears in Belinda's eyes; her hurt must be fresher than I'd supposed.

"No one's cock is *that* big," Mitbu says scornfully. "To compare it to a tree is absurd."

Michael looks pleased with himself. "Just a little hyperbole, man. It beats being compared to carrots."

"Actually, it's not out of line," I tell them. "Have you read the Song of Solomon? He describes his love in very grand terms. Neck like a tower. Breasts like young deer. Et cetera."

"Tell us about the et cetera," Michael urges.

"I'll leave that to your imagination. The point is, a little exaggeration's quite acceptable. Traditional, in fact."

"I like it very much," Belinda says quietly. "You have captured the excitement of first times." She pauses, looks directly at Tina. "It is about a first time?"

Tina nods, and the two women share a half-smile, acknowledging their common experience. I smile with them, though they are not looking at me.

Mitbu closes his notebook. "The hour's up. I have to get back before someone misses me. What's for next time? Love, hate, cherry pie?"

"Whatever you like," I tell them. "As long as it's got at least fourteen lines."

"A sonnet," Michael says. "To Et Cetera."

"If you like."

This week Michael and Tina leave together. Soon all are gone. I gather up my own things quickly, finding Tina has left her poem with me. I dash into the corridor, hoping to catch her, but she is gone. My coat is already on, my hand on the light switch when John Powell rounds the corner. The sight of him is a surprise; he is handsomer than I dared remember. He puts a hand on my shoulder, easily, but I whirl away.

"So it's true," he says. "You *are* avoiding me."

He pursues, smiling, while I retreat.

"No point in that," he says. "Persistence is one of my great virtues."

We continue our circle at least halfway around the room, until I inadvertently get trapped in a corner, and he leaves me no escape.

"That's better," he says. "Now we can talk."

"Talk?" I ask blankly.

"Is it surprising I should want to talk to you, when I've been deprived of your company for three long days? How goes it, my sweet? Where were you yesterday, when I tried to call you?"

"John, back off a bit. Please. I don't like corners."

He doesn't move. "I'll let you sit down on the condition you won't try to run away."

"All right."

"Promise?"

"For heaven's sake, John. I promise."

"Very well." He pulls out a chair for me with a comical flourish, then sits beside me.

"Now, my dear, tell me everything. Has your husband, who is really a rhinoceros and resembles a man only through the blackest of the black arts, discovered our little secret and beaten you? No? Threatened you, perhaps."

John's energy is overwhelming. He is trying hard to make me smile, and I oblige him.

"You're in an awfully good mood."

"Of course I am. My love is like a red, red rose that's newly sprung in June."

"John, don't quote poetry."

He manages to look crestfallen. "But I'm a poet," he says. "Don't tell me that mathematical equations are more to your liking. Take me as I am; I'll never name a new hormone after you, but"—he reaches into his pants pocket and brings out a folded sheet of Mylar—"I *will* celebrate your virtues after my fashion." He unfolds the sheet and hands it to me.

I don't want to read it, but I do. John's letters are neat and strong. They seem to have a sense of humor. But his poem isn't, except for a few throwaway lines that make me chuckle, funny.

"That's beautiful, John." I fold the page and hand it back to him.

"No, that's yours. It's for you. Keep it. And many happy returns."

"Do you have another copy?"

"Of course. Though I blush to admit it. This one I copied over in my very best handwriting, just for you. It took three tries."

I have to laugh. "You print very well."

"Thank you," he says gravely. "I did my best."

"It's a wonderful poem, John."

"The first of many, I hope. The Eve poems, I call them. Nice symbolism in the name, and all that."

"You overwhelm me, John."

"Please don't let me do that. Did the weekend produce any poems for you?"

"No, it didn't."

"Damn. I'd hoped you'd respond in kind. Oh well." He leans closer and takes my hands. "I can't tell you how good I feel, Eve. You've given me all kinds of energy, all kinds of inspiration. I feel like twenty again."

"Just so you don't start looking twenty again. It's bad enough as it is."

"Aha. Then there is an 'us'? I must say, you had me worried for a minute there."

"John, you're impossible."

"Good. Kiss me then."

"John."

"Come on." He leans toward me, eyes closed and lips foolishly puckered, to plant a burlesque kiss somewhere to the right of my nose. Then, being close, he moves his mouth to mine for a real kiss that begins chastely but seduces me into participation, becomes long and tender.

His ebullience is gone when we move apart. He puts one hand on mine. "Now, tell me what's wrong."

"It's a long, long story, John."

"Good. Let's go to my apartment. You can tell me there."

"I can't."

"Why not? Has the mad scientist given you a curfew?"

"No. Of course not. I promised myself I wouldn't."

"That was stupid. Why?"

"John, I'm a married woman."

He looks me straight in the eye. "Tell me honestly you're happy with him, and I'll leave you alone." He waits a moment. "Well?"

"All right. No, I'm not happy. I'm confused, and afraid, and hurt. I feel very much alone. Are you satisfied?"

John puts one hand softly on either cheek. "That'll do," he says. "Now will you come to my apartment and discuss it with me?"

"All right, John."

23

John stalks around the living room. "What an unmitigated asshole. Son of a bitch. Bastard. Why didn't you call me, Eve?"

My mind reaches back over the weekend. "I wanted to Friday night. I punched up your number. And I thought about you Saturday. A lot. But I didn't know how you felt, John. I didn't want to impose. Or worse yet, call and have your other mistress answer."

"There is no other mistress, Eve." Because I look skeptical, he goes on. "That's not to say there haven't been others. I've had a lot of women, Eve, or been had by them. Enough to know when I've found a prize."

"You're crazy, John."

"No, I'm not. I'm an exceedingly rational man. I happen to be trapped in a youthful physique, but I'm really old and very wise. Can't you think of my body as a bonus and enjoy it?"

I laugh. "I could try, I suppose. But what about mine?"

"I love it. Everyone knows women improve with age. You're a great lay."

"John!"

"Well, you are."

"Thank you. You're not so bad yourself."

"At least," he says, "I'm willing *and* able. Tell me honestly, when was the last time the great doctor managed to get it up to your satisfaction?"

"To my satisfaction? Not recently. I think his little mistress wears him out."

"You see? That too. The man's insane. You owe him nothing, Eve, except maybe a kick in the balls."

"You don't understand, John. We've been through a lot together. Fifty years. And I like to finish what I start."

"Yes, you would. I wish you weren't so damn noble. Make a fresh start. I'll promise you a good finish."

"It's coming so soon, John. It's hardly worth it."

"It's worth it to me, Eve. Let me make you happy for whatever time there is."

"You really *are* crazy."

"Okay, I'm crazy, if you want it that way."

"I don't understand you."

"Any more than I understand why you're willing to put up with this man who treats you like garbage."

I sigh, still wanting to explain, realizing the impossibility of it.

"Even if it's only a year, Eve. We'll make it a good year. A fine year. The best." His eyes are bright, his voice fervent. "Or don't you think we'd be happy?"

"John, I think almost any two people could be happy together for a year, if they'd had some practice in living. I'm sure we could have a very good year."

"All right then," he says. "What's the problem?"

"Who's to say that given fifty years, we wouldn't make some pretty big messes ourselves? Maybe worse than the ones I've got to deal with now. People are fragile, John. And relationships are worse."

"Of course they are, if people don't take them seriously."

"Even if they do. Marcus took our marriage as seriously as any man I've ever known. And it's *still* turned out a mess. Not, I'm sure, without some help from me." Suddenly I am weary of talking, of forming thoughts and arranging them into reasoned arguments. I am even tired of being right.

"You insist on being an apologist for the man. Did you write it into your marriage contract that he could do whatever he damn well pleased and it was your sacred responsibility to forgive it?"

"Of course not. But forty years, forty-five years is a long time when time's finite. And we had forty or forty-five good years. If that doesn't mean something, then nothing does."

"You're too loyal, Eve."

I laugh. "No. It's probably not that. I suspect I'm simply

afraid to admit that nothing means anything this late in the game."

John gets up from his chair and comes to me, puts his arms around me. I let myself be held, no longer fulfilled by contact, but alone inside his embrace. He feels the indifference of my body and lets me go, pulls back to look into my face.

"Are you tired of me so soon?"

"It's not that, John. It's the void, staring me in the face. I can feel it in my stomach." I put my hand there, to show him the place that is tight and frightened, the place we feel our essential loneliness. "Do you know what I mean?"

He nods slowly. "I think so. I've been alone all my life, Eve."

"The terrible thing is, so have I. So has Marcus. Even Jason, though perhaps he doesn't mind so much." My voice melts into tears, human but foolish. This piece of information should come as no surprise; I've always known it, sometimes remembered it. By now it should have no power to make me cry. I am ashamed of my weakness. But this central fact of life is the hardest to accept, larger than the capacity of my intellect to deal with it. It is always there, and I am always a little too small to encompass it.

I say, "Excuse me, John, for being so sophomoric. I thought by now I'd be immune to terror. But I'm not."

"Don't be so hard on yourself," he tells me. "No one is. Even their chemical miracles can't dispel it. Though"—he laughs—"they do change it a little. I'm not afraid of dying alone. It's living alone, for me."

I find I am smiling at him. I put out my hand to touch his. "I wish I could help you, John."

And he smiles back. "You can't, of course. But then again, you can. Isn't it delightful, how everything is premised on paradox?"

"You know that, too."

"Sure. And I also know the trick is to absolutely believe both things at once."

"Damn," I say. "I'd like to meet the guy who wrote this play."

"It's just possible," John tells me, "that we wrote it ourselves."

24

My throat hurts from so much screaming. It will force me to stop. But if I stop screaming, then They will never come. And They must come, because I have been here too long. I am unclean. Sometime ago, I felt the pressure inside me, and pushed against it, forcing it out of my body, sure that when I did, They would come to clean me, move me, talk to me, smile at me. Now I sit in it—sticky and slimy, smeared on my bottom. The smell is strong and I can't escape it. It's everywhere around me, on me, of me. And still They don't come.

I try another scream, but it rakes the sides of my raw throat and makes me cry; I feel little spurts of water squeezed out of the corners of my eyes.

Ah, look. The light is different now, bent by the slats, so that it falls on the floor. If only I could reach the place where the light touches the floor. It would be much better there. The rest of the room is brown shadows. They steal the color from the blankets, from the big pieces of furniture, from the walls. They make it nighttime in the wallpaper, where little people dance in some squares, or stand together on a wide lawn, in the others. I know they are people because they look like Him and Her, but they are small, smaller than me, and never move, no matter how long I watch them, hoping to catch them scratching their noses, or changing places when they think I am not looking.

I want to get to the place where the light is, but this thing They have put around me will not move, though it has feet, round ones, and walks nicely when She stands behind it and we go down the street. Now it refuses to move. I push and push and push against it, until it gets angry and bites my legs with its edges, but I cannot make it move.

They have forgotten me. I'm sure of it. Maybe They will never come back at all. I have been alone here in the brown shadows forever. Soon I will be hungry. I know hungry, the feeling inside me that always comes, like a pain, after I have pushed something out of me and into my pants. If They do not feed me, the pain becomes sharper, as if my insides were trying to eat themselves.

It is time to scream again. The situation is becoming serious. I have been sitting here too long.

I throw back my head, and produce a fine, loud noise. It doesn't hurt so much this time; I was right to rest my throat awhile.

Why don't They come?

The light has moved, while I was thinking of other things, and I did not *see* it move. I don't like things to rearrange themselves without my knowing. I must be more alert. I stare at the light place on the floor, daring it to move again while I watch. But it is tiresome. It thinks it can fool me by waiting until I look away to steal a little farther across the floor.

Besides getting hungry, I am getting sleepy too. The brown shadows are closing in around my eyes, sitting on my eyelids to make them heavy, so heavy that they fall down and hide the light. It's some kind of conspiracy against me, between the light and the shadows. There are many enemies in the world, this I know, and I must constantly fight just to hold my own position and not be pushed aside or left to starve.

I am very mad at Them.

There is a flash of light, and at first I think the light outside must have broken all the slats and come inside at last. I think for a moment I am under attack, but then the pain goes out of my eyes, and I see Him standing in the doorway, contorting His face at me. His voice is cheerful, as though he has no idea of what I've been going through.

He makes His foolish sounds at me, and even laughs when He finds the unpleasant mess I've been sitting in for this eternity. The way He wrinkles His nose, I can tell He smells it too. Well, let Him suffer. It is all His fault.

Once He picks me up, I am less mad at Him. I love the feeling of flying when He takes me in His hands and lifts me, high above the floor. Ah. Now we're moving. I need Him, or Her, to move. Soon I will be able to move myself. I am sure, watching Them, that I am able to do what They do, moving Their feet and legs so that all of Them follow. When I try, I fall down. My legs are not equal to the task, yet I suspect they will be someday soon, if I keep trying.

Now I hear Her voice, and when I turn my head, I find Her, dressed in the thing that pleases me, the white, swirling animals, many of them, with red eyes, against a field of dark, dark green.

She smiles and pokes a finger at me. I try to catch the finger because I would like to put it in my mouth. I know from trying that I can't eat Her finger, but that it's pleasant to suck on, and makes me think less about the hungry pain inside me.

I come back suddenly, by myself this time, frightened by how far I have traveled. My mother's face is still vivid in my mind, a younger, prettier face than I can remember her having. It is a face transformed, hidden by the other faces that slowly took its place. The face I remember most often now is the last I saw, my mother's face just after she died, with its strange, nascent smile, her last face. Now I peel off layers of memories, like masks, until I see a face almost as young as the one in my vision. *That* face is beyond my reach, though apparently it is stored away somewhere in my brain.

I am, then, it occurs to me, her immortality, a strange kind, because I have in my brain what no longer existed even while she lived; a young mother, her face almost unlined, smiling. A woman with a husband. My father died when I was rather young; I have fewer memories of him than I would like to have, and those I do are of a relatively young man. He was killed in the last World War. My mother never remarried, and when people asked her why, always responded, "Because there's no point." I always thought it was very romantic of her, but it occurs to me now that hers was a cynical position indeed.

Maybe she felt, as I do now, a need to shore herself up against the invasions of men. It feels *good,* right now, to be alone. I could drink huge draughts of my own company and be sustained by them. Alone I feel whole. There is a certain peace I never quite find in the company of others. It's not that I want to be free to pick my nose or scratch anywhere I happen to itch, though of course I do these things when I'm alone, but more a desire to need no interpretation, to make no apologies. I am what I am, and accept that nicely when I am by myself. There is no fear of being misunderstood, and I am protected from making mistakes that hurt others, or lead others to hurt me.

I am a rather minimal creature in my loneliness, perhaps—do not affect or influence the rest of the world, accomplish little, accept almost all injustices as unavoidable. But oh, it is comfortable here, inside myself, and myself inside time, which moves around me with a steady, not unpleasant tickle. John. Marcus. Suli. Jason. What are they to me? No more than I to them—a shadow passing over the face of their suns. Our crimes don't matter, nor do our noble acts, our loyalties. Nothing matters, and it doesn't matter that nothing matters.

A month ago I longed for human contact, to press my flesh against other flesh and draw warmth from the transaction. I longed to be integrated into the stream of people and events that washed around me, without moving me. And now I want only to regain my watcher's place, the peculiar ease of cheerful loneliness. It would make a fine vessel, I think, to sail for death in.

Though I may change my mind a hundred times yet before the voyage starts.

25

A loud noise wakes me, some large object hurled or knocked down.

"God damn it."

Marcus, swearing as though he means it. A strip of light creeps under the door that joins our rooms. I hear drawers yanked open, slammed shut, and more muttering.

"Marcus?" I call, but receive no answer. I see it is almost midnight. "Marcus?"

I get up now and go to the door, open it, still heavy-limbed from sleep, carrying the warmth of my bed like a wrap around me. I blink into the lighted room, cannot, at first, find Marcus, though I see a chair overturned between the hall door and his bed. Then I spot him, in a crouch, digging through the bottom drawer of his desk. He is hunting furiously for something, leaving what he pulls out of the drawer rudely piled on the floor beside it.

"Marcus, what are you doing?"

He looks up, his brows drawn together and downward in a dangerous scowl. "I'm looking for my gun. There's a prowler in the house."

"A prowler?"

"A big black man. I saw him in the pantry. And I intend to shoot the bastard." His hand keeps digging in the drawer as he speaks. Finally he pulls out an ugly snub-nosed pistol, already fitted to his palm. He brandishes it at me. "This'll stop him."

He gets up from his haunches and starts for the door. I watch him exit, hear his footsteps pounding down the stairs. It takes my sleep-fogged brain longer than it should to grasp the situation, then I, too, start for the staircase. I hear shouting below—Marcus' angry voice spitting expletives. I race through the dark pantry and on to the lighted kitchen.

Alan Wills stands frozen in front of the sink, a glass of water in his hand. He glares at Marcus, who stands some six feet away, holding the pistol in front of him with both hands, pointed in the general direction of Wills' belt buckle. Peering through the other door to the kitchen, opposite me, Suli's terrified face takes shape in the surrounding shadows.

I take a deep breath, then stride into the room; Marcus hears rather than sees me.

"Eve, get back."

I keep walking, until I stand in front of the gun, between Marcus and Wills.

"Eve, for god's sake. What are you doing? Get out of the way."

"You're being rude, Marcus," I tell him. I turn sideways, in order to see both men. "Marcus, this is Alan Wills. Alan, my husband, Marcus Harmon."

"You know this man?" Marcus still clutches the gun.

"Of course I do. Please put that down. It makes me awfully nervous."

Reluctantly he lowers his right arm and points the gun at the kitchen tile. If he shoots it, I think absently, it will be no loss; I've never liked the stuff. Now Suli enters from the dining room, spouting apologies.

"It's my fault, Suli," I tell her. "Marcus mistook Alan for a housebreaker. I guess I neglected to tell him that Alan visits sometimes."

"You mean he's been here before?"

Suli is calm now. She draws herself to full height and speaks evenly. "Mrs. Harmon has given me permission to entertain Alan in my quarters in the evenings, when my services are not needed."

Marcus looks at me. I nod back. "That's right."

"For god's sake, Eve. You'll have Jason's whole special force descending on us. There are regulations, you know. Curfews. Haven't you caused enough trouble?"

I start to explain but Suli, cool-voiced, cuts me off. "Those regulations don't apply to Alan. He's a citizen, just as you are, and free to come and go as he chooses." She pauses. "Of course, if he is not welcome in your home, that's another matter. We had no desire to alarm you."

"Alan," I say, "please sit down and drink your water. Or would you like something a little stronger, after being threatened with a pistol?" I turn to my husband. "The least you could do is offer the man a shot of brandy. It's in the dining room."

Marcus puts his pistol down on the counter and goes into the dining room. With satisfaction, I hear the doors of the liquor cabinet open and close. In the kitchen we wait in silence. I smile broadly into the tense faces of Suli and her friend. When Marcus returns with the brandy, I take glasses from the cupboard and put them in a little square in the center of the table.

"Now, let's all have a nightcap. I'm sure we all could use one." I seat myself at the table and pat the chair beside me. "Come on, Marcus. Sit down." He does, ungraciously. Suli stands beside Wills at the sink, her hand on his arm. "Join us, please," I tell them. Both look at me as though I were insane.

"Come on," I urge. "Marcus didn't mean any harm by it. Nor, for that matter, did I. I should have told him before, so this didn't happen. But the possibility never occurred to me. I'm terribly sorry."

Slowly, unwillingly, they come and sit. I pour out four brandies and pass them around.

"I'm a foolish old woman," I tell them, raising my glass. "But let's drink to disaster averted. In the nick of time." No one drinks with me. I chatter on, under some compelling pressure to fill the silence. "You're awfully lucky, Marcus. If I hadn't wakened when you kicked over that chair, you might have done something dreadful."

He grunts, finally takes a swallow from his glass.

Out of one corner of my eye, I see a slow smile spread like dawn over Alan Wills' dusky, handsome face. It grows until it becomes a laugh, big, hearty, genuine. He leans back in his chair and laughs and laughs, pounding the table once, and his knee several times. Suli resists his mirth at first, but finally there is little she can do but smile. Soon Marcus smiles, too, and I smile.

When there is finally a pause between the bursts, Suli

addresses her lover. A giggle carbonates her question. "Please tell me, Alan. What's so funny?"

He leans forward and puts his hand flat, palm down, on the table. He tries several times to speak, but the words are choked by powerful guffaws. Finally he manages to say, "I almost got my head shot off."

"That's not funny, Alan," Suli says.

"No, no," he agrees. "What's funny is that I'm still alive."

Marcus' eyes are wide, his face rather blank. He raises his left eyebrow slightly, a sign of cocktail party perplexity, questioning but not ready to argue. Suli merely looks pained.

"Surely," I say to my companions, "surely you can see the humor in that."

Our little party lacks momentum. Wills' hysteria passes and leaves him grim. Suli, always the impassive domestic in the presence of the master, does little more than murmur. The discomfort of the situation leads me to play the cheerful fool, while Marcus is embarrassed into awkward silence, and doesn't seem to remember what his hands and eyes are for. Brandy choked down, goodnights said, we part as soon as is decently possible. I regret the scene, of course, but play it out, extending my hand and my apologies to Alan Wills, which forces Marcus to do the same. Without much enthusiasm, the two shake hands.

"Sorry if I frightened you," Marcus grumbles, and Wills responds with a grunt of expiation.

Marcus follows me to my room. I sit in my blue chair while he sinks, weary, on my bed.

"Whatever possessed you, Eve?"

"A spirit of charity, my dear. Oh, I'll admit I rather bungled it. I should have told you. Frankly, it slipped my mind."

Marcus shakes his head, appalled by my folly. I feel obliged to defend myself.

"Those two have been in love for years, Marcus. And they can't get married, largely thanks to our son and his friends. They've been able to see each other exactly one night a week, for all that time. So when a safe, legal solution occurred to me, I just pursued it." I smile ruefully at him. "It never occurred to me you might mistake Alan for a burglar and try to blow his brains out."

"No, I suppose not. Are you sure it's legal?"

I nod. "Alan's a citizen, like you or me. If anyone should ever question it, he's *our* guest."

"Hmm. What about Suli? If Jason ever found out . . ."

"Jason is our son, not our supervisor."

"He's a powerful man, Eve."

"I know. And not a very nice one." My hands, seemingly independent of the rest of me, play with each other in my lap. I watch their nervous antics, thinking of our son. Jason is a failure we've found it convenient to ignore, as much as possible. "I'm not afraid of him anymore, Marcus. I was for years, even after the doctors said they'd cured him. I don't believe he'd hurt us now. He has too much to lose." I sigh. "He's too well socialized for matricide."

Marcus' face is a tired gray. Despite the treatments, he looks old right now, and weary, as weary as I feel.

"I've never understood it, Eve," he says.

"No. Nor have I. But I think it really is all right now. He seems quite friendly to you, anyway."

Marcus nods. "He calls me at the lab sometimes. We had lunch a couple of weeks ago."

Out of old habit, I am sanguine. "Well, that's something, isn't it? Maybe he's coming around. I don't imagine we'll ever be close, but . . ." My optimistic chatter runs down. The pretense is absurd. Instead of continuing it, I ask my husband something I have wanted to know for many years.

"Marcus, do you *like* him?"

He looks at me out of his tired eyes, then shrugs. "What's there to like?" Slowly he gets to his feet. "It's time for bed. Past time."

He stops to kiss my forehead before he leaves the room.

26

I hate the pattern of this linoleum, faded pinks and greens, scored with cracks, but my eyes revert to it anyway, because it is easier than looking at my son. I wish Marcus was beside me, but justice dictates that we form this ragged triangle, three points of isolation. I have never seen a child sit as still as Jason does. He's been like an automaton since I found him on the rocks, saying little, but allowing himself to be directed to eat and sleep, to move from place to place.

Looking at his blank and almost pretty face, I realize I am terrified of my son.

Marcus has been at him for almost an hour now, alternately loud and soft, angry and pleading, to no effect. I haven't listened to it all; I can't. Some portion of my brain stays stubbornly with my baby, my Maria. Gone now. Already cremated. Her ashes are in a box, a little box, on the table beside our bed. We must do something with them soon; we must decide something.

She was dead when I reached her. Dead. Cold. Wet. Her little face was distorted with water, with fear. Her head gashed on one side, by the rocks, and the wound washed strangely clean by the circling tide. When I picked her up, her leg bent in extra places, shattered by the fall. And Jason did not run away, did not move, did not help me, just sat atop the rocks and stared, stared and stared, out at the sea.

Marcus' voice rises and falls; I don't bother to make sense of his words. Violence stirs in me, when I listen. I have felt an overwhelming desire sometimes to hurt Jason, to shake him so hard his humanity breaks loose, even to pound my fist against his fine, expressionless face. My control is shaky. I hold one hand tightly with the other and try to hear the rhythm of my breaths going in and out, in and out of my body.

"Tell me again what happened, Eve." Marcus' voice is dry and dead, his eyes desperate.

"I can't, Marcus. I've told you so many times already."

Jason stares politely, silently at me.

"Ask him, damn it," I say, suddenly angry. "He knows. He was there. Ask him."

I am twisted inside. The pressure is awful. The tendons are pulled tight around my joints; my hands shake. I ache all over; am afraid I will vomit—awful, ugly things. I half rise, trying to relax my contorted limbs before they freeze. My voice soars.

"Tell us, Jason. Tell us. Why didn't you call me? Why didn't you get help?" I'm shouting. Bands of red and black smear across my vision, pulsating. The rage is irresistible. I move toward the boy, my intentions unclear, violent. "Why, damn it. Why didn't you come to me?"

Jason raises his pale, impassive face and sees my rage.

"I was afraid you'd say it was my fault," he says in a quiet monotone.

I did not expect him to speak. His words take me by surprise. All three of us are silent in their wake.

At last, Marcus asks, "Was it, Jason? Was it your fault?"

But the boy has retreated once again; he is gone, gone. My rage breaks and leaves me weak; I return to my chair. Marcus repeats his question again and again, until his words have lost all meaning and his voice no longer sounds like a human voice but pounds like the monotonous drone of the sea outside the cottage. Finally I can stand it no more.

"Go to your room, Jason."

He rises mechanically and walks a neat, straight line to the small room he has been sleeping in. The door closes quietly behind him.

"What now, Marcus?"

He slumps in his chair. "I don't know. Doctors. Tests. Professional help. We'll go back to the city. Is tomorrow too soon?"

I shake my head. "No. The sooner the better. I hate this place."

"So do I. I'll help you pack."

We do not move; it is as though Jason's strange lethargy has infected us all.

"Marcus, do you suppose we'll ever know what happened?"

My husband looks at me. "I don't know. Maybe the doctors can find out. I rather hope not. I'm not sure I want to know. Do you?"

His question does not penetrate to the place where sense is made of words. Instead of answering, I listen to the hated voice of the sea. There are no rocks near the cottage to disrupt its rhythm, only a gentle curve of unobstructed shore. It shouts, whispers, shouts, whispers, threatens and cajoles without a pause, eliciting no more response from the inanimate coastline than we have been able to draw out of our son.

27

It isn't going well today. The momentum of previous meetings is missing; instead of harmony, there is hostility in the air. People are not making the extra effort, not taking the leap of faith required to understand one another. Nothing specific is wrong, but tempers, mine included, are short, and the customary sympathy, the feeling of unity we had magically attained as a group, seems to have deserted us.

Mitbu is restless. Michael's ebullience threatens to show a dark, obnoxious side. Belinda is here in body only, while Tina, unaccountably, is not here at all. Perhaps her absence is what maims us. We limp along like a crippled organism, parodying our usual pace and gait.

"The subways are green," Michael contends. "Any fool can tell you that. Dark, muddy green."

"They're brown," Mitbu says.

"Look, I ride them every day," Michael says. "I should know. You can't call them brown, no matter how blind you are."

"Does it really matter?" I ask. "People do see things differently. It seems to me you can take the color adjective out altogether and not hurt the poem."

"I won't take it out," Mitbu says. "I'm writing about brown cars. It's my poem."

There it is. The standard cry of the criticized. Well, maybe I have been too harsh too soon. But it was working before.

I nod gravely. "Of course it is. If you feel brown is important, by all means leave it. My point is, nothing is ever sacrosanct. You've got to be willing to expand or contract what you write. And if a word's not performing any particular function, it might be just as well to let it go."

Now Belinda speaks, the first time today. "How can you decide a word has no use? If you look too closely, almost nothing makes sense. Why write poetry at all?"

All of the standard answers sound and probably are patronizing. To tell them they'll understand in a few years, if they keep at it, seems too insulting. I remember only too well myself railing against criticism, against the smug certainty of older poets, older people, that there was a rightness, intuited rather than postulated, that I had violated without knowing of its existence until the deed was done. A game with changing rules is hard to play, harder to teach.

"The question is more," I say finally, "why try to write *good* poetry, isn't it? You have a reason for writing it, or you wouldn't be here now."

My back is to the door, but I hear it open now. Across from me, Mitbu tenses and slips to the edge of his chair. Beside me, Belinda turns to look behind her. So do I.

John Powell is in the doorway. Two men in the khaki uniforms of the Importee Police stand behind him.

"Eve?" he begins timidly. "I'm sorry to interrupt, but these men . . ."

The officers have no patience with John's version of academic courtesy, but walk past him into the room, separating at the door, one to each side. Their epaulets twinkle with angry silver stars; their chests are crisscrossed with white straps whose purpose is obscure. They are ordinary men, but seem to draw confidence from their vaguely absurd uniforms. One holds a clipboard, the other a stout, well-polished metal club.

They look from Mitbu to Michael and back again. The man with the clipboard looks from it to both men, then points at Mitbu.

"That one. I'm pretty sure."

As he leaps up, Mitbu's chair falls backward, makes a sharp crack as it hits the floor. The noise startles the police as much as it startles me; I see them tense.

It suddenly occurs to me that this is my class. I'm in charge here. Something is required of me. While trying to decide what it is, I stand up, for more authority. The police have not been watching me. Now they swing sharply at the sound of movement.

"Sit down, lady," one of them tells me.

I have obeyed so long I feel the impulse to do it now, but check myself, and remain on my feet.

"Lady," the IP says, a perfect caricature of exasperated patience.

"Please tell me what you want here. This is a poetry workshop, and you're interrupting it. If you wish to enroll, of course, you can do so through the office."

Someone, I think it is Michael, laughs. With my eyes I try to tell him to shut up, let me handle it.

"We want him, ma'am. That one." The IP points at Mitbu with his club.

"Wanting doesn't make it legal. What do you want him for?"

"We have a complaint from his employer. He doesn't have clearance to be here now."

"What clearance is required to attend a poetry workshop?" I ask.

"This man's a domestic, carded for Wednesday nights. Any other time he's out without permission from the employer, he's breaking the law." He smiles at me, an insolent smile that exposes stubby, yellowish teeth. "And we're here to stop that."

Maybe it's the yellow teeth that get to me. Something does, anyway—a surge of dislike, a desire to rebel.

"I'm afraid I can't let you disrupt my workshop this way. Don't you need a"—I stop, searching for a word—"a warrant, or something?"

"Things is different for importees, lady. We don't need nothing we don't got." The IP waves his clipboard at me, smiling still. "Come on, fella," he says to Mitbu. "Let's go and let this lady get on with her poetry." He says every syllable of the last word slowly, mockingly.

"I thought the government required a literacy test these days," I say, because the thought crosses my mind and I don't stop it. "Or did they waive it for you?"

I feel a pressure on my arm. Just before I vent my instinct to pull away, I realize it's John. He speaks close to my ear.

"Don't, Eve. It's no use. We survive by going along with them."

"You mean you're going to let them waltz in here and arrest someone in the middle of a poetry workshop, for god's sake?"

"If he doesn't have clearance, yes. We warn all the importees who use the Guilds they must have clearance to come here. If they don't have it, they shouldn't be here."

"But John, it's wrong."

"It's practical, Eve. This happens a couple times a year. Now let them take the guy and leave, or we'll all be arrested for interfering with them."

The wind goes out of my sails. There is no graceful way to retreat. While the IPs grin at my impotence, I sit down again, with as much dignity as I can muster. Mitbu glares at me.

"All right," I say. "Please do your business quickly and leave."

The IP with the club walks warily toward Mitbu, who stands tensed, like an angry watchdog. His eyes circle the room, seeking egress. In a sudden lunge, the IP reaches him, seizes his arm, and twists it behind him. Mitbu's lips draw back with the pain; his large, clenched teeth flash white.

"That wasn't necessary," I say. My voice is small and ladylike, absurd.

The IP laughs. "You gonna tell us how to do our job, lady?"

"Maybe," I say coldly. "My son is with your Ministry." Cursed with Jason, I decide to use him. An idea comes to me. I take up my stylus and copy down the numbers on the IP badges. "I've taken down your numbers. I plan to inquire about proper police procedure in making arrests of this kind."

"Sure thing, lady. You check us out." Both policemen laugh. They pull Mitbu, handcuffed, toward the door.

"I promise you, I will."

The IP pokes at Mitbu's back with his metal prod. At the door he turns, grinning. "Who is your son, lady?" he asks.

I look him in the eye. "Jason Harmon," I say distinctly.

For once I am edified to see the shudder my son's name evokes. Apparently I am not the only one with cause to fear him.

The IPs leave. John Powell, Michael, and Belinda stare at me in silence. I rip the top sheet from my pad and crumple it up in my hand, then shrug.

"We've never been close," I tell them.

28

"I'm sorry, Eve. But it'll only put us about three hours behind."

"What about the helicar, Marcus?"

"I called the agency. They'll deliver it at noon." He pauses. "How about you? Are you all packed?"

"Oh yes."

"Good. We'll be on our way by twelve-thirty, then. And the weather's clear all the way. No snow until tomorrow morning at the earliest."

"That's good."

"I've got to run now."

"Okay."

"Hey, you don't mind, do you? I really need the time at the lab."

"No problems, Marcus. I'm used to the vagaries of science by now."

"Good girl. We'll have a fine time."

"I'll see when you get here."

"Got to go now. Goodbye."

So. Three hours more. In a way, I'm grateful for the temporary reprieve—my old habit of wanting to put off unpleasantness. Yet the delay is a disappointment, too. I've readied myself for the trip, which has become, in my thinking about it, not a vacation, but a council of war. There has to come a day that maketh all things clear, and I expect this journey to provide it. More; I've promised myself to make it happen.

For days now I've been making lists, neat outlines, possible scripts. What I Must Tell Marcus. How Marcus May Respond (Versions A, B, C and D). What Marcus Must Tell Me. How I Should Respond. What My Options Are. What His Options Are. Possible Solutions. Future Plans.

List after list. I have tried to face the possibilities in advance. I know it is hopeless. The truth will be slightly, importantly different from anything I have imagined it to be. My preparation is meaningless. I must simply remember to be alert, alive, receptive. I must listen hard. I must remember what I *want* to happen.

Unfortunately, I'm not sure what I want to happen. I've been a realist too long to be able to even compose ideals. Give me a situation, and I'll make the best of it. State me two positions, and I'll find a compromise. Ask me to accommodate and I'll do it brilliantly. Let me react to an existing reality. But don't make me create it.

How I would pray, if I had any gods. I wish beyond anything that there was some power, some order bigger than me, that I could surrender and entrust myself to. It need not be benevolent. It need not be just. The limitations of my own resources stagger me, yet they are all I have, and my only hope is being able to muster them, such as they are, quickly, and to use them well.

John Powell has asked me to leave Marcus, to finish my life with him. He has offered me a home, a place to live and a person to live with. He loves me, he says. He will take care of me.

John Powell is an option, a bit of ammunition, a safety net suspended below the trapeze. I count on it. He said this day before yesterday; he said it yesterday. But perhaps by today he's changed his mind. The offer may be canceled. He may have forgotten it. May not have meant it. Did I really hear him say it, or have I made it up?

Suddenly I'm afraid. I tell Marcus about John. Marcus tells me to live with John. And then I find John doesn't want me. John doesn't know me. He doesn't exist. I come with my suitcases and find a stranger at his door. I'm sorry, Mr. Powell has moved away. My mind is functioning on nightmare logic. My hands are very cold.

I have to talk to John, make sure he exists, make sure he means it. The receiver slips in my hand when I pick it up. Shaking, I put it back in the cradle and try again. Slowly. That's right. Now punch up the number. You can do it.

It's ringing now.

Damn. The secretary answers.

"Is Mr. Powell there, please?"

"May I ask who's calling?"

"This is Eve Harmon."

"Oh, Mrs. Harmon. How are you?"

"Fine. Fine. Let me speak to John."

She leaves the telecom. I hear her footsteps, voices, office noises. Is John in class? I can't see the digichron from here. It was stupid of me to call. He'll be angry. Perhaps I should hang up.

Then warm, reassuring, John's voice.

"Eve. I thought you were gone by now."

He sounds glad to hear from me. No anger.

"A delay. Marcus got held up at the lab."

"You know, I was hoping you were back already."

"John, I'm scared."

"Scared of what, Eve? You don't think he'll try to harm you? If there's any chance of that—"

"No, John. He won't hurt me. Not like that. Do you still want me, John?"

He laughs at me. "Haven't I made that clear? Of course I do."

"Oh good. It seems so improbable. I can't seem to believe it when you're not there."

"Believe it, Eve. Don't forget it. I'll come and get you now, if you say the word. You don't have to put yourself through this."

"No. That's all right. I have to do it. I just wanted to make sure."

"You're funny, Eve. Make sure of what?"

"That I was welcome in your life. That you're real."

"I'm real," he says. "You're welcome. Are you all right? I'll come right now. I really will."

"No, don't. I just had to make sure."

"Are you sure?"

"I think so. Thanks, John."

"Know it. Please. Remember it. Believe. All right?"

"All right. Goodbye, John."

"Eve, I love you. Hurry back. Call me as soon as you get home. Or call from there."

"All right. Goodbye."

29

The splendid old lobby is empty except for us, the desk clerk, and two bored bell captains who slouch at their station. The red carpet is still here, the figured wallpaper, an atrocious, marvelous old clock bedecked with gilded cherubim. The light is very mellow; it comes from ornate sconces on the walls, from the old kind of incandescent bulb. The hotel was quaint when we came here thirty years ago and is quainter still today.

"Uh, were you planning to ski, Dr. Harmon? We have courtesy transportation to the slopes, leaving hourly from six to ten a.m."

"What? No." Marcus laughs. "We're here to relax. Just a room with a bath and a double bed is all we need. I hope your food's as good as I remember it."

The clerk inclines his head. "I hope so, sir. The chef is excellent. Of course, you know how hard it is to get the raw materials these days. But we try, sir. Be assured of that."

"I'll take your word for it."

The clerk takes a key from the pigeonhole behind him and hands it to Marcus. "Front!"

One of the two lethargic bellboys stands and crosses to the desk, tugging at the bottom of his ill-fitting jacket to pull it down in back.

In the elevator, I see the gold braid on his shoulders and cuffs is tarnished, the red of his jacket dulled by many cleanings. Old spots disfigure his splendor. He stops on four and precedes us into the green-carpeted hallway, managing to juggle all four of our bags at once. We turn into a longer corridor, past a polished oval mirror. Our reflection is obscured by a large spray of plastic foliage.

The bellboy puts down our bags and unlocks the door, then bids us enter, hopping along behind us to flip light switches, open doors, and display the closet space for our admiration. He puts our luggage on racks, shows us the bathroom with a certain proprietary pride, then, smiling beside the dresser, awaits his tip. Marcus produces and the man retreats backwards, bobbing thanks.

Still wearing his coat, Marcus bounces on the bed and looks around the room with satisfaction, at the muted green walls, the long impenetrable drapes and the subtle, serviceable carpet of inoffensive gray.

"Marvelous," he says, bouncing still. "It takes me back. This is a proper room."

I must agree with him, though younger folk might not. There is the mirror, square above the dresser, the two sturdy lamps, the matching Naugahyde chairs, almost antiques now, if one has a sense of history and of humor, the two impressionist prints poorly reproduced and cheaply framed. There is a new-style viewer, of course, and controls to summon up strains of computer music, restful or romantic, according to your needs. The room, exactly this room, comes in several sizes and colors. Our present version is a spacious one.

"Tired?" Marcus asks from his perch on the bed.

"No, not really." I take off my coat and hang it in the roomy hotel closet, then busy myself with opening suitcases, arranging our possessions.

"Hungry?" he asks.

I stop and think about it. My body is not hungry, but I would welcome an escape from the intimacy of the room. Unlike a house, it offers no retreat, except the temporary harbor of the bathroom. It is a long time since we have been packed so tightly and forced by space to relate. I sit beside my husband on the bed.

"Hungry I could be. I'm not suffering now. But soon."

"My sentiments precisely. Nice bed. It even squeaks." Marcus bounces while I listen, then bounces to his feet. "Let's have some music." He turns the knobs and the room is filled with the sounds of synthetic violins.

"A little softer, please."

He takes off his coat and tosses it on a chair. "A little cool in here." He looks for the thermostat and adjusts it.

"How about a drink before dinner? I have a bottle in my bag." He seizes the empty ice bucket. "There must be a machine. I'll find it."

He's gone. I bounce a little on the bed myself, check my reflection in the inescapable mirror. The lighting is kind to me; it blurs the lines and creases. My eyes look back at me with a kind of animal panic, pupils wide, the irises dark, bright.

A pounding on the door. I open it to Marcus, ebullient conqueror of the ice machine. I unwrap the stout bathroom glasses, he fills them with ice, then bourbon. We make a good ensemble and play the scene smoothly. I'm grateful for that.

He raises his glass. "Well, to us."

Our toast produces the clunk of cheap glass against cheap glass. We retreat for a moment into the bourbon.

"Excellent, excellent," Marcus says. "This is the life." Glass in hand, he paces the tight perimeter of the room, obstructed by bed and dresser. "Ah, yes."

I stand by the dresser, watching him. He stops in front of me and smiles.

"Turn around, Eve."

"Why?"

"Just do."

I turn. Marcus puts his arm around me. There we are, a mirror-image couple, a corny "after" photograph, Marcus tall, I short; Marcus wide, I slight beside him, our enduring proportion intact. He pats my back. I see his hand move in the mirror.

"Fifty years, Eve." Marcus smiles at himself in the mirror, raises his glass to the image.

"Yes." Self-conscious, I make a face. The woman in the mirror suddenly twists up her features, too. The man beside her laughs. "Enough," I tell him, turning away. "That woman's making fun of me."

He pours us each another drink. I'm glad he's brought the prop. Not only does it give us something to do; the liquor is having its effect, relaxing me. I feel my cheeks grow hot, some of my reservations melt. Why not, after all, enjoy myself? The first night, anyway.

I sidle up to Marcus. "Dance, mister?"

"Who wants to know?"

"I do."

He takes me gallantly, formally. We swoop and swirl, run into the dresser chair, pull back and dip.

"You're pretty good," I tell him. He hums raggedly, behind the violins. We bend low to finish.

"Hungry?"

"Uh huh. The dancing honed my appetite."

"And mine. Shall we?" He proffers his arm.

"Hold it there. Methinks I'll repair the visage before presenting it to the glittering assemblage below."

"I await your pleasure, madame. As long as it doesn't take too long."

"It won't," I assure him. "You can only improve on nature so much." I find my cosmetic bag and retreat into the bathroom, turn on the faucet to seal my privacy. My face, in the cabinet mirror, is flushed. I splash cold water over it and powder my nose.

So far, so good. We do play well together; the practice tells. Our timing is perfect, without the awkward pauses, the missed cues of newlyweds or strangers. I'm a little drunk and having a good time.

Marcus rises when I reappear; I take his arm.

As we sit at our table with another drink, the dining room fills up. Snatches of conversations reach me from nearby tables, talk of good runs and bad falls, chance meetings on the slopes. An occasional clap of laughter rises up and flashes in the darkened room. The people around us seem young, healthy, and attractive. Perhaps it is only a trick of the candlelight, but the illusion is pleasant and I almost feel, without the reminder of mirrors, that I am one with them. Marcus, across the table, is still a handsome man.

We take our time ordering, letting our tastebuds be titillated by the menu, tempted by the many attractive options.

I *like* being Cinderella, suddenly transformed from drudge to belle, enjoying this evanescent fairy-tale world. My husband is a prince among scientists, and now I suspend the skepticism of long familiarity and pay him court.

"What was the excitement at the lab this morning?"

"Good stuff. We're close to another breakthrough. A minor one, of course, but still important."

"From little acorns, and all that."

"To acorns," Marcus says, polishing off his drink.

"And oak trees." I follow suit.

"I have a fine team there, Eve. The best ever. Weeker's not brilliant, of course, but my god, he's thorough. And Curtis has brains. The technologists know their business cold. *And* they care about it."

"It's an exciting time for you."

"It really is. In the last five years, we've pushed the frontiers about three decades' worth. And the next ten will *really* be something." He starts a little, aware of his slip, but I smile back widely, letting it pass. Time for that later.

The waiter comes. We order slowly, relishing the exchange. Marcus orders wine, an extravagantly old cabernet.

"Can't you tell me just a little about the project?" I tease.

"No, I can't. I'd like to, believe me. But I can tell you this. It matters. It really does. Like the cell regeneration work mattered."

"That *is* big time."

"It is." He smiles at me.

"Who'd have thought that serious young man who wandered into my first reading would turn out to be the leading biochemist of his time?"

"Well, that's overstating the case a bit."

"Is it really?"

"Think what you like."

"I shall."

The food is sumptuous. Marcus tastes the wine expertly and nods his approval. Realizing he has an appreciative audience, the waiter performs with aplomb. Dinner absorbs us for a while. The cooking is as good as Suli's, the raw materials much better. Here there are fresh mushrooms, succulent veal, the happy surprise of spices hard to buy, these days, for use at home.

We extend the feast with a liqueur. The wine sings in my veins; its borrowed warmth creeps up my legs, from ankles almost to the knee. It quiets me, and when I speak, my words have soft edges, like velvet.

When at last we head for our room, my fear of going there is gone. I cling to Marcus' arm, out of affection and for support. I am anxious to be alone with him now.

We bolt the door behind us. I totter to the bed while Marcus makes us yet another drink, a nightcap. I put the glass on my head and we both laugh foolishly. When I lie back on the bed, it rocks like a ship.

"Oh oh. Heavy seas. I've had a lot to drink."

"Sit up awhile." He sits beside me on the bed. "Storm warnings, eh?"

"Oh yes. Man the lifeboats, and all that."

He pats my knee. "You'll weather it. A pretty little craft."

"Well, thanks. I hope I'm seaworthy."

"In the meantime, could I interest you in an after-dinner kiss?"

I raise my face to him. His wavers, approaching it. I close my eyes and the pitching motion takes up again, but I attribute it to romance this time and am less undone by it. Our lips are moist and slide against each other. I concentrate on them until they seem separate from our bodies, even from our minds, and become a phenomenon of the universe at large.

We part at last. Marcus stiffens suddenly.

"What's wrong?"

"The message light." He reaches for the telecom. "This is Dr. Harmon, four-oh-nine. What is the message please?" He waves his free hand at me. "I see. I'd like to place a call then. Yes." He gives the number of the lab. "Don? Harmon here. What is it? . . . Terrific. Better than terrific. . . . Right on the nose? You can't ask for better than that. . . . I see. Well, my best to everybody who's still there. . . . Good. Good.

"Great news. It's come out just as Curtis predicted it would. It's a big one, Eve. The ramifications are staggering."

I beam at him blankly. It's a little hard to share his enthusiasm, since I know nothing of the project, but I'm happy for him. I really am. "That's wonderful, Marcus."

"You bet it is. You're going to bed with a happy man, Eve."

"Well, that's better than a miserable one, I guess."

"Come on. Let's do it." Marcus starts to unbutton his shirt. "It's been a long day. And a good one."

"Okay." I get up and unpack my nightgown, then go

to the bathroom. The flush is gone and I'm very pale now. The beginning of a vague apprehension tugs at my stomach and suddenly I think of John Powell. It sobers me and a twinge of guilt mixes with my apprehension.

Poor John. Poor John. I can feel him thinking of me, of us, back in the city and unable to picture this place, this room, this particular me. My stomach lurches, not at peace with me. I don't want to think of John now, but his face remains before my inner eye, no matter how hard I try to erase it, and his voice plays over and over in my ears: "Believe. Believe."

And in the other room is Marcus, who can save the world but not his wife. I am his wife. I no longer know what that means, to either one of us. My god.

I sit on the toilet. The bowl exudes a breath of cold air that makes gooseflesh rise on my thighs. I lean forward as far as I can, doubled over my knees, and pinch the bridge of my nose between thumb and forefinger. My head aches a little; the temple-drum begins to pound. Down my left side, there is the dull ache I've come to live with, to ignore.

John is my pain right now. I wish I could obliterate his image, but cannot. I invited it there and let him spend his tenderness on me. No one is innocent, in matters of love, nor taken unawares. At best, I didn't discourage him. At worst, I led him on.

"Eve, are you spending the night in there?"

The idea hadn't occurred to me, but has its possibilities.

I hurry through my toilet and emerge. Marcus takes his turn. I climb in bed while he is gone, hoping sleep will overtake me very fast.

Marcus, hearty in his striped pajamas, is back before it does. He sits on the edge of the bed to remove his socks. How many times, I wonder, have I watched this man do this, how many times have I waited while he did? Every movement is familiar and predictable, and none is wasted, but performed with the efficiency of a well-established routine. I know this about Marcus Harmon, and other things too—the faces he makes shaving, that he cleans his fingernails twice a day, what brand of underwear he prefers—things only a wife of long standing knows about a man.

I don't know these things about John, could not, perhaps, begin to learn them in the short space of a year. It strikes me that John is not a creature of habit but, most likely, the kind of man who wears jockey shorts one day, boxer shorts the next, with equal indifference.

Marcus draws his legs up on the bed, then slides them under the covers. Smiling, he pats the pillow beside my head. He turns off the light.

The bed grows warmer as he slides his body down beside me. I wait, open eyes staring into the darkness above us, to see what he will do. Does he mean to sleep? I wait, not moving.

Presently his hand reaches out and settles in the curve of my waist, and he pulls himself up on one side facing me, a darker mass in the darkness. Still I do not move. His hand begins to stroke me, up and down, from shoulder to thigh. The fabric of my nightgown slides with it, over my skin.

The tension in his movements tells me what is on his mind. Tonight he means to make love to me. And tonight, I don't want him. I think of all the nights in these last years my needs and I have gone to bed alone, forced to make do with fantasies and the mechanics of habit in the absence of good, warm, man-smelling, living flesh. So many nights that I have taken a lover. My body has forgotten Marcus' ways.

Now I am limp under his touch, empty of desire, except to be untroubled by his probing hand. This body of mine no longer belongs to him, no longer recognizes him. My mind resents the assumptions he makes. It occurs to me that he'll find in my lethargy tonight a posthumous excuse for his neglect, and pride makes me move a little, grow a little hot. I call up certain of my standard fantasies and let them fill my mind; I *will* be adequate, and if it's not for Marcus, well, he need never know. Whatever works.

Yet there is much to overcome. Thoughts of John, of Julie Mitchum, the paralyzing thought of my own death, snipe at my fantasies until they lose their excitement and become merely funny, a little bizarre. I let Marcus pull off my nightgown and my body is naked beside him, but my mind stays clothed in doubt and reservations.

In the darkness I feel the flurry of his fingers opening

the fly of his pajamas, unsnapping the waist. His body jackknifes to remove them, pants first, and then the top. My flesh is neutral. I wait without impatience, without excitement, for what is to come.

His body moves over mine, lowers a sudden breath-stopping weight on my ribs. His mouth seeks mine; under cover of darkness I turn away, so that he tries to kiss the pillow. Far below, he jabs at me, trying to find the opening, and here, too, I use subtle evasions to make it difficult. Finally he frees his hand and sends it down to guide him. His fingers find the place; he takes bearings and then is there, warm, hard, insistent.

I feel invaded, claustrophobic, half sick. His weight, once welcome, pains and stifles me. My body, once fluid, is stiff and awkward. Instinctively the portals close against him. This only makes him push harder, and at last my body betrays me, in its stupidity produces moisture to make it easier for him.

His collarbone batters my chin; my chin will be sore there for several days. His whiskers rake over my cheekbones, making them hot and raw. There is no magic to make these touchings pleasurable; I resent the many small discomforts of making love. The same things, I know, can excite me, and excitement can obliterate the tiny pains. But when the spirit is unwilling, the flesh complains, self-concerned, resentful.

In the darkness, with Marcus on me, I ache for John, for me. I feel guilty, on the one hand; betrayed, on the other. Tears squeeze up painfully, spill silent out of the sides of my eyes, slide down into my ears. In the act of mating, I am utterly alone. The union of bodies underlines the rebellious independence, the isolation of my mind, and makes me realize, too, the complete mystery of Marcus' motives and his thoughts.

I hate him now; I hate myself.

Suddenly, exploring for my ear, his tongue tastes my tears. His body becomes immobile on me, even heavier.

"Am I hurting you, Eve? Is it the pain?"

I pause to feel my body. The pain is there, after a fashion, as it almost always is, but it is dull, insignificant. Passion could drive it out and make me impervious. It is

a good excuse, but I don't want to use it; we have told
each other too many lies already.

The time has come. The evening's enjoyment was only
a brief remission. Our disease continues and must be faced.
I am not ready for what has to be done, but I'm as ready
as I'll ever be. My drunkenness is gone, and has left me
cold, with a residual headache, a dry, unpleasant mouth.

"The pain is there," I answer honestly, so much later
that the question has been lost. "But it's not the pain,
Marcus."

He has gone soft inside me; I have felt him shrinking,
pulling away from my surrounding flesh. Now, with relief,
I feel him exit. He rolls off me and over on his back, lies
silent for a long time, arms crossed beneath his head.

"You were crying," he says finally. His voice is small
and disappointed. I hear his hurt and want instinctively to
soothe it. My hand reaches out and finds his. I squeeze it.
A voice inside me intercepts compassion, though. Don't
forgive him, it says. Don't forgive yourself.

So I tell him, "Yes, I was crying."

It sounds so sad, so ominous. Part of me wants to take
it back, to hold his face against my shoulder, to stroke
his hair. Another part of me wants to hurt him, wants to
make him cry. He *owes* me tears. I have them coming.

Still, I am not anxious to set the wheels in motion. Once
started, they cannot be stopped for a long time, but must
run their course. But I am tired. It is going to be very
hard. I let myself drift awhile in the darkness, postponing
it, gathering strength.

"There are too many lies, Marcus. They get in the way,"
I say slowly.

For some time he gives no sign of having heard me. I
begin to wonder if I spoke out loud.

"You mean Julie Mitchum," he says flatly.

"Partly." I speak to the ceiling.

"You think we're lovers."

"Aren't you?"

He shifts beside me, does not answer.

"Aren't you?" I ask again.

Silence.

"You might as well tell me. It affects me, too. I have a
right to know the situation as it really is."

He waits a long time, then says, "I've made love with Julie, yes." After a pause, his words come faster. "But not anymore. I stopped it all last weekend. I had her transferred. I did it for you. What more do you want?"

"So you've been off Miss Mitchum for what? Five, six days. I suppose that's why your passionate instincts turned toward me tonight."

"Eve!"

I don't mean to be sarcastic, nor unkind. I don't want to be disputatious, because truth doesn't come from argument. Defensiveness is the enemy, yet it is hard, harder than I expected, not to strike out.

"How long, Marcus?" I ask gently, dispassionate.

"I don't know. About eighteen months, I guess."

My mind turns back the calendar, trying to remember Marcus a year and a half ago. "Do you love her?"

His answer is immediate. "No! She's a nice kid. A pretty kid. I enjoy her company."

"Ah. And what does she want from you, Marcus?"

"She wants to marry me." In the darkness his voice is disembodied. It makes the message easier to take, somehow.

"Before or after I'm gone?" It's a bad question. I didn't mean to be self-pitying, but there it is. "Never mind. Don't answer. It doesn't really matter, does it?" I speak to myself as much as to him. "Do you want to marry her?" My damn voice cracks with threatening tears.

"No," he says. Then, "I don't know. You're my wife. I owe you more than that. I decided that last weekend. That's why I called it off."

"You don't *owe* me anything, Marcus. Nothing but honesty, anyway. And that seems to be a big debt by now." My own words make me uncomfortable. There's a great temptation, of course, to keep the upper hand. But honesty has to be mutual to be effective.

"However, I have a debt outstanding myself." I take a long breath. "I've been sleeping with John Powell."

I can feel his surprise; his body starts.

"You've what? Never mind, I heard you." A moment later he mutters, "That son of a bitch."

"Well," I say, slightly cheered, "it does seem we've been getting around."

"I suppose I shouldn't be surprised," Marcus says. "But it never occurred to me. I thought . . ."

"You thought I was too old," I finish for him. "Well, as it turns out, given a chance, I'm not."

"That's funny," Marcus says. "It really is. I've told myself you didn't miss it. You never complained."

"I didn't?" I pause to think. "Well, maybe not. It's hard to force yourself on a man who doesn't want you. I guess my complaints were too subtle."

"Or maybe I chose to miss them."

"Yes. Maybe so."

"But Powell didn't."

"No."

Marcus' laugh sounds. "No wonder you didn't want me tonight. I guess I thought I was doing you a favor. I probably deserved the comeuppance." He sits and turns on the light, gets out of bed. "I think I'll make myself another drink. You want one?"

"All right." I feel on the floor beside me to retrieve my nightgown. When Marcus' back is turned, I get up quickly and put it on. Covered, I am more at ease. I put my legs back under the covers and thank him for the drink.

Marcus sits on the bed. "So. This is a pretty kettle of fish." He swigs his drink. "It's not every day a man finds out his wife has a lover."

"It's the first time, Marcus. In fifty years."

He looks at me for a long time. "You know, I wish I could feel self-righteous. Unfortunately, I can understand. I brought it on myself."

"I'm afraid that's true. It took a lot of pushing away."

His ice cubes rattle. "Would it surprise you to know that this thing with Julie is the first for me, too?"

I think about it. "I don't know. Is it the first?"

"Well, maybe not the first slip. But the first thing to matter, at all."

"Do you love her, Marcus?"

"Jesus, I don't know." He gets up, makes a return trip to the bottle. "She's very young. In some ways, quite shallow. And selfish. Yes, very selfish. Sometimes I feel very alone with her. Very old. She's not you, Eve." He returns to the bed. "On almost every count, she comes up

wanting. We don't talk, we *can't*, the way you and I
always did. And I don't think she has any idea of who I
really am, how I feel." He sighs. "On the other hand,
she's young, she's lovely, she's reckless. Even her lack of
wisdom, her lack of kindness, is appealing, in a way. I do
love her, in a way. I love her youth and her faults. Almost
like a father, I think."

"Incest," I remind him drily, "is against the law."

"Yes. I've often felt strange about it. Guilty." He looks
down at his knees. "But there's a certain ego satisfaction
involved, too."

"I can imagine."

"It sounds foolish, doesn't it?"

"I think it's understandable."

"You know, Eve, this will sound strange, but it's an
enormous relief to talk to you about it. You can't imagine
how hard it is to lie to your best and oldest friend. The
guilt estranges you."

"Well," I tell him, "I've certainly felt the estrangement."
Now I get up to pour myself another shot of bourbon.
"We're going to kill your bottle, Marcus."

"That's all right. I wish I could explain it to you, Eve."

"It's not necessary."

"I *want* to. You know me better than anyone. I'd like
to make you understand. That's selfish, I suppose."

"Yes, I suppose so. But human. Try, if you like."

"Oh, I don't know. It's hard to watch the person you
love, your wife, get old. It's like a mirror of what's happening to you. That's part of it, I guess. Just that gut-
grabbing fear of getting old, of being near the end."

"Sorry, Marcus. I didn't mean to spook you. But some
things are unavoidable."

"It's not *like* that," he says. "Not your changes that
worried me. But they made me so aware of my own. And
then, someone young and lovely seems to find you attractive, desirable. It was almost irresistible." He tries to look
at me but can't, for more than an instant. "You figure, if
I can satisfy a woman like this, then I can't be so old, so
useless."

The vision of this man, my husband, naked and passionate with another woman stabs at me, makes me want to

inflict some wounds of my own. "The treatments must have helped there."

Slowly he turns his glass in his hands, watches it closely as a slide under the microscope. "So you know about that. You weren't supposed to know."

Tears rise. I try to force them back. I can't, but speak through them. "You might at least have let me had the chance to be happy for you." A sob rises and breaks in my throat. "I would have tried, you know."

"Jesus," he says. "You probably would have. I hate to think about it." He shudders. "It's amazing how the mind works, Eve. As long as you didn't know, it wasn't wrong. But the thought of your knowing scared the shit out of me. It made my blood run cold. Do you hate me, Eve?"

"I don't think so, Marcus. I don't know. I don't feel much of anything right now. Except exhausted. Oddly enough, I think I could sleep now."

"Me, too," Marcus says. "It doesn't seem right somehow, though."

"One of the advantages of age, I guess. I've overdrawn my supply of energy for the day. I need to sleep. My body insists. Perhaps I can manage some histrionics tomorrow. I may scream and shout and throw things at you then. But not now."

I put down my glass and slide under the covers. To be horizontal is bliss. The bed relieves me of the need to hold myself erect. When Marcus turns out the light and joins me, I move closer to him so that our bodies touch, all along one side. Already my brain is letting go. I feel the ribbon of warmth where we touch. It is possible now because the lies, at least, are gone.

30

I bob through layers of consciousness from deep, distant
dreams (my father is there, very deep), through semi-
rational fantasies, up to the gray place where I can listen
to the sounds of my external environment without knowing exactly where I am. My father beckons, calls me, and
I go to him for a few seconds, or minutes, I can't be sure,
and surfacing, pass through a crowded room, a peculiar
cocktail party with an improbable collection of guests,
people I have known at different times, in different ways,
some slightly, others well. I am surprised to find people
I thought had died; we laugh together at my mistake.
Others I have not seen for years; I greet them warmly. In
one corner, Marcus is talking to John Powell and I think
it better to avoid them. The two IPs who interrupted my
class circle through the party with drinks on trays, nodding
deferentially at the guests.

Then I am in a spacious gray place, all alone. There is
a faint cracking sound, heating ducts, I'd guess, muffled
footsteps, a distant whine of machinery. It doesn't sound
like my home. My face is buried in an unfamiliar pillow.
It has a foreign smell, is harder and bigger than my own.
My brain sends out exploratory impulses, trying to locate
my limbs. Yes, one arm is folded up under the pillow, and
my toes are just touching the end of the bed. The other
hand is—where? I flex the fingers cautiously, and discover
another body, other flesh, beside me in the bed.

Marcus. Vacation. Hotel. It comes back. Then, like a
sudden, oppressive weight, I remember last night. I try to
travel backwards, to find my father again, buried deep in
my mind, but the gates have closed and he is inaccessible.
The cocktail party has become a collection of tattered

photographs; the guests are two-dimensional and don't move. The holographic capabilities of the subconscious are lost, and whether I wish to be or not, I am awake. There is no flight from this reality, from this day's problems and demands.

I raise my head a little, open my eyes. Marcus is still asleep, on his back beside me. The long gray-greenish drapes muffle the daylight outside, and the dim, powdery light in the room paints Marcus gray. Feeling like a voyeur, I study him. His lips are slightly parted and I just see the precise edges of his front teeth inside them. Deeper shadows carve out caves between his eyes and the tops of his cheekbones. The cheeks are peppered with beard; his moustache curls a little raggedly along his upper lip. From this angle, his nose seems very large.

There's something almost indecent in watching another person sleep, unless it is a child and your own. Adults asleep are so undefended, so vulnerable, it seems unfair to observe them, when the flesh is unguarded and the spirit traveling abroad somewhere. I hope Marcus doesn't wake to find me watching; it would embarrass both of us. He would wonder; I would know.

I roll to my side, away from him. In response to my movement he stirs slightly, sighs. I try to lie quietly, not wanting to wake him. My motivation is selfish, not kind. We will relate awkwardly; it will be tiring. I am not anxious to begin what must be done today.

Perhaps if I lie very quietly, breathe very slow, I can tease myself back into sleep.

"Good morning," Marcus says tentatively, to my back. He has been awake for some time, so have I. I heard his breathing change, the shifts of his body become deliberate, and I could feel it somehow when his mind surfaced and became engaged in rational, wakeful thought. Each of us has been waiting, patient, polite, unsure, for the other to speak first.

"Good morning."

"Any idea what time it is?"

"None."

He leans over and picks up the telecom. "Time, please. . . . Ten fifteen? Thank you."

It is earlier than I had hoped, later than I'd feared.

"Well," Marcus says, "do you want the bathroom first?"

"No. Go ahead."

I get up and go to the single window, peeling back the heavy curtains and the gauzy ones beneath. There is a glaze of mist on the glass. Through it I see snow falling, big flakes, lots of them, coming silently and straight down because there is no wind. I wipe the fog from a patch of window and the picture beyond gains clarity. Shapes emerge, white on white, blanketed trees and pillowed vehicles, a whiteness that rises and falls gently according to the contours of what's beneath.

Behind me I hear Marcus come out of the bathroom.

"It's snowing," I tell him. He comes to stand beside me, and clears the fog from another bit of window, higher up than mine. We watch in silence, our breathing hushed by the snow.

"Let's take a walk after breakfast. Can we, please?" I want to be out there, not to despoil its purity but to absorb what of it I am able.

Marcus takes up the idea. "Let's. I'd like that. Make sure you dress warmly."

We carry our heavy coats and gloves and hats to the dining room with us and breakfast with minimal conversation, excusing ourselves and each other on the grounds of a slow waking, a morning lethargy. What we have, really, is a willing truce.

The snow is still coming down when we go outside. It takes only a few moments to dust us both with white. Flakes land on our faces and turn to water, dribble down our cheeks. Our breath comes in clouds. The snow under our feet is too soft to make a sound. The silence here is unimpeachable.

My foot comes down crooked on something hard, hidden in the drifts and my ankle turns over on its side. Marcus catches me as I slip and tucks my hand under his arm. We walk a long time, even after I am cold clear through, because walking is peaceful and a postponement. At last, by mutual consent, we turn regretfully back.

Inside there is a further postponement as we dry and warm ourselves with towels and a drink. Finally, out of excuses, we sit facing each other in the ugly Naugahyde chairs. We look at each other and we smile, to acknowledge our common discomfort, then both begin to speak at once.

"Go ahead," Marcus says.

"No. You."

"I just wanted to say," he stops. "God, this is awful, Eve. It feels like the end of the world. That damn snow doesn't help."

"I know. Here at the end of all things. Well, we could defer it. Go on as we have been. It won't be for too long."

"No," he says. "That's impossible. We haven't lived that way. Not till recently. I don't like it."

"Nor do I."

"We used to share everything," Marcus says. "We had the best relationship I could ever imagine."

"Uhmm."

"I don't know why I let myself be seduced away, Eve. I really don't."

"I'm sure I helped. I don't know how. But I must have."

"I ask myself that. What could she have done? I don't know, Eve. Just after so many years of plodding along, discarding alternatives that didn't work, I finally hit on something big. So much bigger than I am that it just naturally took me over. I lived it, and breathed it, and dreamed about it when I slept."

I nod, not understanding, but urging him to go on.

"I'll tell you what it is. I have to. It is secret, though. You mustn't tell anyone."

"I won't."

"For the first time, we're able to make new tissue. Living tissue. Not from existing living cells, but from the chemical components. We're learning to create viable new life."

"That *is* a breakthrough."

"*The* breakthrough, Eve. Man has dreamed about it for centuries. The capability could be horribly misused. It's frightening, when you think about it. That's a big reason our work is classified."

"Yes. I can see that."

"But the potential for good is boundless. We'll be able to create skin for grafts, correct defects with perfect living limbs. Eventually we'll be able to create whole new organs."

"New people, too?"

"Possibly, yes. That's beyond the scope of our current work. I'm not sure it should be attempted. But theoretically, it's close to possible now."

"That *is* frightening. Would you do it if you had a chance?"

"I don't know," he says slowly. "The Government's beginning to ask that, too. They want to bring a team of geneticists into our lab."

"And?"

"And as a scientist I want to, of course. It's a problem to be solved. Science suspends morality. A good scientist pushes against the problems. He doesn't think about consequences, or applications. As a man, I have some reservations."

"Who's going to win?"

He shrugs. "If it's going to be done, I want to do it. I want to be in charge. That's why I took the treatments. Or why I tell myself I did."

"I'm curious about something, Marcus. Why did they let you take the treatments? Because of your work?"

"I suppose so. I'm not sure. The Director of the Ministry of Health contacted me and said that because one of our children had died, one of us was entitled to take the treatments, and it was me because I was the younger. I suppose if I'd refused they might have made you the same offer."

"To a poet, Marcus? Do you really think so?"

"I don't know. He said it was the law."

"I think the law is made for special cases. Do you think they bother to seek out plumbers in the same situation?"

"I honestly don't know, Eve."

"So you accepted."

"Yes."

"Before or after Julie?"

He sighs and will not look at me. "During," he says finally. "In those first rosy stages."

"Did you talk to her about it?"

"Yes."

"I see."

"It wasn't like that, Eve. It wasn't. I believed it was for my work. I still believe it. Julie was pleased, of course. And in a way, that made me think less of her." Now he looks up at me. "I wanted to tell you, Eve. Sometimes I wanted to stop the treatments. I can't tell you how many nights I haven't slept because of this. I've felt so cut off from you. And it's only gotten worse."

The numbness I feel now is not unexpected; I have been through enough crises to know the strange calm that overtakes me in their midst. My reactions are delayed for days, for weeks, or years. I seem to suffer in a different time frame than I live in. Now I merely sit very still, legs crossed, hands on my knees, and wait for Marcus to go on.

"That's why I've been so awkward, and so cold. I knew it was hurting you, confusing you. But what could I do? How can you make love to a woman you've betrayed like that? How can you accept her love, when you don't deserve it? It's been terrible."

Marcus begins to cry, and it seems terrible to me, not because I believe men shouldn't cry but because he is so totally undone by it. My father cried, and it did not seem terrible to me. One of my clearest memories of him is crying before he left the last time for the war, and I remember thinking he was very beautiful with tears glistening on his cheeks and in his eyes. His cheek was wet when I kissed him goodbye.

But Marcus doesn't cry easily. It tears him up. Loud, dry sobs shake him; his tears seem painful, as though they were acid. Worst of all, it seems to give him no release, only to torture him more. My sympathy is held at bay by this coolness, this strange detachment. I try to summon it, telling myself "I love this man," but part of me wonders if it's true.

My husband gets up from his foolish chair and comes to me. For a moment he looms above me, his face contorted, speckled with tears. Then he drops to his knees before my chair. My hands reach out to him, and he buries his face in my lap. I stroke his hair.

He lifts his face to mine. "I'm sorry, Eve. I'm sorry."

Perhaps this is all I needed to know, to hear. I cannot bear his anguish or withhold myself from him. Suddenly, overwhelmingly, I *need* to comfort him, to protect him, to relieve his pain, if I can. It is not a question of forgiveness.

This is Marcus. This is my husband. I slide forward and put my arms around him, press his face against me, between my ancient breasts. I will my body to give him peace.

"My baby. My baby." A terrible tenderness overtakes me. I hold him tight. I would take him up into my body if I could. "Oh, Baby. Marcus. It's all right."

After a long time, his sobbing stops, his body is quiet in my arms. His voice, flat, thin and close, comes to me; I can feel his warm breath through my blouse.

"Eve, tell me. What would you have done?"

31

"So," Marcus says. "How much does Powell mean to you? Would you stop seeing him?"

"Would you stop working six twelve-hour days a week at the lab?"

"I can't promise that." Marcus sighs. "I wish I could, but I'd be lying."

"In that case," I tell him, "I don't think I could stop seeing John. I enjoy his company too much. Especially when the alternative is being alone."

"I guess I have no right to object."

"No, you don't. Nor do I have any right to stop you from carrying on with Julie, if you want to. What's fair for the goose is fair for the gander." I laugh. "Aren't *we* being mature?"

Marcus shakes his head. "I still don't understand how this happened to us. It's nightmarish. I don't like it."

"Cheer up, Marcus. At least it's real. We're talking about it. That's something."

"I guess so. I think I preferred being twenty-five and idealistic. It seems so cold-blooded to confer about our respective affairs. It hurts me, Eve."

"It hurts less than being lied to. At least we can close it out friends. Or would you rather not? We *could* separate, Marcus."

He shakes his head emphatically. "No, I couldn't take that."

"Why not? Because people would disapprove, or something else?"

"I'd miss you too much, Eve. You can't just cut it off after this long. If nothing else, we've got fifty years behind us. That's got to mean something. It has to. Besides, where would you go? The house is ours, not mine."

"John Powell has offered to take me in. I wasn't just bluffing."

"And where does he live? Some rathole in the old part of town. No, Eve. At least our house is clean and warm and safe." Marcus clenches and unclenches his fists. When his hands are open, I see the crescent imprint of fingernails against his palms. "It may get rough for you, Eve. I want you in a decent place. Powell can even visit you. All right? But I want you to stay in our home."

"I'm ready for the rough," I tell him. My thoughts, not clear before, sort themselves out as I speak. "If it gets too bad, I'll ask for euthanasia." It's the first time I've used the word not as a concept but as a personal option; it sends a little tremor through me. "At least, I think I will. I can't quite imagine not hoping tomorrow will be better. But I suppose there comes a time when you know it won't."

Marcus sighs audibly; his face is pained.

"You can ask for it, too. If I lose consciousness. Do it, Marcus. Please. I have no desire to be a living vegetable."

"I don't know if I could."

"Promise me, Marcus. Don't let guilt or sentiment or anything stop you from that."

"I'd ask the same of you, of course," he says, weighing his words. "But that's a lot different from making the decision."

"Promise me you'll make it if the time comes. I deserve that much. I don't want you to *see* me that way. If that's false pride, okay. But there it is. Now, promise."

"All right. I'll try, Eve."

"Thank you."

"Jesus."

"No, I mean it. Thank you. That settles one of my worst fears."

"Are you afraid of dying, Eve?" Marcus asks.

"Of course I am." I laugh. "I'm more afraid than I ever dreamed I'd be. It's so easy to deal with intellectually, especially when you're young. But let me tell you, that bravado is ignorance, not courage."

"I felt that too," Marcus says, matter-of-factly. "I couldn't stand it."

"Well, you don't have to worry about it anymore now, do you?"

"You know, that's the funny thing. One on me, if you like. The treatments haven't stopped the fear. Now I'm sure a car will run me over, or a building will fall over on me, or I'll electrocute myself. It sounds stupid, I know. Guilt speaking, I suppose. I have terrible nightmares."

I try to imagine it. "That is rather ugly."

"That's one thing I've learned," Marcus says. "They're *all* afraid of dying. Maybe worse than mortals. Somehow you can be braver if you *know* your number's coming up. But once the natural causes have been eliminated, you get terribly afraid of the random fluke. It approaches paranoia."

"So. Damned if you do, and damned if you don't."

"Something like that."

"Except that it's not going to happen to you, Marcus. It's happening to me." I say it not because I want to but because I have to. I want to be strong, realistic and not self-pitying. Yet it's impossible to pretend our situations are equal, or that I can have as much compassion for Marcus as I do for myself. He's going to live, and I am dying.

I believe that now, and it makes me impatient with time. Each minute I want to be full as it can be, with meaning, with feeling, with effect. I have squandered huge pieces of my life, waiting, being uncertain, weighing two acts so carefully that neither was performed. Now I want results; I want to know exactly what I'm buying with my time, and I haven't a great deal to spend feeling sorry for Marcus.

I tell myself this because the habits of decades pull me the other way. It is easier to react than to initiate, easier to give than to take, easier to offer him my sympathy than to make demands on his. Perhaps poetry has helped to cripple me this way; my curiosity to see how things unfold themselves has kept me from influencing them. Marcus, on the other hand, is used to applying conditions and controls.

I can sit still no longer, but get up, restless, wanting to move. This room offers me few options, little to focus my wandering attention. I go to the window and burrow through the drapes. When my pupils open wide enough, I see the snow still falling imperturbably through the black night air. A little wind has risen to give the snow a new angle as it falls, a uniform and gentle slant.

After a while I feel Marcus' arms come round me from behind. He speaks softly, into my hair.

"I'll be there, Eve. Right to the end. I'll take care of you. Live your life however it pleases you. I won't interfere. But I'll be there. I promise I will be, if you'll let me. We'll finish together. It may not mean much to you now, Eve. But it does to me."

My mind wandered as he spoke. For so many years listening to Marcus received my full attention; I was always wholly there for him. Now it doesn't seem to be enough. I must watch the snow fall, too. I must feel the feelings it calls up in me.

Marcus, the snow, both are irrelevant, but taking them both in at once makes me feel more alive. In due time, I put one of my hands over one of his and say, "Of course it means something to me, Marcus. Of course it does."

32

"Can't you stay till next week?"

"No."

"Till tomorrow?"

"No."

"Till nine o'clock tonight?"

His fingers dart out and find my ribs to tickle. I wriggle and kick with my feet.

"Daddy, stop!"

My father is an expert tickler; no matter how I try, his persistent fingers dig at me. He laughs and laughs.

"There now," he says, and stops as suddenly as a summer shower. I have fallen from my perch on his knees and am lying now across his lap. He puts his big hands around my waist and sets me upright, facing him.

"Now, promise me you'll be a good girl."

A new thought comes to me. "Take me with you, Daddy. Please."

"No, honey. That's impossible."

"Why is it impossible?"

He unfurls his fingers, poised to tickle again. I scoot up a little farther on his knees, away from the threatening fingers.

"Why can't I come?"

"Because it's dangerous," he says, poking the soft middle of my stomach with one big finger. "War's no place for little girls. Besides, you have to look after your mother for me." He smiles somewhere beyond me. I turn around and see my mother has come in. I wave at her and turn back to my father, who winks at me. "Think you can handle that?"

"I don't know. What do I have to do?"

"Well," my father says, very serious, "you have to mind her. When she asks you to do something, you do it, right away. And you have to be pleasant and smile and give her big kisses, like this." He puckers up his mouth and makes a loud, wet kissing noise that makes me laugh. "And if any strange men come sniffing around, why then I want you to bite them." He growls and shows his teeth. "Like this."

"Oh Daddy. Do it again."

He bounces me on his knees. "No. Once is enough. You get the idea."

"How about Uncle John? Do I have to bite him? And Mr. Vellors?"

"No, Eve. They're safe. Only strange men, who want to take your mother out to dinner."

"Uncle John takes us out to dinner."

"That's okay. He's Mommy's brother. You be nice to Uncle John."

"I can see the headlines now," my mother says. "Child bites mailman."

My father smiles at her and shrugs. "Somebody has to look out for my interests when I'm gone. We'll call her off as soon as this damn war is over."

I watch his smile fade when he talks about the war.

"What's war, Daddy? Why do you have to go there?"

"Eve," my mother says, and I hear a warning in her voice. "We've been through that already."

"But it doesn't make *sense*," I tell her. "I don't see why Daddy has to go to it."

"We'll talk about it later," she says. "Don't bother Daddy with it."

"It's all right, Martha," my father says. "It must seem very strange to her. It seems very strange to *me*." He laughs his short laugh that isn't really a laugh. "I have to go, little one, because if I didn't, they'd send soldiers to come get me, and they'd put me in jail and throw away the key, most likely."

"How can they do that, Daddy?"

"It's the law."

"Do you like the war, Daddy?"

"No. I hate it."

"Do the other soldiers like it?"

"Oh, some do, I guess. Most everybody I know is just scared."

"Are you scared?"

"You bet I am."

My mother comes toward us and puts her hand on my shoulder. "Climb down now. Lunch is ready."

The thought of food makes all my other questions shrink. "What's for lunch?" I ask her.

"Go to the kitchen and see."

I find a platter of sandwiches on the kitchen table. By prying just a corner of the bread apart, I discover tuna fish inside, a real treat. I run back to the living room to tell my father about the tuna, but when I get there he is busy kissing my mother. They have their arms around each other, and I decide it's best not to disturb them. They look very pretty that way, like people in the movies.

I go back to the kitchen and help myself to a sandwich. Normally I would get in trouble for that, but with Daddy here, my mother may not notice at all. It's worth the chance.

No one talks much over lunch. I concentrate on the tuna fish. I love it. When I look up, I find my parents looking at each other as they eat. My mother doesn't take her eyes off him, as though she's afraid that if she looked away, he'd disappear.

After lunch he gets his big brown bag out of the bedroom, and puts on his tie. I watch him tie it.

"Are you sure you don't want us to come to the airport with you?" my mother asks.

"No," he tells her.

"I don't like it," she says. "It gives me the willies. I'm afraid."

He tucks his tie under his jacket. "Straight?"

"Perfect. The hateful thing."

"It won't be long," he says. "Neither side can afford it. It's too expensive."

"I think that's why I'm afraid," my mother says.

He laughs his sad laugh again. "Me too. Well, I've got to go. I've cut it too close already."

We follow him into the living room. Beside the door

he crouches to my height, and puts one of his hands on each of my cheeks.

"Remember, you're going to be a good girl."

"And bite men," I tell him.

"Strange men."

"Oh yeah."

He pulls me close to him. I put my arms far as I can reach around his back. With my face against his shoulder, I can smell the foreign smell of his uniform, not like him or his clothes at home.

"You take care of yourself, Muffin. I love you."

"I love you too, Daddy."

I squeeze him tight as I can, then he stands up and looks at my mother. They hug each other for a long time and don't say anything.

Then suddenly he is picking up his bag and putting on his hat, opening the door, stepping out into the hall.

Already outside, he lifts his hat to us. "I'll write," he says. "A lot."

"Hurry home," my mother calls after him. "Hurry home."

The elevator comes and takes him away. My mother pushes me inside and closes the door. I stare at it for a long time, wondering what we'll do now. Then I look up at her. My mother's cheeks are wet, and her eyes are red. It makes me afraid, to see her look so sad.

"You're crying. Why are you crying?"

With one finger my mother wipes at her eyes. "I'm not crying," she says. "It's just . . ."

She doesn't finish what she was saying, but crouches down beside me, like my father did, and puts her arm around my waist.

"Yeah, I'm crying, Eve," she tells me. "I miss him, honey. I already do."

33 ⌐⌐⌐⌐⌐⌐⌐⌐⌐⌐⌐⌐⌐⌐⌐⌐⌐⌐⌐⌐⌐⌐⌐⌐⌐⌐⌐

Class was good today. *I* was good. The general tenor of
my life isn't bad; if the truth didn't exactly succeed in
making us free, it has at least done a lot to make us easy.
We are not lovers now, Marcus and I, but we are friends,
and that word has a special flavor, a special meaning after
fifty years.

The mysterious and paradoxical obstacle of sex, being
at once the means to union and, more often, the thing that
makes it impossible, no longer divides us. We have by-
passed it, miraculously, and can touch each other freely,
fraternally, as family members do, with no conditions or
demands either present or implied in the action. My body
is my own at last, and I grant Marcus sovereignty over his
as well. Of the possible ways there are to be, given the
situation, given ourselves, this way, I think, is the best.

Even the pain, these last few days, has eased its grasp
on me somewhat. Marcus calls it a remission and warns
me it will be temporary. But summer is temporary, too, and
that has never lessened my love of its warmth, its smells
and sounds.

The hire-car—Marcus is paying for it, not wanting me
to waste my strength on the subways—drops me off at
home. My stomach growls as I fit my key in the lock; my
days at the Guilds leave me hungry, ready for a sugar fix
to hold me up till dinner. Like a child after school, I must
have my afternoon snack. Suli indulges me with cookies
or rolls and a pot of hot tea when I get home. She joins
me at the kitchen table more often than not, and is glad,
I think, for the company, though she never says so.

We talk aimlessly of the little issues that make up our
days, and I take it for a good sign, too, that we have

learned to laugh together. I was able to have her leaves extended to the maximum of three nights a week. Marcus agreed to it, after some persuasion. Alan Wills comes here to see her sometimes still, and when they meet, always by chance, Marcus is civil to him, and he to Marcus.

Feelings of hunger and well-being propel me quickly to the kitchen, pausing only long enough to shed my coat, a lighter coat, now that spring approaches. I hang it over the banister knob at the bottom of the stairs and make tracks for my tea, salivating like a well-conditioned dog.

There it is, the pot steaming, a plate of tiny pastries beside it, and two cups waiting to be filled. Suli sits at the table, her back to me as I come in. I put my hand briefly on her shoulder, because I feel good, and because I am brave enough to touch her now without fearing she'll recoil or think me patronizing, then swing around and take a seat across from her.

"These look beautiful," I say of the tarts, not hesitating to snatch one up and stuff it in my mouth.

She pours our tea, and the aromatic steam rises, warming the late-winter outside chill still clinging to my cheeks and chin. The pastry is superb and I concentrate on letting its delicate flavors separate on my tongue, tasting the individual ingredients and the exquisite small tensions set up between them.

"Wonderful, Suli," I tell her, despite the crumbs still lingering on my tongue.

"I'm glad you like them," she responds gravely.

"You've really tamed that monster." I motion at the sound-wave range. Never quite at peace with machines, I'm thoroughly intimidated by its lethal speed. But Suli makes it perform small miracles on a daily basis.

"Any calls, Suli?"

She shakes her head. "None."

"Well, that's only to be expected, I guess. I've already seen everybody today I talk to willingly." Suli's gravity begins to make an impression despite my self-absorption. "How was your day?" I ask, cheerful and bullying.

Her answer doesn't come immediately, not even an "all right," or an "okay," or any of the meaningless sounds people normally make in response to stupid, meaningless questions like mine.

There is trouble in Suli's eyes, and they seem to search my face for something. The intensity of her look makes me nervous, so that I have to drop my eyes.

"Is something wrong, Suli? Have I done something to offend you?"

Her gaze persists, as though she's judging me, or trying to. She folds her hands on the table in front of her, now looks at them, knit into a single, steady fist.

"I had a letter from home today. My mother is dead."

Perhaps because I'm feeling good myself, my empathy is readily accessible and my sympathy quick to rise. The news shakes me somewhat less selfishly than it might and makes me want very much to be of some use to her.

"That's dreadful, Suli. I'm very sorry." I reach out and put my hand on her two folded hands. They are cool to the touch, and steady. Feeling as inadequate as such news always makes me feel, I search for something to say, not just to fill the silence, but something helpful, something meaningful. I am arrogant enough to suppose that there is something I could say, one right thing, if only I were not clumsy, or selfish, or stupid. There isn't, of course; I make myself remember my own bereavements and realize that only time, not I, can cure a deep and natural grief.

"Was it a long illness, Suli?"

She shrugs. "I don't know. My brother's letter was heavily censored. To me that says she died of starvation, or by violence."

"My god."

"Perhaps," she says thoughtfully, "they have had another plague. They would censor that, too, I think."

"Is there anything you can do?"

"No," she says. "I can write to my brother. I can send money for burial. But it will arrive too late to help, if it arrives at all."

"There must be a way," I say, seizing on a specific problem to worry at. "Maybe Jason could find out something."

"No." Her voice is sharp, emphatic. "There is nothing. You don't understand the chaos. The difficulty of finding anyone, even if they live in the same city. Your son is powerful here. But in my home, men no longer have power. Disease has power. Hunger has power. Numbers have power. People do not have power anymore."

"I'm sorry, Suli. I didn't mean to interfere. I guess I'm very naive about some things."

"You were only trying to be kind. Don't apologize."

"I sure as hell don't want to make things harder for you, Suli. I remember what it was like when I lost my mother."

"I did not have my mother, to lose her," Suli says gently. "It's nine years now, since I left. My mother did not write. I got her news from my brother. I have no photographs of her."

"But you have memories," I say.

Suli laughs, a short, hard, humorless laugh. "Very few," she says. "Perhaps because I've chosen not to. Do you know I can't make a picture of my mother in my mind? When I try to remember her face, it slips away. I can't get to it." She pauses, opening her folded hands slowly and spreading her fingers fanlike in front of her. She looks at them and so do I. "I see your face instead," she tells me. "I expect to see black, and I see white. I try to see my mother, but I see you." Now she looks up at me. "When you die, I will feel more sorrow than I can find for my own mother. If I grieve now, I grieve because that's true."

Her words stun me, with a small stab of pleasure that she honors me thus, with pain for the situation she describes. I don't know what to say to her.

"My mother was an ignorant woman," Suli says. "Perhaps she was smart. I don't know. She never knew. She spent her life bearing children. Most of them died. Love was a luxury beyond her reach."

"That can't be true, Suli. Loving is part of being human."

"You *are* naive," she tells me with a grim smile. "Think about it. What comes first, food or tenderness? Kindness, or shelter for the night? I know. I lived there almost twenty years. And I know that even though I'm an importee with no rights and no hope of being anything else, I am better off than she."

And what does Jason say of me? Suli's honesty frightens

me; I must protest. "I'm sure your mother loved you, Suli. She must have."

Her dark lips twist in an ironic smile. "Perhaps so. Who knows what love is? Alan says I'm very cold sometimes. I tell him I am merely realistic. But maybe he's right." She stops. "I feel nothing now. Only emptiness. My mother isn't real to me. How can her death cause me tears?"

Suli's eyes may be dry, her hands steady, but the pain I hear in her voice is real.

"Don't demand them from yourself, Suli. The dead don't ask for tears. People cry because they need to, for themselves. It's an entirely selfish thing. Use it, if you need it. Otherwise, forget it."

She listens attentively, so I blunder on. "Emptiness is real too. It's a valid way of feeling. Only I think it scares people, so they don't talk about it much. They whip up a tempest, instead, to convince themselves they're human."

She looks directly at me, takes in my words and weighs them. I have no idea if what I'm saying makes sense, or if I'm right.

"Suli, I loved my daughter Maria, probably more than anything. But when she was killed, I couldn't cry for days. I was just numb. I'm sure Marcus thought it was strange of me. *I* thought it was strange. And I wish I hadn't, because things were hard enough, without wondering if I was some kind of monster." As I speak, my eyes fill up with foolish, unbidden tears. They make me laugh out loud.

"There. You see. I started feeling sorry for myself, and wham, there they are. One hundred percent genuine wet salty tears." I wipe at them, then hold out my hand to her. "There. Have some. I've got plenty to spare."

I get up from my chair, half laughing, half crying, and spread my arms theatrically. "Watch this. Nice, huh? Self-pity, that's the trick."

Suli laughs a little hysterically at my performance. I drop my arms and go to her where she sits, pull her, laughing, up tight against my side.

"You're all right, Suli," I tell her. "You're just fine."

She raises one slim, shapely brown arm and puts it lightly around my waist. I put my hand over hers.

"You're very good to me," she says. "I don't want to lose you, too."

When she looks up at me there are tears in her eyes, and laughter and sorrow are at war in her face for possession of her features. I can't help but chuckle a little, to see my theory proved.

Then I put my hand on her short, thick, curly hair and say, "Cry, Suli. Go ahead. You cry for all of us."

My voice is happy and strong. I press my eyelids down tightly, to clear my eyes of tears.

34

The alarm on his digichron sounds at last. Thank god.

Now the alarm stops, shut off, having summoned him from sleep. I've waited this long, I tell myself. Let him go to the bathroom first. Predictably, I hear the door close, the water begins to run.

Don't read on the toilet, Marcus, I pray. Don't have to defecate.

The toilet flushes. I listen for the door to open.

Now.

I call him. My mouth is so dry it desiccates his name, and I am speaking dust. I gather up saliva and try again. The effort intensifies the pain and makes me breathe quickly. A film of sweat breaks on my face.

I think he hears me. His footsteps follow him around the room.

Softly the latch slips, the connecting door opens, and Marcus stands in the doorway.

"Eve. Did you call me?"

He looks toward the bed. I lift my hand to show him I'm awake. He comes to me.

"You look terrible."

I nod slightly against the pillow. "I feel terrible."

"Have you taken anything?"

"No."

"Has this been going on long? Why didn't you call me?"

My voice is like dead leaves. "I couldn't wake you. I was afraid to get up."

"We'll have to rig up some kind of signal. I should have thought of it before. But you were doing so well."

"I know."

"Where's your medication?"

"In the desk. Bottom drawer."

He goes to the desk and opens the drawer. "I don't see it."

"It's buried."

I can hear him digging, then, standing, he comes into my field of vision again, the box in his hands.

"Why didn't you take it?"

"I can't use needles."

"I'll show you how. It's not hard. A little unpleasant shooting yourself, but you'll get used to it."

"No, Marcus. I'll never get used to it. I hate them."

"Are you kidding?"

"Do I look like I'm kidding?"

"I guess not. I'd better call Suli, then, and show her how to use the syringes." He activates the intercom on my desk and calls Suli's quarters. "I didn't wake you? Good. Could you come upstairs, to Mrs. Harmon's room?"

Marcus sits in my blue chair to wait for Suli, crosses his legs easily and opens the box in his lap.

"Oh, they gave you this. Good. It works very quickly."

Suli's footsteps sound on the stairs. Soon she knocks, then enters the room, a white bathrobe wrapped around her.

"Excuse me," she says. "I didn't stop to dress."

"Neither did we," Marcus says. "I want to show you how to give Mrs. Harmon this medication. She may need it anytime from now on. You're not afraid of needles, are you?"

"No. Of course not."

"Good. It's really very easy. They're prefilled, and disposable. All you have to do is find the right place to stick it."

She nods at Marcus. He hands her one of the syringes and she examines it, then hands it back.

"Okay. Come over here."

Together they approach my bed. I am in limbo, longing for relief. Marcus pulls the right sleeve of my nightgown up above the elbow, then sits on the bed and takes my arm in his lap, inspecting the inner crook of my elbow.

"She's got good veins. We're lucky. You see them?"

She nods.

"Okay. You just have to shoot the stuff in one of them." He takes the plastic needle cover off between his teeth. It makes his speech unintelligible, and he takes it out, smiles. "What I said was, aim the point at the vein. Then slide it in sideways, like this." I feel a small prick of pain as the needle punctures my skin. "Not too deep," Marcus says. "And the faster the better. Now"——he pulls the plunger back a bit and all three of us watch a drop of my red blood rise up inside the tube and mix with the fluid there—— "if you get blood, you've got the vein. If not, take her out and try again." He depresses the plunger now, all the way, and drives the fluid into my arm. I try to feel it enter or start working, but nothing happens.

"See?" Marcus says. "It's simple. Think you can do it?" Suli nods.

"Good, because she's going to need another one in four hours."

Suli looks at the digichron. "At ten-thirty."

Marcus stands up and puts the box down on the desk, then returns to my bedside. "Get her some juice, and see she gets some food down, all right?" At this, Suli leaves. "This may make you drowsy, Eve. It does some people. One of the fellows who developed it worked for me some years back. Rodney Kent. Remember him?"

"No."

"Well, it's an efficient painkiller. But it does have that side effect."

"Good. I'm exhausted." I try to smile at him. Something *is* happening now; I begin to feel it. Actually, it's more like something not happening. The pain is slowly disappearing, and I realize how tired I really am.

Marcus' voice wakes me. When I drag my eyelids up, I see he is combed and shaven, dressed for work. Strong, attractive, he stands at the foot of my bed.

"Is it working?"

"Uh huh. I may sleep all day."

"That's good. Do. I just wanted to say goodbye, and see how you were."

"Better. Thanks."

He seems to give off energy, to exude health. I *am* grateful for his help, but I resent his strength a little and

wish he didn't have to see me like this, so weak. I must
look terrible. Vaguely I try to raise my head, do something with my hair, but realize how useless it is, at this
point.

"I may have to stay late tonight. Sorry."

"That's okay. Have a good day."

"I will," he says, coming around to give me a quick and
token kiss on the nearest cheek.

As soon as his back is turned, before he leaves the
room, my heavy eyelids drop back down, and I return to
a dark and painless place inside my head.

35

My legs are weak and shaky, so long disused, but I race along on them as soon as I see John slouched carelessly, like a good poet, against the concrete façade of the Ministry of Culture. It's Saturday and the Ministry is closed, its thin strips of windows dark. When he sees me, John stands up straight and smiles his greeting across the remaining space of sidewalk.

He loops his arm around my shoulders when I reach him. "It's good to see you," he says.

I smile up at him timidly, knowing that my face is worn by the disease, more than when last I saw him. I am afraid it will frighten him, that he'll find me repulsive. His expression changes a little when he first looks at me, but he gives me a warm squeeze and my smile relaxes, becomes more at home on my face.

"You've lost weight," he says. "It's lucky I like skinny women." He takes my arm and laces it through his. We begin to walk, away from the Government complex. "I missed you, Eve. Why wouldn't you let me come to the house?"

"I was asleep most of the time. Besides, I looked like bloody hell."

"That doesn't matter."

"Well, I figured since I was neither charming nor attractive, you'd do best to stay away."

"*He* gets to see you."

"*He's* a very old friend. Not my paramour."

"Is that what I am? That's nice." He looks sidelong at me. "I just feel so disenfranchised, that's all. I want to be there. To help."

"I appreciate it, John. But I'd rather have it this way,

for now. When it gets really bad, you can bring me flowers, if you like, and pretend you're visiting your batty grandmother."

"Eve, don't talk like that. Besides, do you know what flowers cost these days?"

"I meant it figuratively. You can bring poems and read them to me. They're cheap enough."

"That's why I can't afford the flowers."

He *does* struggle to make ends meet; I know it. Now I feel a little guilty. "Listen, we don't have to go out to lunch, John. I'm hardly hungry at all."

"Shut up and keep walking, then. You will be. I'll take you out to lunch if I want to. Enough depressing talk. I intend to enjoy myself."

"So do I."

It's a fine false spring day, a preview of the poignance to come. Even here, in the cavernous city streets, the pale gold sun penetrates with its promise of renewal. The gray streets and sidewalks don't respond to it, but we do, our steps light and brisk, our spirits believing the promise, despite evidence to the contrary.

"It *is* good to see you, John." I squeeze his arm and laugh at the little wind that's playing with my hair.

"I'm glad," he says.

We pass other couples walking arm in arm. I smile at them, though they don't notice us, absorbed in each other, as they ought to be. As we approach the commercial downtown, traffic thickens around us. People waddle about, made clumsy by the fat packages they carry. At last we come to the restaurant, a crêperie, nice but not extravagant.

The hostess, a bit too ripe and brassy for the peasant costume she's stuffed herself into, looks speculatively at John, in passing at me.

"Two?"

"That's right. Someplace dim and intimate, if you can manage it."

She looks at us and laughs. "Anything you say."

She leads us around a corner, the foot of an L, into an almost empty area with smaller tables and less light than in the front of the restaurant. John seats me.

"You want a drink?"

"Sure. Two bourbons."

"You got 'em." She writes the order down and goes.

"She thinks I'm your grandmother," I tell John across the dancing flame of a red candle.

He laughs. "What she doesn't know. Actually, probably my mother. Or my aunt."

"You're such a good boy, Johnny."

"Shut up," he says cheerfully. Then, "You mind if I say something?"

"I haven't been able to stop you yet."

"Okay. Eve, I think you're wearing too much rouge."

"I am?" I put my fingers to my cheekbones. "I looked so pale this morning. I thought it might help."

"The problem is, it looks like that's what you thought. You were wrong. Pallor becomes you, my love."

I look around for the ladies' room, and when I find the sign, get up.

"Where are you going?"

"To wash it off."

"That's not necessary. Sit down. For future reference only."

"No, John. I don't want to look stupid. Let me get it off. I'll feel better."

"I'm sorry I mentioned it. I didn't mean to upset you."

"I'm not upset."

In front of the washroom mirror I scrub my cheeks. The towel is so rough it leaves them redder than before. Around the spots of color, my face is deadly pale, almost translucent. I look so tired it makes me want to cry—self-pity again. Only my eyes have color or life in them. I *could* be John's mother, the way I look. And he's right; it doesn't help to paint myself up like a clown. It's a measure of my terror that I tried at all.

I wish I could change my face; if the devil were to appear in this particular washroom and offer me a new one for my soul, I'd gladly strike the bargain. My soul is worth very little to me, if indeed I have a soul. It's never evidenced itself, sick or well, never spoken up in a crisis, never bothered to introduce itself to the rest of me. I wouldn't miss it if the sale were made.

The devil, being no realer, fails to appear, and I must

take my old face back to the table. I am so dissatisfied with it, so disappointed, that it unnerves me when John looks at me. My skin is sensitive to his gaze, as sunburn is to the sun, and wants to shelter itself from his eyes.

I am disappointed in myself, too. All my life I have done battle with vanity, not wanting to be one of those women who trade on the lay of flesh over bone, not wanting to make myself, as they do, so terribly vulnerable to the devastations of age or the caprice of fashions.

No, I have been deliberately reckless with my small store of beauty, spent it on poems and passions. I've tried to welcome each line as it came, to wear my face with pride. I held it up to time and invited time to write there. What did it matter to me? I was to be Something More, to acquire Something More Valuable than mere beauty, to compensate my courage.

Now time has written, with a vengeance, whole volumes around the eyes, across the forehead and down the cheeks, carved deep for every smile I have smiled and, with each surprise, scored wonder deeper in my flesh. What More I am in recompense is hard to figure out, unless it is More Wrinkled, More Neurotic, More Self-Despising than my careful sisters. It seems I have neither beauty nor a soul.

"Eve, why are you looking at me like that? It's as if you expected me to spit at you."

My laugh is small, nervous. "You mean you're not?"

"Did I start this by mentioning the rouge? I'm sorry if I did."

"The trouble is, you're absolutely right, John. It was stupid. Tasteless. Weak."

"No," he says. "I wouldn't go that far. It was just a little too red. That's all. No reason to be upset."

"Yes it is. It's a symptom of something else. I always wanted to grow old graciously, and I've failed."

"Oh, I don't know. You look pretty gracious to me."

"You don't understand, John. I'm not sure if it's because you're an immortal, or a man, but you don't."

"Okay. I don't understand. Do you doubt that I find you attractive?"

I need my hands to help me talk; I present my answer with the palm of my hand. "Yes! I'm *not* attractive. I'm an old woman and I look like hell." My voice is small when I finish, and I drop my hands to my lap.

John laughs at me. He throws back his head and laughs. It makes me angry.

"It's not funny."

"Sure it is," he says. "In an awful kind of way. Don't you realize that one of the reasons you're so appealing is that you look like you've lived? Like you know the score?"

"Either you're crazy, or you're lying."

"I'm not lying. I don't know about crazy. But I do know that this eternal springtime stuff really puts me off. Who wants a perennial eighteen-year-old?"

"Lots of men. Stop trying to make me feel better. You're making it worse."

"All right," he says, infuriatingly cheerful. "Have it your way. You're positively hagridden. Unsightly. It's my peculiar perversion that I can stand to look at you at all. Are you satisfied now?"

I have to laugh, at myself. "I'm ashamed of myself. This whole thing is very silly. I shouldn't take it out on you. Let's talk about something else."

"One more round. Tell me why you're so insecure. Is this more of Dr. Harmon's good work I see before me?"

"I don't think so. I'm going to die soon, and it's not as easy to deal with as I'd hoped. That's all. I'm not as strong and sensible as I thought I was."

"It must be hard to look at him every day and know he's going to go right on living. Or at me, for that matter."

I'm grateful for his honesty; it makes mine possible. "Yes. It is hard. It's my problem, and I don't want to lay it on anybody else. But yes. I resent you all." It feels good to say this. I pick up my glass and drink the watery bottom of my drink, a toast to resentment.

The waitress comes back and positions her ample breasts directly in John's line of vision. He blinks at them.

"Ready to order now?"

We do. After this hiatus, I'm able to change the subject. "You know, John, I'd like to schedule a reading for my poetry workshop. I'd like them to have a chance. Is that possible?"

"Sure. That's a fine idea. Why not?"

"I think they could manage a decent twenty minutes apiece. Not great, but certainly interesting."

"You don't have to sell me. We'll get the auditorium."

We plan the reading. In a little while the waitress returns with our meal. After it's served, she looks at John studiously, one hand on her hip.

"You know, I'd swear I've seen you somewhere before. Now where could it be?"

"Gee, I don't know," John says. "I was just released from prison last week."

The waitress picks up her tray from the serving stand. "My mistake. Sorry. Maybe you got a double."

"Maybe so."

The meal is pleasant, and I enjoy myself, but when John invites me back to his apartment, I decline. My sensual appetites are strangely silent; more than that, I find I do not want to be touched today, nor entered, nor filled. I don't even want to come, but to divert whatever sexual energy I possess right now to other purposes. It feels *good* to refuse.

"I think I want to write this afternoon, John. I need to. My mind's been muddled by painkiller for almost a week."

"That I can understand. How about Monday? After class."

"Maybe," I tell him. "Probably. You don't mind, do you?"

"I don't mind about the writing. Not if I get to see the results on Monday. I just wish we could go home together. I don't like being kept at a distance, Eve."

"No." I manage a sigh. "I'll call you tomorrow. Okay?"

We leave the table, settle up with the cashier.

"Shall we call you a car?"

"Don't bother. I'll take the subway home."

"Are you sure?"

"I sort of enjoy it," I tell him. "And I feel fine."

"I'll walk you there."

"Oh, John. Don't bother."

"No bother. I want to." He helps me on with my coat. Because he wants to be gallant, I let him. We stroll arm in arm to the nearest station, several blocks away.

"Thanks for lunch, John. I had a good time."

"So did I." John pulls me close to him and kisses me. "Till Monday, then," he says. "Don't forget to call tomorrow."

"I won't. Till Monday." I touch his arm, then turn and start down the stairs.

"Safe journey," John calls after me, his hand raised in farewell.

Some stairs down, I turn and wave at him. "Safe journey yourself." I don't look back again.

I am relieved to be alone. By the bottom of the stairs, I begin to feel a little guilty for giving John short shrift, but the feeling of freedom that follows so surpasses the guilt that it is soon forgotten.

Alone I can forget about my face. I needn't worry if I'm attractive, or charming, or being kind. Simply, selfishly, I can exist with no anxieties and no apologies for what I am or what I seem to be. Other times, I know, I need John very much, but at this moment, I'm oddly sick of love.

36

The subway stops just four blocks from my house. It extends here not to serve the residents but to carry their servants to and from their homes. A few hoary clouds have appeared to challenge the weakening sun, but the air is still mild for a while yet, the breeze still gentle. Here there is no traffic in the streets; few of the privileged choose to walk, either for transportation or for exercise. The big houses keep their secrets and reveal nothing of the lives played out inside them. I am not above trying to see something of interest in my neighbors' windows, but they have pulled their drapes against my curiosity.

I am strangely happy, walking home. Unfettered, for the moment, by either pain or passion, I feel compact, self-sufficient and whole. My joy in being alone persists. For the first time in my life, perhaps, I feel free of men. If no man loves her, a woman is enslaved by wanting one. If she has one and loves him, then she is afraid of losing his love and must do what she can to nurture it. A woman bound to a man she dislikes suffers another kind of bondage. Now, old and indifferent, I have my victory. Now I can choose to refuse; I can be ugly or disagreeable, quiet or voluble. It doesn't matter what I do; my actions can gain or lose me nothing. People will love me or not, as they see fit, but their love can no longer enslave me; I am wholly independent of it.

As I round the last corner, I see a police car parked at the curb, in front of my house. A hundred explanations present themselves at once. I am going to be arrested for working at the Guilds; Alan Wills is being arrested; Suli. Or someone has broken in, smashed things or taken them. It occurs to me that Suli may be hurt, and concern overcomes my apprehension and makes me hurry up the steps.

I call for Suli. She comes out of the living room to meet me in the hall.

"You're all right. Good. What are the police doing here?"

"Is that Mrs. Harmon?" a man's voice calls from the living room.

Suli takes my arm protectively. "I think you'd better come in here."

"But what do they want, Suli?"

When we come in, a policeman gets up from the sofa. His hat falls to the floor.

"Mrs. Harmon? I'm Officer Rogers."

"Let her sit down," Suli says. "Mrs. Harmon has been ill."

"I'm fine, Suli. What's the matter?"

"You *are* Mrs. Marcus Harmon."

"Of course I am. What's Marcus done?" My question is pleasant, but the fear that follows it is not. I become certain that Marcus has tried to steal some cancer drug for me and gotten caught. "What is it?"

"I hate to say this, ma'am. But I guess there's no other way to put it. Your husband's dead, Mrs. Harmon."

"That's impossible." I say it and think it at the same time.

"It should have been, ma'am. The laboratory had Class AAA security. The tightest. But something got by us. The lab was bombed this afternoon."

Suli stands close beside me; I feel rather than see her there. "Bombed?"

"Yes, ma'am. It was quite an explosion. Multiple charges. Gone. It looks political."

"And Marcus?"

"Everyone who was at the lab, Mrs. Harmon. There's a crew in there now, trying to . . . collect the remains, I guess you'd say."

I watch dumbly as he takes a notebook from his pocket and opens it.

"As a matter of fact, you might be able to help us some, with the identification."

I shake my head, trying to obliterate the picture he's made in my mind. "No. I couldn't do that."

"Oh, I see what you're thinking. No. Not like that. The

security log was destroyed by the bombing. I thought you might know who else was there, with your husband."

"You don't have the log?"

"No, ma'am. It was destroyed."

"You mean you don't know for sure that Marcus was there?"

The policeman consults his notebook. "Well, strictly speaking, I guess not." He turns to Suli. "She said he went there this morning. But we haven't got the log. And none of the remains have been identified so far." He pushes at his hair. "It's going to be tough."

I get up from my chair. "Excuse me. I have to make a call." Suli follows me to the kitchen. I ask her for the directory and she takes it from a drawer.

"I have your son's number written down."

"I'm not calling him." I leaf through the directory, J, K, L, M, praying that Marcus' passion was not for his work today. I have not questioned him about his arrangements with Julie Mitchum, nor he about mine with John. With any luck I'll find him safe in her bed. At last I find her number, take a deep breath and punch it up. It rings a long time and I wait, making myself imagine not an empty apartment, but my husband caught in the act, unwilling to answer the ring.

"Hello?"

"Is this Julie?"

"Who's calling?"

"This is Eve Harmon. I'm trying to find my husband. I'm sorry to bother you, but it's very important."

The voice is cool and wary, coming back. "Why should you call here? Why not try the lab?"

"Julie, listen. I know you've been seeing Marcus. It's all right. Just please let me speak to him if he's there."

"You *know?*"

"Of course. Didn't Marcus tell you? Look, this is urgent. Is Marcus there? Please say he's there."

"He was here earlier," she says reluctantly. "But he left."

"When did he leave?"

"About eleven, I guess. He stopped by early, on his way to the lab."

"Oh god."

"What is this? Is something wrong?"

"Are you sure he went straight to the lab, Julie? He doesn't have any other young ladies he visits?"

"No," she says coldly. "Why would he? What are you trying to do?"

"Julie, the lab was bombed this afternoon. Everyone who was in it is dead."

I break the connection. Maybe he wasn't there. Maybe he decided not to go there after all, went downtown shopping, or for a drive. He may walk in at any minute, or call me. Maybe he has another mistress. Hope after hope occurs to me.

I go back to the living room. "Was Dr. Harmon's car in the lot?"

"Yes, ma'am. It was there."

Suddenly my legs are very weak. I sit on the sofa, and face the incomprehensible news. It makes no sense. It wasn't supposed to happen this way. I am supposed to die. Marcus is supposed to live. This random, absurd thing cannot have happened. Yet one small part of me believes it is true.

I appeal to the policeman. "Isn't there anything I can do?"

"I don't think so, ma'am."

I take my head in my hands and my eyes go out of focus on the carpet below. Dimly, I hear Suli guide the policeman to the door. Then I feel her touch my shoulder, a ghost of a touch.

"Can I do anything?" she asks. "Do you want to go to your room?"

I look up at her. Her face seems very large. "What?"

"Do you want to go upstairs now?"

I try to think about it, but I have no opinion, no desire at all.

"You might be more comfortable there. You could lie down."

"All right."

Suli helps me to stand, and together we head for the stairs.

37

He finishes, deep and unexpected. The feel of it completes my circuit and I flower around him, petal by petal, in those small, soft, feathery contractions I always seek but can't control. My mind goes black and deep as space, but I cling to the one word as I hurtle through it.

Baby. Baby. Baby.

My brain repeats it like a mantra. I hold fast to Marcus, to keep him with me on my ecstatic journey. At last I am quiet inside, and the blackness is transformed into the everyday shadows of our bedroom once again.

"We'll do it again later, just to make sure." Marcus rolls off me and lies on his back beside me. I hate to relinquish his weight, his warmth so soon. The coming apart after lovemaking seems to me the saddest breach imaginable. I find his nearest hand and fit my own inside it.

"Do you think it'll work? Do you think I'll really get pregnant?"

"I don't see why not. We're both young and healthy. And this is the day, right? October fifteenth."

"This is it. The doctor said it's not a hundred percent certain, though."

"It's close enough. Besides, if we don't make it this time, we'll try again next month."

"And in between, too."

He squeezes my hand. "And in between."

The street lamps outside dust the ceiling with a cold, silvery light. I sigh up at it.

"It seems like such an improbable way to procreate a race."

Marcus laughs. "It would be, except for one very ingenious feature."

"What's that?" I adjust my brain for "explanation," expecting my scientific husband to give me some complex and irrefutable bit of knowledge.

"It feels good," he says. I wriggle appreciatively against him.

"That's true, isn't it?"

"Sure," he says. "Can you imagine doing this if it felt bad? Or even just all right?"

"No. I guess not. I wonder why amoebas haven't picketed for a better deal?"

"Hmmm," Marcus says. "Just because *we* call it asexual reproduction doesn't mean the amoeba doesn't get a big thrill out of it. It could be positively orgasmic to split in two."

"I wonder."

"Don't wonder too hard. I like our way well enough."

"Me too." I spread my palm flat on my stomach. "I wonder what's going on in there."

Marcus puts his hand beside mine. "The little bastards are swimming like hell."

"I hope one of them makes it."

He pats my stomach. "It will. This stomach won't be flat for long, my love."

I turn over onto my side and put my cheek on Marcus' chest. He shifts a little and brings his arm up around my back. I close my eyes, feeling his body rise and fall as he breathes, listening to the reassuring tick of his heart.

"No regrets?" he asks softly, close to my ear.

"No. None at all. Since we finally decided, I've felt very good about it, very strong."

"So have I. We're doing the right thing."

"I think so, Marcus. I love you too much not to want to have our child."

He draws his arm tighter around me. "We may fix them all yet. Our kid could be running the whole show someday."

I smile against his chest. "Hey, I thought we agreed not to be pushy parents."

"I'm not being pushy," Marcus says. He lifts his head up from the pillow and addresses my lower abdomen. "You hear that in there? It was only a suggestion. You can be anything you want. As long as you're brilliant and beautiful."

"Stop that. You're going to be impossible. What are you trying to do? Make junior a compulsive overachiever in the womb?"

"What's wrong with that? We overachievers do quite well."

"Ugh. Just so long as I don't overconceive. I'd hate to end up with a ten-pound baby."

"I was aiming for twins, actually. Then we could get it all over with at once. Statistically, of course, the odds are against it."

"Marcus?"

"What?"

"Shut up, will you? I want to love you quietly for a while."

"Shut up, indeed," Marcus says. "Is that any way to speak to the father of your child?"

38

Beside me, Jason is dry-eyed and dignified. Suli, expression-less, holds fast to my arm. I have long since stopped try-ing not to cry. The tears come and come, from some inexhaustible supply. I thought I had used them all up yesterday and the day before and the day before that. It is not for Marcus that I'm crying now, nor for myself, but because the organ music being piped into the chapel is exploiting me somehow, striking tears as surely as a drill-ing rig hits oil. Cruelly, mechanically, these awful sounds have tapped a spring in me. I flow and flow. It makes me furious, to be so used that my last tribute is turned into a sham.

I wish like Jason I were impervious and could listen with polite attention to what these people, one by one, are saying about Marcus. Perhaps someone is saying some-thing I would like to hear. Maybe words are being said that I could cherish later. Perhaps one of these men *knew* my husband and is able to say something that touches on the essence of the man.

I hate this building, the Government chapel, with its borrowed pomp. When the Catholic Church went bankrupt, they took it for back taxes, and the saints in the windows have been replaced by geometric shapes, the crucifixes by flags, but the intention of the building remains the same—to intimidate, to terrify. I hate it, and them.

More than anything, I am angry at Marcus, furious with him for dying. This is the most unspeakable betrayal of all, the very worst of his transgressions against me. It is far, far worse than him living while I died. It is the worst thing anyone has ever done to me.

It is comparable to the North Star falling out of the

sky, or the laws of gravity suddenly failing to apply. Some basic force has been subtracted from the world. In my personal universe, the ensuing chaos is calamitous. Our first conversation was about negative space, and the negative space where Marcus used to be is now bigger than anything else in my world, bigger than any space or time I can fill up alone. I imagine amputees must feel this way. My phantom limb aches horribly. If it existed, I would punish it for paining me so.

Jason nudges me. "Mother, it's over. Come along." He pulls me to my feet and Suli rises beside me, her support physical and real. The synthetic organ swells grandly, trying to wring one last sob from my desiccated heart. I follow Jason out of the pew, and turning, am stunned by the multitude of eyes that stare at us. The damnable chapel is nearly full. Why do they lack the decency to let me grieve in private?

Somehow we sail past them up the dividing aisle. I hear it fill behind us, like the rush of the Red Sea closing up. There is a moment's respite before they descend on us, to wring our hands and murmur at us.

"It was a fine memorial," Jason says. "Tasteful. I especially liked the Minister of Science's remarks."

I can only shudder. People I have never seen before crowd up and peer into my swollen eyes, take my limp hand in theirs and tell me how they share my grief.

Like hell, they do. I hate them all.

A few familiar faces swim up to mine out of this deafening ocean. I simply nod at everyone, let myself be condoled dumbly. To my right I hear Jason explaining, over and over, "You must forgive Mother. It's been a terrible shock. She isn't well."

Some almost extrasensory perception leads me to see Julie Mitchum emerge from the chapel and hurry for the door, avoiding our tribunal. Her pretty face is blotched with angry red spots, the wounds of sorrow. Oddly, my heart goes out to her because, among so many mourners, I know her grief is real. Just at the door, she pauses to look back. Our eyes lock for a moment over the many intervening heads.

John Powell takes my hand firmly in both of his. I see Jason notice and turn to look.

"Eve, my god, how are you? Why haven't you returned my calls?"

"I couldn't, John."

"I want to help, Eve. We have to talk. What can I do?"

"Not now, John. Later. Please. I'll call you."

"Promise you will."

"Okay. I promise. If I don't, call me."

"None of this 'Mrs. Harmon isn't receiving any calls' business?"

"No, John. I promise. I want to talk to you. Okay?"

"I'll call you tonight."

"Fine. Whatever."

"Mother," Jason hisses, "who is this man?"

"A friend of your father. John, I don't believe you've met our son. Jason Harmon, John Powell."

Reluctantly, each clearly mistrusting the other, the two shake hands.

"It was kind of you to come, John. Give my best to Celia."

"Celia?" I hear John mutter as the crowd elbows him away.

Jason looks questioningly at me.

"Celia," I tell him. "His wife."

There is not time to discuss it further, because the Minister of Science himself is approaching, to offer us his deepest sympathy.

"It seems indecent to be hungry now." I bite into my sandwich. "But I'm starved."

"You've eaten almost nothing for days," Suli says. "I'm glad to see you with an appetite."

Even Jason gnaws at a sandwich, managing to look as though he does so only because there is no more fastidious way to acquire sustenance. "Yes. Quite good," he says. "Mother, did you hear the Minister of Science say they intend to rebuild the laboratory and name it after Father?"

"Frankly, I'd rather they rebuilt your father and named him after a lab."

Jason puts down his sandwich. "So. Your sense of humor returns. I suppose I should welcome it back."

"I wasn't trying to be funny, Jason. I miss the man immensely. More than you're capable of imagining. And I wish they wouldn't try to elect him to the godhead. At least not before I'm dead, too." Suddenly I'm very tired.

"I'm sorry, Mother," Jason says levelly. "That was uncalled for on my part."

"Everything's uncalled for. Don't apologize."

Suli does not eat but simply sits across from me, inscrutable as always in Jason's presence, and watches me closely.

"I suppose it's too soon to think of what you'll do now," Jason says. "Though I think it would be well to settle things as quickly as possible. This house, for example. You'd be wise to consider something smaller now."

"I intend to die here, Jason. It won't be long. Then you can do what you want with the house."

"Father's estate may be tied up in litigation for quite some time. Have you any money of your own?"

Weary, I nod. "My piggy bank is full."

"And there's the question of a servant. I think one trained as a nurse would be more appropriate."

"Suli stays," I say, with an energy that surprises me. I look at her. "If she wants to, of course. I suppose it's a lot to ask."

"I want to stay," Suli says.

"That's settled, then. What else, Jason, shall we put to rest? Oh, I know. When I go, Jason, please spare me, yourself, and others the ignominy of a memorial service. I'll come back and haunt you if you don't."

The doorbell rings so unexpectedly it makes all three of us start. Suli gets up to answer it.

"Tell them to go away. There's absolutely no one I want to see."

"Yes, ma'am."

Though I'm no longer hungry, I take another sandwich from the tray and am playing with it idly, much to Jason's disgust, when Suli ushers a man into the room.

I look sharply at her. "I said no guests."

The new arrival cuts me off. "Your woman tried to deter me, but I insisted. Pardon the intrusion." He bows slightly toward me. The man is wearing a black and formal suit and though he looks deceptively young, his manner indicates authority. I have the vague recollection of having seen him before today, at the chapel.

"Who are you?"

"My name is J. D. Rigby, Mrs. Harmon. I am currently the Deputy Minister of Health. And I am, as I say, sorry to intrude on you at a time like this."

"You want to name a hospital after Marcus. All right. Go ahead."

Rigby smiles unctuously. "That's a fine idea, of course. I understand the Ministry of Science has some plans of that sort. But my business has to do with you, Mrs. Harmon." He beams at me.

"What do you want with me? I've been taken off your rolls. And I wear my death's-head, just like they told me to." I pull the damn thing out of my dress.

"Uh, yes. That is, more or less, what I wanted to see you about. After your husband's unfortunate accident, I accessed your health records at the Bureau of Geriatrics and found we had little time to spare. That's why I took the liberty of coming today."

"Get to the point, Rigby. I'm very tired."

"Yes, of course. The point is this. As you know the law stipulates that a couple may choose to have two children and remain mortal, or to take the IMM treatments."

"I know."

"As you may also know, when it was brought to our attention that you and Dr. Harmon had lost your second child, we were able to make the IMM treatments available to one of you. Your husband, in fact, being the younger. He accepted them."

"I know all that, Rigby. A lot of good it did him."

"Sadly, we're powerless in such instances," Rigby says, spreading his hands out in the air before him. "What I wanted to discuss with you is simply this. Since the death of your husband, *you* are now entitled to receive the IMM treatments."

My eyes are fixed on the bureaucrat, but I hear both Jason and Suli make little sounds of surprise.

"Because of your condition, I felt there was no time to waste. We would have to treat your cancer first, of course. I am prepared to admit you to our hospital as early as tomorrow morning. Sooner, if you like. I think it can be done if we begin at once."

"That's damned decent of you, Rigby," Jason says.

"Thank you. We do try to be just. This is a very difficult set of laws to administer. But tell me, Mrs. Harmon, what do you say?"

"What do I say?" I look from Rigby to Jason to Suli. "What do I say?"

Laughter comes over me as inexorably as did my tears, and comes so hard it ultimately produces more of them. Above my own roar, I hear Jason's cries of "Mother, stop it!" and "She's hysterical." Gradually the fit passes.

"I'm sorry. It just strikes me terribly funny that I've finally come to some kind of peace with dying and you suddenly appear like a *deus ex machina* to offer me life everlasting."

Rigby smiles his perfect government-issue smile. "Well,

yes. I suppose that is rather funny, in a way. But what do you say, Mrs. Harmon?"

"My first inclination is to tell you to take all your laser guns and needles and other junk and shove them up your ass, Mr. Rigby. You see, I'm not afraid of dying anymore."

"I see," he says. "Well, perhaps this was a bad time to broach the subject. You've been under terrific strain. Under the circumstances"—he brightens again—"I won't accept that as your final answer. Think it over, Mrs. Harmon."

Suli gets up to see him out. Jason stands. I stand myself. We walk in a pack toward the door. At the foot of the stairs, I stop.

"All right, Rigby. I'll think it over. Jason, you'll pardon me, but I'm exhausted."

I nod at them, then turn, and clutching the banister, begin the slow climb up the stairs to my room, where my blue chair waits for me.

Lexington, Massachusetts
October, 1975

THE BIG BESTSELLERS
ARE AVON BOOKS

☐ **Humboldt's Gift** Saul Bellow 29447 $1.95
☐ **To Jerusalem and Back** Saul Bellow 33472 $1.95
☐ **The Moon Lamp** Mark Smith 32698 $1.75
☐ **The Auctioneer** Joan Samson 31088 $1.95
☐ **Laura: The Life of Laura Ingalls Wilder**
    D. Zochert 32938 $1.75
☐ **The Viking Process** Norman Hartley 31617 $1.95
☐ **The Surface of Earth** Reynolds Price 29306 $1.95
☐ **The Monkey Wrench Gang**
    Edward Abbey 30114 $1.95
☐ **Beyond the Bedroom Wall**
    Larry Woiwode 29454 $1.95
☐ **The Eye of the Storm** Patrick White 21527 $1.95
☐ **Jonathan Livingston Seagull**
    Richard Bach 34777 $1.75
☐ **The Bellamy Saga** John Pearson 30874 $1.95
☐ **Working** Studs Terkel 34660 $2.50
☐ **Something More** Catherine Marshall 27631 $1.75
☐ **Getting Yours** Letty Cottin Pogrebin 27789 $1.75
☐ **Confess, Fletch** Gregory Mcdonald 30882 $1.75
☐ **Shardik** Richard Adams 27359 $1.95
☐ **Anya** Susan Fromberg Schaeffer 25262 $1.95
☐ **The Bermuda Triangle** Charles Berlitz 25254 $1.95
☐ **Watership Down** Richard Adams 19810 $2.25

Available at better bookstores everywhere, or order direct from the publisher.

AVON BOOKS, Mail Order Dept., 250 West 55th St., New York, N.Y. 10019

Please send me the books checked above. I enclose $_____(please
include 25¢ per copy for postage and handling). Please use check or money
order—sorry, no cash or COD's. Allow 4-6 weeks for delivery.

Mr/Mrs/Miss_____

Address_____

City_____State/Zip_____

BB 7-77